Wrongly Accused
By Erin Wade
Copyright 11/2018

Edited by Susan Hughes

Erin Wade
©11/2018 Erin Wade
www.erinwade.us

DEDICATION

To the one who has always supported me in everything
I have ever undertaken. You have encouraged me and have
always been my biggest fan. Life is sweeter with you. Erin

To Valerie who gave me the idea for this book. I hope
this is what you had in mind and enjoy reading it. It took
several turns I didn't anticipate, but all my books seem to
leave me wondering what is going to happen next. Love
you bunches.

Acknowledgements

A special "Thank You" to my wonderful and witty "Beta Master," Julie Versoi. She makes me a better storyteller.

A heartfelt "Thank You" to Laure Dherbécourt for agreeing to beta read for me. She has added insight and an incredible knack for catching incorrect homophones.

She Is

She is the softness in my life
The whisper in my night.

I believe in her and she
Makes me believe in me.

Erin Wade
Wrongly Accused

Chapter 1

"I can't believe you're doing this to me!" Richard Wynn screamed at his now-ex-fiancée. "Two years I've invested in you, and now you tell me you don't love me. Give me the damn ring. At least I can get my money back on it."

Doctor Dawn Fairchild removed the engagement ring from her slender finger and dropped it into his hand.

"Please, Richard, I've tried. I just don't love you like I should. You deserve more than a loveless marriage."

Richard downed his scotch and motioned to the waiter for another one.

"You're getting drunk," Dawn mumbled.

"You're damn right I'm getting drunk. My world just went up in smoke. It's someone else, isn't it? You've fallen in love with that Latin Lothario in the emergency room. I saw the way he can't keep his eyes off you. Are you letting him put his hands on you too?"

Richard tossed down his sixth scotch of the night and ordered another one. "You're just like all the other doctors who think they're God. You think you can control life and death, break hearts or mend them, whichever strikes your fancy. You think you're the judge and jury. You'll pay for this, Dawn. If it's the last thing I ever do, I'll make you pay for this."

"Richard, there's no one else in my life. You know I can't condone what you're doing at the hospital. I think it borders on illegal."

He staggered to his feet. "Come on, I'll take you home. I'm sick of being with you."

"I should drive you home," she said. "You're too drunk to drive."

Dawn paid the check and then supported Richard as he weaved his way to the valet. His car was one of the last left on the lot as the restaurant prepared to close for the night.

"Dr. Wynn, I've already brought up your car." The smiling valet held out Richard's key fob.

"I'm driving," Dawn said as she grabbed the fob. "Dr. Wynn isn't feeling well." She maneuvered Richard into the passenger's seat, fastened his seatbelt, and slid behind the wheel of the Mercedes.

She tried to tune out the tirade Richard was launching at her. She was certain he had invented some of the profanities he was spewing.

"Pull over," Richard yelled. "Pull over now. I'm going to puke all over my car."

Dawn pulled to the curb and watched as Richard bolted from the car and vomited all over the sidewalk in front of an elite men's apparel shop. He threw up until he began to dry heave, then slid to the sidewalk, resting his back against the store's wall. He massaged his temples.

She got out of the car and tiptoed through the trail of stomach contents Richard had regurgitated. When she stood in front of him, he looked up at her and burst into tears.

"Please don't do this to me, Dawn. I love you."

She held out her hand to help him stand. He got to his feet and leaned against the wall. "Feel better now?" she asked.

He took a deep breath and then exhaled loudly. "Much. I'm sorry. I didn't mean to go off on you like that. I know you're just trying to be honest with me. I've known for a long time that things weren't right between us." He wiped his mouth on the sleeve of his suit jacket and walked to the car.

She watched as he slid into the driver's seat. "Are you certain you can drive?" she asked as she settled into the passenger seat.

"Yeah, I'm good."

He pulled the car away from the curb and accelerated to make it through the intersection before the light turned red. The squealing of brakes and the screeching of metal against metal were the last sounds Dawn heard before sinking into total darkness.

##

"Please help me! Please, someone help me," a woman's voice cried out in the darkness.

Dawn heard the plea for help through the fog and pounding in her head. She unbuckled her seatbelt and opened the car door. She stumbled toward the voice. The woman was on her knees, bent over another woman lying on her back. She was crying into her cell phone. Dawn knew without touching the prone woman that she was already dead.

Dawn placed her hand on the other woman's shoulder. The wail of an ambulance told her the woman had called 911.

"Where did you come from?" the woman asked, brown eyes peering up at Dawn.

"The other car," Dawn replied.

The ambulance and police arrived at the same time. Dawn was hustled into the emergency vehicle as another ambulance arrived at the scene.

So sleepy, she thought as she stretched out on the ambulance cot. The attendant pulled a sheet over her.

Chapter 2

Valerie Davis pulled the collar of her coat tighter around her neck to ward off the bitter November wind. The priest handed her a single rose and nodded toward the coffin that filled the gaping hole in the ground.

"Toss it on the coffin," Val's mother whispered. Val obeyed and watched the red petals separate and cover her sister's casket just as Mary's blood had covered the pavement.

She spent the rest of the day consoling her parents and accepting condolences from relatives and friends. She wanted to get back to work to get her mind off the incidents of the past week.

"Val, look who's here," her mother said as she dragged Val's high school boyfriend toward her.

"I'm so sorry about Mary," Detective Bobby Joe Jones mumbled as he shook her hand. "I wish I could do something to make it easier for you."

"Just make sure the person who did this pays," Val hissed.

The next person to console her was her secretary, Lillian Cribs. "I'm so sorry about your sister."

Lillian was an excellent secretary, but she left a lot to be desired in the tact department. "Boss, we've got an influenza outbreak. When are you returning to work?"

Val cocked her head and glared at Lillian.

"I'm just asking," Lillian snorted. "How else will I find out?"

Dawn Fairchild awoke in a room that was very familiar to her—the intensive care unit of All Saints Hospital where she practiced.

"About time you woke up, Dr. Fairchild." Martina, a friendly Spanish nurse, smiled at her. "You've been in la-la land for a few days."

"What am I doing here? What's wrong with me?"

"You're here because we have no empty rooms," the nurse said, "and there's nothing wrong with you but a concussion."

Dawn struggled to sit up and almost fainted, the nausea and pain between her eyes forcing her to lie down again.

"May I see my chart?" Dawn motioned toward the laptop Martina was using to enter information.

"Sure." Martina turned the rolling table so Dawn could see the report.

Dawn studied the information attached to her name. "I see no reason for me to be here," she said, smiling. "I'm discharging myself."

"I'll take care of the paperwork," Martina said. "I'll leave it at the nurse's station. Don't forget to sign it."

Before the door closed behind the nurse, a man dressed in a neatly pressed suit stepped into the room.

"Dr. Dawn Fairchild?"

"Yes," Dawn replied as she continued to search for her civilian clothes.

"I'm Detective Bobby Joe Jones," the man said. "I'm investigating the death of Mary Davis."

"Mary Davis?" Dawn processed the name and could find nothing familiar in her mental data banks. "I'm afraid I don't know a Mary Davis."

"She was the young woman involved in the accident you were in seven days ago."

Dawn swayed and lowered herself onto the hospital bed, trying to stop her head from spinning. The memory returned like the reoccurrence of a horrible nightmare. Fog, dizziness, blood everywhere, and a gorgeous brunette calling for help as she sobbed over a dead girl.

"Yes, yes! I remember." Dawn took a drink of water to alleviate the dryness in her mouth. "That was awful. I . . . I couldn't help her."

Detective Jones gave the blonde doctor time to gather her composure and then pulled his notebook from the inside front pocket of his jacket.

"According to the traffic report, you were the driver of the other vehicle involved in the accident."

"No." Dawn shook her head as if clearing the cobwebs. "Dr. Richard Wynn was driving. We were in his car."

Jones studied his notes and flipped the page. "According to Dr. Wynn, you were driving. He said he'd had too much to drink and that you drove him home and took his car to your place."

"That isn't true." Dawn sighed. "I was driving when we left the restaurant, because Richard was inebriated. But he became ill and demanded I pull over so he could throw up. After he vomited he forced his way behind the wheel and took over driving the car."

"The car belonged to Dr. Wynn?" Jones started writing in his notebook.

"Yes."

"The valet at the restaurant said you took Dr. Wynn's keys and insisted on driving."

Dawn took a long time to answer. She was beginning to have a bad feeling about the detective's questions. "Yes."

"Dr. Wynn says you dropped him off at his home and took his car. He says he was not even in the car at the time of the fatal accident."

And there it is, Dawn thought. *Fatal accident.*

"I was in the passenger's seat. Richard was driving. Surely someone at the scene of the accident must have seen him."

"The only people at the scene of the accident were you and the two women in the other car. One of them was dead on arrival, and the other said you were the only one in the car that T-boned them."

Dawn closed her eyes. *And just like that, Richard has made me pay. He killed a woman then ran away, leaving me to pay for his crime.*

"There must be some way to prove Richard was driving," Dawn sobbed. "Security cameras at the scene . . . his fingerprints on the steering wheel? Someone must have seen him returning home on foot."

"I've run down everything you just mentioned." Jones frowned. He didn't like the idea of the beautiful, blue-eyed blonde being incarcerated with hardened criminals. "I found nothing to support your story. Only two security cameras on the corner were working, and they didn't record the accident. Fingerprints belonging to you and Dr. Wynn were lifted from the steering wheel. That only proves that both of you had driven the car. The best thing you have going for you is there was no alcohol in your system at the time of the accident."

"The most damning information comes from the valet, who heard you insist on driving and witnessed you drive away, and the sister of the victim who swears you were the only one in the car.

"You ran a red light and broadsided the passenger side of the car, killing Mary Davis."

Detective Jones pulled a pair of handcuffs from his pocket. "Dr. Dawn Fairchild, you're under arrest for vehicular manslaughter. You have the right to remain . . . ."

Dawn stared in horror at Bobby Joe as he Mirandized her. Then her mind began to work. "May I change from this flimsy hospital gown before you take me to jail?"

Bobby Joe nodded, and she pulled her clothes from the cabinet. She laid them on top of her cell phone and prayed it had a charge.

"I'll just be a minute." She faked a smile, scooped up her clothes and cell phone, and headed for the bathroom. She locked the bathroom door, dropped her clothes on the floor, and called Libby.

"Libby, I can't talk long. I'm being arrested by a Detective Bobby Joe Jones. Please be there when he brings me in."

"I'll be waiting for you at booking," Libby promised. Dawn's mind raced as she considered her options. She wasn't even sure she had options. *This can't be happening. How could the gods be on Richard's side?*

True to her word, Attorney Libby Howe was waiting when Bobby Joe Jones led his prisoner through the door. She had already spoken to someone and arranged for Dawn to be released into her custody. She didn't want her friend to go through the dehumanizing process of being booked into jail.

"In Texas the penalty for vehicular manslaughter is two to twenty years," Libby informed her best friend and client as they got into her car. "We can go to trial or plead guilty and throw yourself on the mercy of the court."

"I can't plead guilty, Libby. I could lose my license to practice medicine."

"I can probably get it reduced to a misdemeanor," Libby thought out loud. "You could lose your license if the judge declares it a felony, but you're okay if it's treated as a misdemeanor. I'm pretty sure I can make that happen."

"Libby, I won't plead guilty. I'm innocent. I didn't kill that woman. I don't care what her crazy sister says. I've been wrongly accused."

##

Valerie Davis watched her sister's killer as she followed her attorney into the courtroom. Val could tell the blonde doctor was nervous. *Who wouldn't be?*

The trial lasted two days. Two days to destroy a woman's life. The prosecuting attorney presented his witnesses in chronological order, leading jurors to the death of Mary Davis.

The valet testified that Dawn was the one driving Richard Wynn's car. Richard swore Dawn had dropped him at his home before continuing to her house. Valerie Davis was the most convincing of them all as she described Dawn getting out of the other car.

Before giving closing remarks, attorney Libby Howe recalled Valerie to the witness stand.

"Remember, you are still under oath, Miss Davis," Libby reminded her. "On the night your sister was killed in the automobile accident, are you positive, beyond a doubt, that you saw Dr. Dawn Fairchild get out of the driver's side of the vehicle that struck your car?"

Val locked eyes with the beautiful blonde doctor and hesitated before answering. For one split second, she admitted to herself that she had only become aware of the other woman when Dawn had placed her hand on Val's shoulder. "Yes, I am positive," she said.

The jury returned a guilty verdict.

"Court will reconvene at eight in the morning for sentencing," the judge declared.

Dawn fought back the hot tears that threatened to run down her face. Anger flooded her body as she stood and screamed, "Valerie Davis, you are a liar."

Val's gaze locked with Dawn's. She had never seen such loathing in anyone's eyes in her life. Dawn Fairchild hated her with a passion.

The bailiff slapped the handcuffs on Dawn and led her from the courtroom.

##

Dawn paced in her holding cell. She was still traumatized by the booking process. The matron had instructed her to strip, and then she'd searched every orifice of Dawn's body. Dawn shuddered as she recalled the invasive search. She had never been so humiliated in her life. The icing on the cake had been the delousing spray. She had given thanks when she was shoved into a communal shower with a handful of shampoo. She had scrubbed her body as long as possible before the matron instructed her to move on. A tan, two-piece prison uniform had been shoved into her arms while she was still wet from the shower.

She was terrified of prison. How could this happen to her? She'd been raised by a loving Christian family. Her parents and older brother, Flint, doted on her. She had been the perfect daughter, the perfect scholar, graduating at the top of her class in high school, college, and med school.

She was the epitome of prim and proper. She picked her friends based on perceived cleanliness, socially accepted conversation, and character. Prison was so far out of her realm that it was like a foreign universe.

God, she prayed, *please help me.*

Dawn surveyed the prison that was to be her home for the next two years. Federal Medical Center, FMC Carswell was a U.S. federal prison in Fort Worth, Texas, for female inmates of all security levels with medical and mental health problems. It also housed 600 minimum-security female inmates.

The facility sprawled across eighty acres near the southeast corner of Lake Worth and was home to over 1,400 prisoners.

As a teenager, Dawn had heard horror stories about the prison. It was Fort Worth's dirty little secret. Women inmates were often raped by prison guards and denied medical treatment. Belligerent prisoners committed suicide under questionable circumstances.

During her residency at All Saints Hospital, she had heard about a new prison administrator who was turning the facility around. She prayed the stories about the current operations of the prison were true; otherwise, she was about to be dumped into the cesspool of all prisons.

Chapter 3

Dawn kept her eyes down, avoiding eye contact with the prisoners who made salacious remarks to her as the guards led her to her new home, a six-by-eight cell.

I can do this for two years, she thought, sitting down on the hard bed in her cage. *I'll keep my head down, do my time, and get out.*

A movement in the cell next to Dawn made her jump.

"Hi, I'm Niki Sears." A scrawny young woman stuck her hand through the bars. She pulled it back when Dawn made no move to touch it. "What're you in here for?"

"Vehicular manslaughter," Dawn mumbled.

"Drugs." Niki shrugged. "I'm a drug addict."

"How long have you been in here?"

"Six months," Niki said, flashing a snaggletoothed smile. "Eighteen more months and I'm outta here."

"You've been in here six months and you're still using drugs. I'd think you'd be clean by now."

"I am." Niki smirked. "That doesn't mean I wouldn't take a hit of something if I had a chance."

"Did the hospital give you something to help you withdraw?" Dawn couldn't suppress the doctor in her.

"Yeah, a cell with nothing but a paper sheet. I'm sorry to say I ate it, used it for toilet paper, and tore it into small pieces to make a nest in the corner."

Dawn studied the skeletal woman. She was certain Niki must have been beautiful at some point in time. Her green eyes had a haunted look, and her lips were the perfect

Cupid's bow. She had no eyebrows, and her nose had been broken. Missing teeth and a scar down the left side of her face reflected the hard life Niki had chosen.

"Listen," Niki whispered. "Keep your head down and your mouth shut. Try to be as unobtrusive as possible. They'll come after a looker like you."

"They who?"

"Gotta get my beauty rest," Niki scoffed. "It also helps to pretend to be crazy. They don't bother crazies."

"They who?"

Niki appeared to be asleep.

Chapter 4

For the thousandth time Val picked up her cell phone to call Mary. Mary! Her twin sister. Her best friend. Her confidant. Her rock. Mary had always been the one to make her laugh and see things through rose-colored glasses instead of the dark gray of Val's world. Mary had convinced her she could make a difference.

Val shuffled through the stack of files on her desk. She knew she was making a difference, but God it was so slow. She had inherited the mess from hell when she accepted her present position two years ago.

A Harvard graduate with a double major in law and medicine, she had quickly made a name for herself. Her rise in the ranks had been phenomenal. Her battles had been hard fought and usually won. Losing her sister was a battle wound that might never heal.

One stupid woman not paying attention and poof, just like that Mary's life was snuffed out. Val had heard that Dr. Dawn Fairchild had been transferred to a prison out of state. That was good. Texas prisons were notoriously hard on prisoners.

Still, it's a shame, Val thought. *Dawn Fairchild was one gorgeous woman. It's amazing how three lives were destroyed in the blink of an eye.*

And then she heard it, that little voice in her head that wouldn't stop tormenting her: *And you lied.*

##

Dawn followed Lucky, a trustee inmate who had been assigned to show her the routine. Over six feet tall, Lucky was tattooed on every inch of skin Dawn could see. The tattoos ran the gamut from crosses to skulls. The sides of her face were tattooed with flames, making her look like a race car. They were obviously prison tattoos—all one color, different shades of black. She wanted to ask Lucky where she got her name but remained silent. *No one has ever learned anything with their mouth open*, she thought.

"What are you in for?" Lucky asked as she led Dawn to the kitchen.

"Something I didn't do."

"Yeah, they all say that," Lucky snorted. "Me, I'm in for murder. Plain and simple. My girlfriend cheated on me, and I slit her throat with a kitchen knife."

Dawn didn't respond. *Silence is the safest response. What I really want to do is run screaming from this hellhole.*

Lucky chuckled. "Don't worry, I'm not a killer. I just don't like cheaters."

Dawn gulped and followed the six-foot Amazon to the next room.

Lucky showed her the layout of the kitchen and then took her to the laundry room. "Don't come in here alone," she warned Dawn.

"This is where bad things happen to pretty women." She trailed her fingers down Dawn's arm. Then she moved her right hand up to touch the cleavage between Dawn's breasts.

Dawn stood still, maintaining eye contact with Lucky. *Oh God. Please don't let this happen.*

"You're going to need a protector in here," Lucky murmured. "A pretty woman like you. They'll gang up on you if you don't belong to someone."

Lucky slid her hands from Dawn's shoulders to her wrist and caught Dawn's hands in hers as she pinned her against the wall of dryers with her body.

Suddenly, Niki shoved her way through the double doors leading into the laundry room. "Lucky, there's a fight in the kitchen."

Lucky's eyes darted from Dawn to Niki. "Stay with her, Niki. Don't let anything happen to her."

"Should we call the guards or someone to break up the fight?" Dawn asked as Lucky left the room.

"Nah, there's no fight. I was just trying to stop Lucky from staking her claim on you."

"Oh," Dawn squeaked. "Thank you. Did you have to cut it so close?"

Niki shrugged. "I was her bitch until I stopped complying with her demands. Then she beat me up, knocked out my front teeth, and threw me back into the shark tank. Traded me for a pack of cigarettes. I haven't always looked like a skank. This place has a way of changing women. I'll keep you safe as long as I can, but I'm not very strong . . . and Lucky is a hulk."

"What do you expect of me in return?" Dawn whispered.

"Nothing," Niki said. "But if you get out of here alive, please get me out too."

"I will," Dawn promised.

"I've been instructed to take you to the assessment center," Lucky said as she blasted back into the room. "Niki, you need to get back to the library. You gotta be there when it opens."

Niki nudged Dawn toward the double doors. "I was just telling Dawn that you're someone important here. She's lucky to have you showing her the ropes."

Dawn was surprised at the way Lucky preened over Niki's compliment. Niki continued to praise Lucky all the way to the assessment center. Then she waved goodbye to

Dawn and winked at her. Niki knew her way around the prison and its inhabitants.

##

Dawn squirmed in the hard straight-backed chair as the woman across from her studied her file. "You're a doctor?"

"Yes, ma'am."

"What's your specialty?"

"I'm a surgeon and a pretty good diagnostician." Dawn tried to be brief and to the point.

"Hmm." The woman slid the papers back into her file. "How would you feel about working in the hospital here?"

"I'd be happy to help in any way I can." Dawn wondered what kind of archaic equipment the facility would have.

"Fill this out. I'll pass your request on to the warden."

"My request?"

"If you want to work in the hospital, you must request it. If not, I'll have someone escort you back to your cell."

"Yes, yes, I'll fill out the request."

##

"How was your first day?" Niki whispered as they leaned against the bars between them.

"Scary."

"Did they assign you a duty?"

"Not yet. I think they're going to use me in the hospital."

"God, I hope so." Niki sighed. "That would get you out of harm's way. You'd be housed in the hospital instead of this place."

The clanging of iron doors announced the arrival of the guards for their last check of the night. "Pretend you're asleep," Niki whispered, pulling her sheet over her head as she turned to face the wall away from the guards.

Dawn did as she was told and held her breath as two guards stopped in front of her cell. "Hey, blondie, you awake?"

Dawn didn't move. One of the guards clanged his nightstick between the bars. "You awake?"

Niki sat up. "What the hell do you want?"

"Nothing you've got," the female guard huffed. "Go back to sleep, skank."

"She's sleeping," Niki yelled. "She's worn out. Leave her alone."

"What's going on down there?" A voice from the other end of the cellblock echoed through the unit.

"They're messing with your woman," Niki called out as Lucky sprinted toward them.

"Is there a problem here, officers?" Lucky asked.

"No. We were just making sure she's okay," the female guard answered. Then she pointed at Niki. "And you . . . you're a troublemaker."

"Everything's good here," the male guard growled. "Let's move on. You need to get back to bed, Lucky."

The three walked away, bantering about the blonde.

Dawn waited until the steel doors locked and then scooted to Niki's cell. "Oh God, Niki! I've never been so scared in my life. Thank you."

"Sooner or later they'll get to you," Niki cautioned. "Don't fight. They'll only hurt you more to teach you a lesson."

##

Later that night a strangling sound pulled Dawn from a deep sleep. Her body was rigid as she tried to identify the noise. *Choking! Someone is choking Niki.*

Without thinking Dawn rushed to the bars between their cells and started screaming. Two figures were bent over Niki.

"Help! Help! Somebody help her! They're killing Niki."

A loud pop and bright light filled the cell block as other prisoners began yelling. The two muggers ran from Niki's cell and disappeared through the door at the end of the cellblock.

Lucky and two guards Dawn had never seen before ran to Niki's cell.

"Jesus Christ," Lucky yelled, "she's been stabbed."

Dawn watched as blood flowed from Niki's stomach. "Let me help her," Dawn begged. "I can help her."

The two guards looked at one another. "She's a doctor," Lucky yelled. "Let her help Niki. I'll get a stretcher."

By the time Lucky returned, Dawn had located the cut artery and pinched it off to stop the bleeding.

"Lift her onto the gurney," Dawn directed. "I'll hold the artery until we can get her to the hospital, otherwise she'll bleed to death."

The four of them rode the elevator down to the first floor, and Lucky led the way to the infirmary. "This is closer than the hospital, Doc. Everything you'll need is in here."

Dawn located the clamps and looked around for suture. She was surprised to find the infirmary well-stocked with swaged needles, prepackaged with the needle attached to the thread. She carefully cleaned the wound and neatly sutured the artery back together. She located a punctured intestine and sutured it. She cleaned out the leakage from the intestine to keep Niki's stomach cavity from becoming infected. She checked to make certain the nicked artery and intestine were the only damage done by the would-be killers. Certain she'd done all she could, Dawn removed the clamps, watching to make certain her sutures held as blood pumped through the veins. Satisfied, she closed the wound.

Niki moaned. "That hurt like hell, Doc."

Dawn patted her patient's hand. For the first time she realized that she had performed a major operation on a patient who wasn't sedated. Her admiration for the pitiful woman on the gurney went way up.

"You must have a pain threshold that's off the charts," Dawn said. "You never made a sound."

"I didn't want to startle you," Niki murmured, groaning. "You had your hands in my guts. Is there any chance of getting some pain meds? I'm really hurting."

"I'll take it from here," the hospital doctor said as he touched Dawn's arm. "I watched what you did. You're one hell of a surgeon. I'll make certain the warden moves you to the hospital housing when we finish here. I'm Dr. Lance Reynolds, by the way."

She shook his hand. "Dr. Dawn Fairchild."

##

Dawn looked out the window and realized a new day was beginning. *I've survived two days*, she thought. *Taking it one day at a time.*

"You want some coffee?" Lucky caught Dawn's elbow and steered her toward the doctors' lounge.

"That sounds great. Will they put a guard on Niki? Whoever tried to kill her is still loose."

"Did you get a good look at them?" Lucky filled two cardboard cups with hot coffee.

"No, it was too dark, but I bet Niki knows who did it. Will there be a full inquiry?"

"Probably. Our new warden is a bitch about this sort of thing. She'll go ballistic, and you can bet heads will roll. I'm just glad they didn't go after you."

"Will I meet the warden?" Dawn asked.

Lucky shrugged. "I doubt it. She's not a real hands-on administrator, but she knows how she wants things to run, and if the people under her don't do as they're told, she fires them"

"Have you met her?"

"Yeah. Once a month she holds a luncheon for the trustees. We get to eat with her and answer her questions. She even answers ours."

"What does she look like?"

"She's a knockout. The kind of woman you'd give your soul to spend one night with. Like you."

Dawn grunted. The thought of spending a night with Lucky made her nauseous.

Chapter 5

Dr. Reynolds immediately arranged for Dawn to transfer to hospital duty. "She's too good to live with the animals," he informed Assistant Warden Ray McDonald. "She really knows her way around an operating room, and I could use the help."

Dawn settled into the routine of managing the infirmary. She had convinced Dr. Reynolds that she could train Niki to assist her. "She's very smart and has a degree in biology."

"She's also a drug addict," Reynolds countered but had given in and granted her request.

Dawn shared her room with Niki since rooms in the medical suites were scarce. Niki had lived up to Dawn's expectations and was thriving in the new surroundings. Both woke an hour early every morning to work out in the hospital gym. "We don't want to get soft," Dawn said. "Besides we need the endorphins to make it through the day."

Niki took to exercise with the same zest she had taken to drugs. "Our workouts make me feel like a million dollars. Tell me about endorphins again?"

"They're hormones secreted by the brain and nervous system. They're peptides which activate the body's opiate receptors, causing an analgesic effect, almost like drugs. They have several physiological functions."

"Humph, go figure." Niki smiled. "I do remember some of that from my biology classes.

Over the next six months Dawn and Niki became a cohesive surgical team. Niki quickly learned what instruments Dawn needed during surgery. It was as if their minds melded, and Niki anticipated Dawn's every need.

Inmates requested the "dream team" as they had named their resident doctor and nurse. Lance was more than happy to turn over the surgery and potential fatal injuries to Dawn and Niki while he handled the less serious needs of the inmates.

"I've spoken to the dentist on staff," Dawn said one morning. "He has agreed to cap your teeth that are broken and replace the missing ones."

"They can do that?" Niki beamed. "They can make me look normal again?"

"Yes, but Niki, I want you to take a good look at yourself in the mirror and know that the reason you're here, the reason you look like you do now, is because of drugs. You must never do drugs again."

"I promise," Niki pledged. "I feel that God has given me a second chance, and I'm not going to mess it up. Dawn, I don't know why you did this for me, but I appreciate it."

"You risked your life for me."

Loud screaming in the hallway and people scurrying in all directions drew Dawn's attention. Suddenly, the door was shoved open, and two guards carried in a neatly dressed woman. Blood was oozing across the white blouse she wore.

"That loon on the fourth floor shanked her," the guard explained. "She's hurt bad, Doc."

Niki helped the guards lift the woman onto the exam table as Dawn washed her hands and slipped on surgical gloves. The shank was still buried in the valley between the woman's breasts. Dawn tried to ignore the perfect breasts as she wiped the blood from them.

"Doc, it's the warden!" Niki stood slack-jawed, staring at the injured woman as if she were the second coming.

"Niki, call the anesthesiologist. We've got to move quickly to stop the bleeding when I pull the shank out of her chest."

A bloody hand gripped Dawn's arm. "Please don't let me die!"

The blood in Dawn's veins turned to ice water as she stared into the woman's face. "You! You're the warden?"

"Yes," Valerie Davis sputtered.

Dawn leaned closer so only Val would hear her words. "I should let you die, but I won't because I've never killed anyone in my life."

"You're a lucky woman," Dr. Lance Reynolds said as he removed the sutures from Warden Davis's incision. "You won't even have a scar. Dr. Fairchild is an excellent doctor. She's a highly trained surgeon, you know. I don't know what she did to land in here, but you're lucky she was here. She saved your life."

"She hasn't followed up with me on my surgery," Val said, her stoic expression emphasizing her disapproval.

"She asked me to take over your follow-up treatment," Reynolds said. "She said she didn't think an inmate should be treating the warden."

"I'm sure that was said tongue in cheek," Val huffed.

"No, I believe she was sincere," Reynolds mused. "She has been an incredible asset to our hospital. She's a very dedicated doctor.

"I can't tell you how glad I am to have someone of her caliber," Reynolds said. "You know I'm old enough to start drawing my pension and social security. I'd really like to retire before some nut shanks me. Is there any chance Dr. Fairchild would stay on here after she serves her time?"

Val snorted. "I doubt it. I don't think we could pay her enough money to get her to work for me."

Chapter 6

From the observation box suspended over the operating room, Warden Valerie Davis watched Dr. Fairchild as she performed an appendectomy on a prisoner.

Reynolds was right. Dawn did know what she was doing. Her self-confidence and knowledge were apparent in every move she made. She was at home in the operating room. Whether she was performing a routine appendectomy or an emergency intubation to get air into the lungs of a patient with a crushed larynx, Dr. Fairchild moved with the calmness and assurance of one who knew how to handle any situation.

Dawn completed the surgery and handed her scalpel to the woman who had assisted her during the operation. The two exited the operating room and headed for the doctor's lounge.

##

"We get to attend our first trustee meeting with the warden this afternoon," Niki said as she handed Dawn her coffee.

"Must I?" Dawn asked.

"Yes." The younger woman furrowed her brow. "Why wouldn't you?"

"I just thought my time could be better used elsewhere," Dawn said with a shrug. "I have sutures to take out, tonsils that need removing, and an ingrown toenail to take care of."

Niki laughed. "While I can't argue that the warden is more important than an ingrown toenail, I do think you'd be well served to attend her meetings."

Dawn secretly smiled at Niki's efforts to speak properly. The young woman had come a long way in a month. "I'm very proud of you," she said.

"Me?" Niki raised nonexistent brows. "You're the one that got us out of hell's toilet. I'm just happy to be riding on your coattails. I'm not sure I would have survived much longer. You've taught me so much in a short time."

"But you saved my life," Dawn reminded her. "If you hadn't started screaming that night, God only knows what those two would have done to me."

Niki scowled as she nodded. "I know what they would've done to you. The same thing they did to me. I was prepared to die to keep that from happening to you."

"And you almost did."

"Then you saved my life. We're even." Niki shrugged. "Let's not talk about it again. We're in a safe place, so let's keep the warden happy and attend her meetings. Okay?"

Dawn nodded.

"May I ask you a personal question?" Dawn said, lowering her voice. "You don't have to answer if you don't want to."

"Sure." Niki steeled herself at the thought of revealing the abuse she'd suffered in prison.

"What happened to your eyebrows?"

Niki laughed at the simple question. "I removed them with duct tape."

"Why?" Dawn said, wide-eyed.

"After several encounters of the worst kind," Niki said, "I realized that the uglier I looked, the less they would want to . . . to rape me."

Anger flared on Dawn's face. She squeezed her eyes shut, trying to block the image of the smaller woman being molested. "I'm sorry, I didn't mean to—"

"It's okay." Niki shrugged. "I lived. You know the old saying, 'What doesn't kill you makes you stronger?' In prison that is the truest statement you'll ever hear.

"Anyway, a plumber left some duct tape in the laundry room and I took it. That night in my cell I ripped off my eyebrows. It hurt like a son of a gun."

"They're beginning to grow back." Dawn touched the other woman's brow with her fingertips. "I have some cream that will help."

Chapter 7

Warden Davis double-checked the seating arrangement for the trustee luncheon. She had Dr. Reynolds on her left and Dr. Fairchild on her right. Lucky had asked to be seated next to Dawn. The table was set up in a horseshoe shape, so she could easily answer questions from anyone in the room.

Dawn's smiling face danced through her mind, making her heart skip a beat. Even in prison garb Dawn was one of the most gorgeous women Val had ever seen. A woman like Dawn Fairchild should not be in prison. *She's here because you lied*—the thought crashed through her mind.

Val was haunted by the thought night and day. She justified her little lie with the knowledge that Dawn had been the only one to try to minister to Mary and her, the only other person at the scene of the accident. But the truth was, she had not seen Dawn get out of the driver's side of the car.

Why the hell did she end up in my prison?

##

Dawn stayed close to Niki as they searched for their places at the table. "I'm here in the curve of the table," she said as she located her place card next to Warden Davis.

"I'm the last place on the end," Niki said.

Dawn picked up Lucky's place card and exchanged it with Niki's. "Now you're seated next to me," she said.

Niki beamed as she pulled out her chair and sat down. The table was filling quickly as others filed into the room.

Niki and Dawn were discussing stocking the infirmary when the warden and Lucky entered the room.

The warden took her place at the table, while Lucky looked menacingly at Niki. "I believe you're in my chair," Lucky said.

Warden Davis was immediately aware of the altercation. "Oh Lucky, I placed Dr. Fairchild and Niki beside me, so I could introduce them to everyone. I believe your chair is—"

"The one on the end," Dawn said, flashing her most innocent smile.

Lucky continued to glare at Niki as she swaggered to her chair. Dawn placed a reassuring hand on Niki's leg.

Warden Davis asked and answered questions throughout the luncheon, agreeing to some of the requests made and explaining why other changes weren't possible.

Dawn was surprised at how patient and genuinely interested the warden was. As the meal was served, the inmates talked among themselves and let the warden dine in peace.

"What about you, Dr. Fairchild?" Val said, turning her attention to Dawn. "Surely you have some suggestions about improvements in our system."

"I'm not qualified to give you suggestions," Dawn answered without emotion. "Ask me again when I've served my time."

"I wanted to thank you for saving my life." Val spoke softly so others wouldn't hear. "Dr. Reynolds tells me I would have died if not for you."

"Yes, you would have." Dawn's blunt reply caused Val's eyes to widen. She opened her mouth as if to reply but apparently thought better of it.

"Warden, ma'am," Niki said, leaning around Dawn. "This food is delicious. Thank you for sharing it with us."

Val frowned as she appraised Niki. She wondered why Dawn had pleaded to train the girl as her surgery nurse. She was certainly nothing to look at.

"You're welcome," Val said. "I'm sure it isn't any better than the regular cafeteria food."

"Now you're just being cruel," Dawn mumbled.

"I beg your pardon?" Val glared at Dawn. "What did you say?"

"Surely you know the gruel fed to the prisoners in no way compares to the meal we've just eaten." Blue eyes locked with brown as Dawn tried to ascertain if the warden was as uninformed as she tried to pretend. "The coffee we just drank was delicious. The coffee served to the inmates this morning tasted like they boiled an old sock to make it."

Val stood and addressed the women. "Thank you all for coming today. Thank you for expressing your concerns and ideas. I look forward to seeing you next month."

The women knew they had been dismissed. They rose, thanked the warden, and then filed out of the room.

Dawn mumbled a "Thank you," and led Niki from the room.

##

"Are you sure it won't hurt?" Niki whimpered as Dawn led her to the prison's dentistry department. "When Rooster had her tooth pulled, they almost killed her."

"I promise," Dawn reassured her. "I'll make certain it's painless. The dentist is going to use nitrous oxide. You probably know it as laughing gas. You won't feel a thing."

"I know what nitrous oxide is," Niki grumped. "I'm not stupid."

"I . . . I didn't mean to imply you are." Dawn bit her lip and looked away. "I didn't mean to insult you. I was just trying to reassure you."

"You're really beautiful when you do that." Niki grinned, flashing her gapped teeth. "You didn't insult me.

34

I'm just nervous about this. I didn't mean to be rude to you. I know you're just trying to help."

Dawn patted her arm. "That's understandable."

"She'll have some swelling and slight discomfort for a couple of days," the dentist informed Dawn. "Just let her rest, and give her the pain meds I gave you. She'll be fine."

Dawn put Niki to bed and placed icepacks on her jaws. Niki was sedated enough to sleep twelve hours. Dawn made one last check on her and then headed to the hospital where a tonsillectomy was waiting.

From the viewing room, Val watched Dawn as she removed an inmate's tonsils and set another woman's broken arm. There was no doubt the beautiful blonde doctor had been a godsend for the prison hospital.

Val sat in the viewing room for a long time after Dawn had left the operating room.

"There you are," Dr. Reynolds said as he entered the room. "Your office said I'd find you here."

"I like to observe what is going on in my prison." Val smiled up at him. "How may I help you?"

"We have several patients who have blockages and need a bypass and stents inserted. We need a heart-lung bypass machine."

"We have no doctors who can perform open-heart surgery," Val pointed out. "Can you?"

"Me? Oh no, I'm not qualified, but Dr. Fairchild is."

"Of course she is." Val wrinkled her brow.

"We send the inmates to All Saints Hospital, and for what they charge us for two surgeries, we could purchase a bypass machine."

"I'll look into it," Val promised.

"How long will we have her?' Reynolds asked.

"I'm not sure."

"What's she in for?" Reynolds inquired.

"Why don't you ask her?" Val stood and left the room.

She had a meeting in ten minutes with the prison dietician. As she hurried to her next meeting, Val replayed Dawn's trial in her mind—something she had done a thousand times, and each time she came to the same conclusion. She had lied about seeing the doctor exit the driver's side of the car. The truth was, she hadn't even been aware of Dawn's presence until the doctor placed her hand on her shoulder to console her.

Val reached her office to find Sue Creighton, the prison dietician, pacing the floor of the waiting room.

"Did you bring the information I requested?" Val asked as she ushered Sue into her office.

"Yes, ma'am." Sue held out the prisoners' menu for the past thirty days.

Val settled in her desk chair and studied the information as Sue shifted from one foot to the other.

"Do sit down, Sue. I want to be certain I'm understanding what I see."

After several minutes, Val closed the file and stared at Sue. "I have to wonder why there is no variety in the menu and also why the nutritional value is so poor."

"I work hard to stay within the budget you allow me," Sue answered. "And to stay within the director's mandates."

"Hmm. I'll keep these. I appreciate you visiting with me." Val stood, dismissing the woman.

After Sue left, Val called the prison's accounting department and requested a review of the cafeteria's operations. "I want to know if the items we are being charged for match the items being served to the prisoners."

Chapter 8

Pacing their room Dawn anxiously waited for the matron to call her. Her parents visited her every week. Their love and reassurance were all that kept her going. They were a reminder that life went on outside the prison, and there was a clean, safe world waiting for her. She worried about Niki, who seemed to have no one on the outside.

Although the warden had been hesitant to allow Niki to work in the hospital where drugs were readily available, Dawn had convinced Val to give the girl a chance.

"One slip up, one indiscretion, and she'll go back into general lockup," Val had threatened. Niki had become the model prisoner.

"You're lucky to have someone visit you every week," Niki said. "I wish my mom would visit me."

"Why doesn't she?" Dawn asked.

"My family washed their hands of me when I was picked up the last time. I can't say I blame them. I was a mess. I would do anything for a hit."

"What did you do?" Dawn wasn't sure she wanted to hear the answer to her question.

"I was picked up for prostitution." Niki grimaced. "My folks said they wanted nothing to do with me. My mom did try to visit me about six months after I was thrown in here, but I'd already been beaten, had my teeth knocked out and my nose broken. I didn't want her to see me looking like that."

"Well, you look good now," Dawn said. "In fact, you're beautiful. The dentist gave you a lovely smile, and your eyebrows have grown back nice and dark. The cream we've been putting on your scar has almost made it disappear. A little makeup will hide it completely. You look nothing like you did when I arrived."

"Thanks to you." Niki flashed her beautiful smile. "You made all this happen for me."

"When you get out you'll need a safe place to go," Dawn reminded her. "You should try to contact your folks. Write them a letter. Reach out to them."

"I'll try," Niki said.

"Now!" Dawn insisted. She pulled stationary she had purchased in the prison commissary from her dresser drawer. "Here's a pen and some stationery. Write them and ask them to visit you."

With Dawn's encouragement Niki wrote the letter and addressed the envelope. "I'll mail it for you," Dawn said.

##

Dawn had started talking about Niki Sears on her parents' second visit, and they were aware of Niki and the progress she'd made since Dawn's incarceration.

When Dawn asked her parents to contact the Searses, Ruth Fairchild was hesitant. "Where do they live?"

"They live in Dallas, Mom. About an hour's drive from your home. This is important to me. Niki has turned her life around. She deserves another chance. She'll be released and will need a place to go. I'm afraid she'll end up on the streets, and it's so easy for a drug addict to get hooked again."

Dawn gave her mother the Sears's address. "Next week, could you sign in to visit Niki and let Dad sign in to visit me?"

"I won't be able to come next week," Phillip Fairchild said. "Flint will accompany your mother."

"I'll miss you, Dad, but it'll be great to see my brother again." Dawn smiled.

"We'll do everything we can to help your friend, dear," Ruth assured her daughter. "She did save you from a fate worse than death."

Val looked up when Lance Reynolds entered her office. "I'd like to take Dr. Fairchild with us to look at the heart-lung bypass machine we're considering," he said.

Val tried to ignore the warm feeling that spread through her body at the mention of Dawn's name. "That's fine with me. Why don't you ask her to clear her calendar all day tomorrow? We'll check out the machine and go to a late lunch."

"I'd like that," Reynolds said. "I'll check with her now and get back to you."

"Lance, be sure to inform her that she must wear a tracking anklet."

"That should make me popular with her," Reynolds grumbled.

As soon as the door closed behind Reynolds, Val called her beauty salon and made an appointment. She wore her hair in a bun or a French braid and had let it get unusually long. A nice stylish cut would be good.

Dawn smiled at Val's secretary as she entered the warden's reception area. "I think Warden Davis is expecting me."

"Oh yes, Dr. Fairchild, she said to send you in when you arrived."

Dawn opened the door and stepped into the warden's office. She was unprepared for the gorgeous brunette silhouetted by the window. Val turned and smiled. Dawn was certain the room got brighter.

Dark curls curved their way onto the woman's shoulders. She tossed her hair back and broadened her smile. Dawn hated herself for the feeling that was stirring in her stomach. Warden Davis was stunning.

"Dr. Fairchild, thank you for agreeing to join us today."

"Only a fool would miss the chance to get out of this place." Dawn hoped her contempt for the woman was obvious.

Val lowered her eyes and then turned away from Dawn. "Dr. Reynolds will join us in a few minutes. He's running late. Please sit down."

Dawn sat in silence as they waited. She didn't want to talk to Warden Davis. *Lying Warden Davis.*

"I'm looking into the food situation in the cafeteria," Val volunteered. "I have discovered some problems."

"That's good," Dawn said.

Val's secretary entered the room and informed her that Dr. Reynolds had been involved in an accident. "He said it was nothing serious and he's fine, but he's waiting to file an accident report. He suggested you two go, and he'll meet you at the manufacturer's showroom."

"Shall we?" Val retrieved her purse from the bottom drawer of her desk and ushered Dawn out the door.

##

Val pulled her car through the prison gates and exhaled softly. She realized that she always breathed a sigh of relief when she left the prison grounds. She could only imagine how an inmate must feel when released from the institution.

"How are things going in the hospital?" Val said, finally breaking the silence.

"Good," Dawn replied.

"Your roommate is due to be released in a few months," Val noted. "I've already initiated her paperwork."

"Good."

Dawn's monotone was driving Val crazy. "Look, Dr. Fairchild, I understand you're angry at me, but can't we at least pretend to be civil with one another?"

"That was me being civil toward you," Dawn mumbled.

Val chewed her full bottom lip. *Damn, she's infuriating. It would help if she were ugly as a stick, but no, God, you sent me the most gorgeous prisoner imaginable.*

"I know you think I'm to blame——"

"I don't *think*!" Dawn said, her voice dripping with venom. "I know that you destroyed my life. I know you're the reason I'm in that hellhole. I know you lied, and you know you lied. And I loathe liars."

Val held back the tears that burned behind her eyelids. No one had ever spoken to her in such a manner. The biggest problem was that Dawn was right. She did know she had lied, though it had seemed like the truth at the time.

She was still hurting over the death of her twin sister, and she wanted someone to pay for all the pain she was enduring. Unfortunately, she knew the wrong person was paying for something she didn't do.

Mary was all Val had. All her life, Mary had been there to applaud her triumphs and comfort her during bad times. Now all she had was a prison full of criminals. Some were insane, and some were just evil.

Then there were the Dawn Fairchilds and Niki Searses. Women who didn't really belong with the others. Val wondered how many innocent women she had incarcerated.

She glanced at Dawn. The blonde was staring out the passenger window. *You're so damn beautiful*, she thought.

##

Val was impressed with Dawn's knowledge of the equipment needed for open-heart surgery. The heart-lung bypass machine Dawn selected was a few thousand dollars over budget, but Val would find the extra money somewhere, even if it had to come out of her own salary.

She gave the salesman her purchase order and signed the sales contract. "I'd love to take both you lovely ladies to lunch," he said.

"We're on a tight schedule," Val quipped as she escorted Dawn toward the exit.

Dawn's empty stomach growled as she fastened her seatbelt. "I am hungry," she thought out loud.

"There's a nice new restaurant on University," Val said. "It's called Bread Winners. It's extremely successful in Dallas and has received rave reviews in Fort Worth. I made a reservation for us. Lance will join us there for lunch."

Dawn nodded and offered a begrudging, "Thank you."

The restaurant was nice with white tablecloths and red napkins. *I took places like this for granted*, Dawn thought. She looked around, admiring the artwork and elegant statues placed around the dining area. It was two hours past the lunch-hour rush, and the restaurant was quiet. Soft music played in the background.

They both ordered iced tea and perused the menu while they waited for Dr. Reynolds.

"I like the dress your mother brought you for our outing," Val said. "When we return you should hide it in your room. We do have a few thieves in the hospital wards."

Before Dawn could respond, Val's phone rang, and Dawn listened as the warden spoke with the caller. "No. No, really Lance it's okay. We'll discuss it when we get back to the hospital.

"He had trouble getting in touch with someone to give him a ride," Val explained as she shoved her phone back in her purse. "His son just showed up, so he's going to the hospital. He said he can't wait to see what we bought."

The mention of the new equipment made Dawn smile. "I'm certain he'll be pleased."

"You should do that more often," Val said, beaming.

"What?"

"Smile. You're breathtaking when you smile."

42

"I don't have a lot to smile about right now," Dawn snapped.

"There's these little muffins." Val grinned as she held out the basket filled with mini blueberry muffins.

Dawn took one and placed it on the butter plate in front of her.

"And whipped butter," Val said.

Dawn accepted the offering and spread the butter on half of the muffin. She closed her eyes as the taste of the warm muffin and butter overwhelmed her senses. "This is delicious." She ran the tip of her tongue along her bottom lip. She opened her eyes to find Val staring at her. She couldn't stop herself from falling into the dark eyes that held her mesmerized.

"Have you ladies decided what you'd like to order?" the perky waitress asked as she tapped her pen on the table.

Dawn looked at her menu as she tried to tamp down the flush that had spread from her chest up to her cheeks. "You go ahead," she told Val. *While I regain my composure.*

Val ordered and then raised an expectant brow at Dawn.

"Chicken Caesar Salad." Dawn cleared her throat and sipped her iced tea to alleviate the dryness that gripped her tongue and lips.

"May we talk, or would you prefer silence?" Val asked as the waitress departed.

"Whatever makes you happy. You're the warden."

"If I ask questions will you answer them?"

"Depends." Dawn shrugged. "If I answer yours, will you answer mine?"

"I've nothing to hide," Val said. "Tit for tat."

Dawn tried to keep from making eye contact with Val. She didn't want a replay of her breathless reaction to the gorgeous brunette.

"Why did your fiancé testify against you?"

"He wasn't my fiancé," Dawn sneered. "I had just broken our engagement and returned his ring. That's why he was too drunk to drive. He testified against me to avoid prosecution."

"How long were you engaged?"

"Two years. Now I get to ask two questions," Dawn reminded Val.

"You're Harvard educated. How did you end up running a women's prison in Texas?"

"I wanted to do something that would matter, something that would change other women's lives."

"You certainly changed my life, Warden."

Val's lips moved, but no sound came from her mouth.

"My second question," Dawn said. "If you really want to make a difference, why do you let women like Lucky run amok in your prison?"

"Lucky is my liaison with the other inmates. She brings their concerns to me." Val tilted her head and watched Dawn.

Dawn snorted. "Surely you aren't that naive."

"I . . . what do you mean?"

"Lucky is a criminal. She terrorizes the other inmates and rapes anyone who catches her eye." Dawn was surprised by the dark expression that crossed Val's face. "She had already declared I was hers. If you hadn't moved me to the hospital quarters, I would be one of her victims by now."

"Excuse me," Val said, pushing back from the table and making a mad dash for the ladies' room. The waitress was placing their order on the table when she returned.

Val's pasty face convinced Dawn she had thrown up.

"Are you okay?" Dawn asked.

"I've had better days," Val growled. "Are you sure about Lucky?"

"Positive. I was just a night away from being Mrs. Lucky. If Niki hadn't charged into the laundry room my second day there, I have no doubt that Lucky would have raped me then.

"The reason Niki was stabbed is because she started screaming when two of your guards tried to pay me a midnight visit."

"The guards?" Val shook her head. "Are you sure they meant you harm?"

"I'm positive they weren't planning a wine and cheese tasting for me," Dawn drawled.

Val leaned her head from side to side and rubbed the knot at the base of her skull, trying to loosen the tension that had settled in her neck.

"Why don't you talk to Niki? She was Lucky's favorite until she refused her demands. Then Lucky beat her up, knocked out her front teeth, and traded her for a pack of cigarettes."

Dawn noticed Val aimlessly moving her salad around her plate. "You're not eating, Warden."

Val shuddered. "I've lost my appetite."

For the first time, Dawn almost felt sorry for Warden Val Davis, almost wished she could help her make a difference.

"We should go," Dawn said. "I worry about Niki when I'm not there to watch her back."

"Surely no one would bother her in the hospital," Val said as she signaled for the check.

. "You give Lucky free run of the place. Believe me, if she finds out we're gone, she'll pay Niki a visit."

"She is quite beautiful now," Val said. "It's amazing what a difference a pretty smile, hair, and eyebrows can make."

Dawn agreed. "Once she gets her broken nose fixed she'll be perfect."

"We don't have a plastic surgeon on staff," Val said. "I could make inquiries and locate a good one. Her nose was broken in my facility. I should have it fixed."

"You would do that?" Dawn tried unsuccessfully to stop her frown from turning into a smile. "You'd do that for Niki?"

Val placed her hand on top of Dawn's. "I'd do that for you."

Dawn scanned the other woman's face. Her sincerity made it soft and beautiful.

"Thank you," Dawn said. She didn't pull her hand away from Val's touch.

On the way back to the hospital, the two women discussed the conditions at the prison.

"I'm obviously out of touch," Val huffed. "If you could keep me informed, that would help me make changes."

Dawn couldn't believe she was agreeing to help the woman who was to blame for her incarceration.

"Why did you break your engagement?" Val asked

"I caught Richard taking drugs from the hospital pharmacy. I don't know if he was using them or selling them. I just know it's illegal."

"You're a very right-or-wrong person," Val said.

"Either one is honest, or they aren't."

Val ignored Dawn's dig. "So, Richard greatly benefited by your being found guilty and imprisoned."

"Yes!"

"Did you . . . um . . . cohabitate?" Val cleared the hoarseness from her throat.

"We didn't live together," Dawn said, glancing at Val, "but I did sleep with him, if that's what you want to know. I was planning to marry him until I discovered he was a thief."

"Oh." Val exhaled the breath she had been holding.

Chapter 9

"I'm going to make my rounds before I go to bed," Dawn informed Val as the prison gates swung closed behind their car. "Would you like to join me?"

"I'd better go by my office and see if there's anything that can't wait until morning. I'll drop you at the front door of the hospital."

"Thank you for getting me out of here, if only for a day," Dawn said as she opened the car door. "I did enjoy it."

"I did too."

Dawn signed in at the guard's desk. "Have you seen Niki?" she asked.

"She was here this morning," the woman said, her brow furrowed in thought, "but I haven't seen her since lunch."

Dread seeped into Dawn's bones as she checked for Niki in her office. She wasn't in the infirmary or the storeroom. The operating room was empty. The young woman was missing.

Dawn went to the nurses' station. "Have any of you seen Niki?"

"I haven't," the head nurse said. "You might check with Lucky. She was looking for her just before lunch."

Dawn ran to her room to change. Val was right; wearing a nice dress in the prison was asking for trouble.

She grabbed a pair of jeans and a pullover prison shirt. "Dear God, please let Niki be okay," she prayed out loud as she searched for her shoes.

"I am." A mop of glorious auburn hair poked out from under Dawn's bed.

"Oh Niki!" Dawn fell to her knees and pulled the young woman from under her bed. "Are you okay? I was so scared when I couldn't find you . . . and . . ." Dawn realized she was sobbing. "I was so afraid something had happened to you."

"I hid," Niki whimpered. "Lucky was looking for me, so I hid. I didn't think she would come in here, but I was wrong. She did, but she didn't look under the bed."

"I'm just so thankful you're all right." Dawn hugged Niki to her. "I shouldn't have left you alone. I wasn't thinking. I had no idea we would be gone so long."

Niki put on a brave face. "I'm okay. You're back. Everything's right in my world."

Dawn stood, pulling Niki to her feet. "Why don't you get ready for bed? You take your shower while I remove my makeup. Then I'll shower. It's been a long day."

"I'll hurry," Niki muttered as she scurried into the bathroom.

Dawn locked the door of their room with her keycard, removed her clothes, and slipped into a terry cloth robe she had purchased from the prison commissary. Her hands shook as she removed her eye makeup. Niki's disappearance had shaken her to the core.

She's so close to being released, Dawn thought. *I'd die if anything happened to her. She's young. She deserves a second chance at a good life.*

"All yours," Niki announced as she stepped from the bathroom. "I left you plenty of hot water."

Niki always insisted on showering first. Dawn knew that Niki showered in lukewarm water to save the hot water for her. Niki Sears was probably the most selfless person she had ever met.

Dawn let the steam fill the shower as the semiscalding water washed away the last remnants of her fear of losing Niki. She dried her hair and then slipped on an old T-shirt that now functioned as pajamas.

Niki's light was out, and the soft glow from Dawn's night-light was the only illumination in the room. Dawn was glad that Niki had fallen asleep quickly. Sleep always made things better.

Dawn slipped into bed and turned off her light. She lay on her back, replaying her day with Valerie Davis. She hated to admit that she found Val attractive. She suppressed the urge to touch herself as the warden's beautiful, brooding face floated through her mind. She jumped as Niki sat down on the edge of her bed.

Sobs racked Niki's small frame. Dawn threw back her sheet and held out her arms. "Come here, baby."

Niki wasted no time slipping into Dawn's bed and burying herself in the blonde's arms.

"You're trembling, Niki. It's okay, honey. There's nothing to be afraid of. I'm here."

"I was so afraid," Niki cried. "You've helped me so much. Made me pretty again. I knew Lucky would destroy everything. I would have fought her hard. I couldn't stand her touching me, and she would have beaten me."

"Shush, sweetie," Dawn cooed. "None of that happened. You're safe, and I won't leave you alone again. I promise." Dawn stroked Niki's back, calming her and reassuring her she was safe.

Niki sighed as she snuggled into the fragrant softness of her friend. No one had ever held her without demanding more from her. Finally, her body relaxed, and she slipped into a deep sleep.

##

Niki awoke at dawn. She lay still, afraid to move. It took her a few minutes to realize the protective body wrapped around her was Dawn. She inhaled, loving the scent of the woman sleeping with her. *I could stay right here forever*, she thought.

Dawn moved then inhaled sharply. Niki knew Dawn had just realized that she was holding her. Niki didn't move. She didn't want the feeling to end.

"Are you awake?" Dawn asked.

"Yes."

"Are you okay?"

"I'm more okay than I've ever been in my life," Niki murmured.

"Did you sleep well?"

"Yes."

"You should move to your bed," Dawn suggested.

"I should but I don't want to."

Dawn sighed as she tightened her arms around Niki and drifted back to sleep.

Chapter 10

Val poured her first cup of coffee and carried it onto the terrace of her two-story townhouse. The moon had disappeared, and the sun's rays were peeking over the horizon. The strong black coffee was just what she needed. She hadn't slept much. Dawn Fairchild had haunted her sleep.

She replayed the day she had spent with the gorgeous doctor. Dawn was right; she didn't belong in prison. Val had wrongly accused her. *If I retract my statement*, she thought, *I'll leave myself open to a perjury charge. A perjury conviction would discredit any warden in the prison system.*

Val's recommendation often meant the difference between parole and continued incarceration. If her reputation were impugned in any way, she would become a leper in the legal system, and her word would always be questioned. She would be transferred to some hole-in-the-ground human garbage dump where no one would even care about her innovative ideas, much less provide the funding to implement them.

She thought about some of the women who called her prison home.

FMC Carswell had the dubious distinction of housing the only woman in the U.S. with a federal death sentence. Lisa Lee Morgan was convicted of strangling pregnant Frankie Jo Starnes from behind and then cutting the woman's unborn child—eight months into gestation—from her womb. Morgan had been on death row for fourteen years.

Starnes had become Facebook friends with Lisa Morgan. Starnes and her husband raised French bulldogs and were expecting their first child. Morgan made an appointment to visit Starnes, pretending to be a buyer for one of her dogs. She traveled to Missouri where she killed Starnes, took the baby, and returned home to Kansas where she was arrested the next day.

The fast rescue of the baby and capture of Morgan were attributed to the use of computer forensics, which tracked Morgan and Starnes's online communications. Both bred French bulldogs and had attended the same dog shows.

Val wondered why women were so quick to give out personal information on Facebook.

Women like Lisa Morgan belong in my prison, Val thought. *The Dawn Fairchilds of the world do not. I can't destroy my own reputation, but I must restore Dawn's. No wonder she hates me.*

As Val dressed to face the day, she vowed to find a way to get Dawn out of her prison.

##

Visiting day was always abuzz with excited inmates waiting for their call to visit with family and friends. "Did you hear back from your mother?" Dawn asked Niki.

"No, but I didn't expect to." Niki gave her a faint smile. "You're lucky. Your folks come every week."

The drone of the prison intercom continued as the announcer rattled off the names of those who had visitors.

"Dawn Fairchild, Louise Palmer, and Niki Sears," the intercom squawked.

"Did you hear my name?" Niki jumped up and down. "Did they call my name?"

"I'm sure they did." Dawn laughed at her friend's excitement. "Come on. Our time starts when they call our names."

Niki followed Dawn to a large room furnished with metal tables, each surrounded by four chairs—all bolted to the floor. The guard looked at the sign-in sheet. "You two are at table twelve," she barked.

"We're both at the same table?" Niki asked the guard.

"Yeah, now move it. I got a line behind you."

Dawn grabbed Niki's hand and led her to the table where her mother and brother were waiting. "Mom, Flint, this is Niki Sears. Niki, this is my mother and brother."

Ruth Fairchild stood and hugged her daughter. Then she embraced Niki. "Dawn said you were beautiful."

Ruth's warm welcome relaxed Niki. *Dawn thinks I'm beautiful,* she thought.

"And she's right." Flint held out his hand to shake Niki's. Then he hugged his sister.

They spent the next hour discussing what was happening outside the prison. Ruth told Niki about her visit with Sylvia Sears Niki's mother. Dawn and Niki told them about the new equipment the hospital had received. "Dawn can do open-heart surgery now," Niki said, beaming.

"Do you work in the hospital too?" Flint asked.

"Yes. Dawn has taught me so much. She is a joy to work with. I have a degree in biology, and I'm delighted to put it to practical use."

Flint's eyes gleamed as he listened to the auburn-haired beauty sitting across from him.

Dawn was surprised when the intercom announced their time was up. Time had passed faster with Niki in the group. They said their goodbyes and hugged Ruth and Flint.

"I'll see you next week," Flint promised as he hugged Niki.

"I don't know if your mother will visit you or not," Ruth said. "She's a cold person."

Niki scrunched her nose. "I know."

"I'm sorry," Ruth mumbled to Niki as the guard waved her toward the exit. She hugged both women one last time and hurried for the door.

##

The hospital public address system crackled, and Dawn heard her name as she returned to the hospital. "Doctor Fairchild, report to the emergency room STAT."

Dawn sprinted to the ER with Niki close behind. "What's wrong?" she asked the head nurse.

"Thirty-four-year-old white female," the nurse rattled off. "Hung herself. Possible suicide. She turned blue."

The nurse had already put the woman on oxygen. Dawn checked the marks on her neck. "This looks more like someone choked her than a suicide. Unless, of course, she choked herself, which has been known to happen in prisons." Her sarcasm wasn't wasted on the guard.

Dawn picked up the dead woman's hand and examined her blue fingertips. "Cyanosis is obvious. She was without oxygen for more than ten minutes. She has bruising on her chest and torso."

Dawn proclaimed asphyxiation as the cause of death. "The body shows all the signs of burking."

Two male guards started to remove the inmate's body. "Leave it," Dawn commanded.

"Yeah, right," one of the men snorted as they continued to push the gurney from the room.

"Where are you taking the body?" Dawn demanded.

"Coroner," the guard grunted.

"I need to see the warden," Dawn told the female guard as the men left the room with the body. "Now!"

The guard glanced around and then spoke into the mic attached to her shirt. "Dr. Fairchild has requested to see the warden."

"The warden isn't on the premises," a voice answered back.

"When will she be back?" Dawn said.

The guard relayed her question.

"I have no idea," the voice replied.

"Ask her to call for me when she returns, no matter what time it is." Dawn was determined to give Val her views on the death of the prisoner.

"What were the names of the two guards who whisked away that woman's body?" Dawn asked the remaining guard. "What was the dead woman's name?"

"I don't know," the woman said, scowling as she edged toward the door.

Dawn took a step toward the guard, and Niki caught her arm, pulling the doctor back into the room as the guard fled.

"We need to go to our room," Niki muttered so no one could hear.

Dawn's jaw dropped as she whirled around to face her friend.

"We need to leave now!" Niki rasped.

The hard glint in Niki's eye startled Dawn, and she followed her friend from the room without further questions.

##

"What's going on?" Dawn closed the door to their room and locked it. Niki wedged a straight-backed chair under the doorknob.

"You called the cause of death perfectly," Niki whispered. "They'll come after us. Especially since you called for the warden."

"What do you mean?" Dawn glared. "She was murdered, and you know it."

"Of course I know it," Niki hissed. "But I didn't want them to know you spotted it so easily. Her body will probably disappear."

55

"Do you know who she was?"

"Yes, her name was Terry Shipman. She has all kinds of mental problems. The psych doc diagnosed her as bipolar. She had all the severe symptoms that accompany the disease: hallucinations, psychosis, grandiose delusions, paranoid rage, and days without sleeping." Niki paced the floor, listening for noises outside their door. "She was due to be released in a couple of days. She bragged that she was going to expose this place for the hellhole it is. Her family had already retained an attorney to sue Dr. Merrick for malpractice. That is probably what got her killed. I'm sure your warden is involved."

"She's not my warden." Dawn gritted her teeth.

A loud knock on their door sent Niki scurrying into Dawn's arms. "They've come for you. You hide. I'll tell them you're headed for the warden's office."

"No. I won't leave you alone," Dawn whispered.

"Who is it?" Dawn called out.

"Dr. Fairchild, it's me. Warden Davis," Val replied, her voice strong and confident.

"Don't open the door," Niki whispered. "She isn't what she seems."

"Lock yourself in the bathroom," Dawn said, pushing the petite woman toward the door. "I'll talk to her."

"Okay, but I'm shooting out of there if they try anything with you."

Dawn waited until Niki was in the bathroom before unlocking the door to their room.

"May I come in?" Val asked.

Dawn looked around her and down the hallway. "Are you alone?"

"Of course. I doubt I need a guard to visit you."

Dawn stepped back and motioned for Val to enter. Then she locked the door behind them.

"I'm sorry to come unannounced," Val said, "but I wanted to talk to you."

Dawn frowned. "You aren't here because of my request?"

"What request?"

"I just had the guard contact someone to ask if I could see you," Dawn explained. "I was told you were off the premises."

Anger flashed in Val's eyes. "I've been here all day."

"Are you aware that an inmate has been murdered?" Dawn asked.

"Murdered? A prisoner has been murdered on my watch?" Val said, all color draining from her face. "I've heard nothing about any murder."

"Have you been informed of a death?"

"No." Val's body was limp as she sat down in the chair that had been used to reinforce the door.

"About forty-five minutes ago, a woman was brought to the hospital. She had already turned blue from asphyxiation. Her body showed all the signs of burking."

"Burking?" Val said, nearly choking on the word. "Are you certain?"

"I know the symptoms when I see them." Dawn furrowed her brow. "I'm positive, and I have every reason to believe the culprits will seek me out tonight because of my call on the cause of death. I'm concerned for Niki's safety too.

"I also believe the body will disappear. The guards hustled it out of the hospital. They said they were taking the body to the coroner."

Val stared at Dawn as if she would disappear too. "We need to get you out of here."

"Do you have a safe room in the prison?" Dawn asked. "Someplace only you can get into?"

"Yes, but I've never felt threatened. I've never used it."

"Do you always walk around the prison without bodyguards?" Dawn asked in disbelief.

"I'm not walking around the prison," Val said in self-defense. "I'm in the hospital. I came to discuss something with you."

"It's still a prison hospital filled with corrupt guards and violent patients," Dawn said. "You're not that careless." She began to back away from the warden.

"You're actually afraid of me." Val gasped. "You don't trust me!"

"Why should I? Your lie is the reason I'm in this cesspool."

Val pulled her cell phone from her pocket and tapped the screen. She turned on the speakerphone. "Warden's office," squawked the person answering the phone.

"Penny, this is Warden Davis. Do I have any messages?"

"No, ma'am," Penny replied. "Everything's quiet on the home front, boss."

Dawn raised her brows and nodded at Val as if to say, "Told you so."

"Okay. Thanks, Penny. I'm heading home. See you tomorrow."

"Who do you trust in this place?" Dawn demanded after Val ended the call.

"I trusted Penny. She's the chief operator who mans the prison switchboard," Val fumed. "But I'm beginning to feel like I'm in an asylum where the patients are in charge. I don't know who I can trust."

"Do you have guards who are your personal bodyguards?" Dawn asked.

"Yes, but they go off duty when I leave the prison. I sent them on their way and then dropped by here to talk with you before I left for the day."

"Do you have some protocol in place if there's a riot or something you can't contain?"

"Yes, but I can't activate it from your room."

"Your cell phone . . . can't you call the police or sheriff's department?" Dawn reasoned.

"I . . . that would make me look foolish," Val argued. "Like I can't control my own prison."

"Warden, you don't have control of your prison," Dawn pointed out. "You have no officers under your control that you can trust. You don't know the good ones from the bad ones.

"You need some other law enforcement agency to help you sort out the ones who need to be fired or prosecuted and the ones you can trust."

"You're right." Val clenched her fist in anger. "But first we've got to get you out of here. If there has been a murder and they think you'll testify against them, your life isn't worth a plugged nickel."

"Niki was there when they brought in the woman's body," Dawn said. "We've got to get her out too."

"Where is she?"

Dawn walked to the bathroom door and knocked on it. "Niki, it's safe to come out."

Niki opened the door and joined them. "I was eavesdropping," she said, wrinkling her nose. "How do you plan to get us out of here?"

"My car is parked in the garage by my office," Val said. "If we can get to it, I'll go directly to the sheriff's department and come back with enough firepower to make certain I have control here. Then I'll conduct a thorough investigation into the woman's death.

"I encountered no one coming in the back way. The inmates are in their cells, so maybe we'll be lucky enough to get out unseen."

Chapter 11

Ducking into corridors and hiding at the sound of voices, the three women made it back to Val's office.

"The door to the safe room is inside my office." Val hesitated and then unlocked her door. "Come in here."

Dawn and Niki followed her as she scurried to the safe room and keyed in the access code. She opened the steel door, flipped on the lights, and motioned for them to enter the room.

Dawn looked around the safe room. It contained rations and water to sustain four people for a month. Sleeping bags were rolled up and stacked in the corner. A wall thermostat indicated a dedicated central air system, and a commode sat beside a sink in the far corner.

"I don't think—" Her sentence was interrupted as Val shoved Niki into her back. The safe room door slammed shut.

"What the hell?" Niki howled. "That bitch has locked us in here."

Dawn fought the rising panic. *If anything happens to Val, we're stuck in here. No one knows we're here.*

"I told you not to trust her," Niki huffed. "She's evil."

##

Val wasted no time activating the button that put her prison in lockdown. No one could open the doors but her. The guards were locked in the prison units they patrolled, and all prisoners were locked in their cells. Val was the only one who could move freely about the prison. She called Jerry Ridder, the leader of the police riot control team assigned to the prison, and explained her problem to him.

"I'm sure I can handle this situation," Val said, doing her best to sound confident. "But I'd like your team on standby just in case things get out of hand."

Jerry assured her he could have his men in the prison in under thirty minutes if necessary. "I'll call if I need you," she added.

Val unlocked her gun case and took out her Glock, shoved a clip into it, and racked it. As much as she hated wearing it, she slipped into a Kevlar vest and secured it. She put a full clip in each vest pocket.

She placed her gun on her desk and walked to the window of her office that overlooked the exercise area. No one was in sight.

Seconds later, her office door swung open and slammed against the wall as Flo Menton filled the doorway. The six-foot black woman looked menacing on her best day. Today she was terrifying. Val knew that Lucky didn't like Flo and had warned her about the woman on several occasions.

Without a word, Flo strode to Val's desk and picked up the warden's Glock.

"Flo, what are you doing here?" Val mustered as much bravado as possible as she walked to her desk.

Flo inspected the Glock as if she'd never seen a handgun. "As your trustee, I was in the kitchen making my nightly inspection when everything locked down. I thought I'd better come see what's going on. Make sure you're all right." She aimed the gun at a vase across the room and looked down its sights to the end of the barrel.

She held out the Glock to Val. "You should keep this in your hands at all times, Warden."

It took all the strength Val had to keep her hand from shaking as she reached for the Glock. "You came to help me?" she asked.

"Yeah," Flo muttered. "What's going on?"

Val told Flo about the murder in the prison and her fear that inmates and guards were after Dr. Fairchild and Niki. She watched Flo's face as she related the story. The trustee seemed genuinely concerned.

"You might want to send this to your cell phone." Flo held out a cell phone showing a picture of Terry Shipman crumpled in the corner of her cell. The words "The Rapist" were scrawled across the cell wall.

"How'd you get this?" Val demanded.

"I was the one who found her," Flo said, glaring at her. "She chewed on her arm until it bled. Then she wrote those two words in blood."

"How'd you get this cell phone?"

"Really, Warden?" Flo snorted. "I'm here to help, and you want to know how I got a damn cell phone?"

"I don't know who to trust," Val confessed.

"For starters, you can trust me." Flo grinned. "Don't trust Lucky. She's ninety percent of your problem. I know she bad-mouths me."

Val nodded.

"Most of the women on my cellblock are just trying to keep their heads down, do their time and get out of this place." Flo walked to the door and looked down the hallway. "Your problems are with the lifers. They've got nothing to lose. Why don't you call in the riot squad?"

"Flo, I've been here two years," Val said. "Have things improved over the past two years?"

"Yes, ma'am. The food just got better, and we always have the things we need, like toothpaste and soap. We still have guards that are meaner than hell, and some of your trustees abuse their power, but you are making a difference, Warden."

Val grimaced. "If I call in the riot squad, there will be a long-drawn-out investigation, and I'll be removed from this prison because I'm not capable of running the place. I want to make a difference, Flo. I really do."

"What can I do to help?" Flo asked.

"Help me identify the troublemakers," Val said. "I need to know who I can trust. Then I need them to help me. I need to put the dangerous ones in solitary confinement and return the prison operations to normal as quickly as possible."

"You have some guards you need to put in solitary confinement too," Flo reminded her. "They're just thugs in uniforms."

"What about my bodyguards?" Val held her breath waiting for the answer.

"They're all straight arrows," Flo said, grinning. "You did good on that."

Val pushed the video button that allowed them to observe each hallway in the prison.

"It looks like the inmates are asleep," Flo muttered. "They don't know there's a problem. Look! There!" Flo pointed out a group of two male guards and four women hurrying through the prison hallway. "They're trying to figure out what's going on. It's just a matter of time before they arrive here."

"Do you know them?" Val asked.

"Yeah. Lucky and her three henchmen and two of the most brutal guards in the place. They won't be easy to subdue."

"Can you use a gun?" Val whispered.

"Yeah, I'm good with a gun."

"Rifle or handgun?"

"Handgun. I can keep it hidden until I need it," Flo said.

Val reopened the gun case and handed the woman a Glock and two clips. "It's loaded. You'd better wear this vest too.

Flo checked the gun, racked it, and then pulled on the Kevlar vest. "We're ready."

"It looks like we can diffuse this problem by arresting the six roaming the hallways," Val noted. "They're our immediate threat."

Flo nodded. "We need to split them up. As long as they're together, we don't have a chance."

Chapter 12

Dawn pushed the buttons on the control for the central air conditioning. "It's like an oven in here," she said as the system kicked on and air started circulating in the small room.

"We have plenty of water and rations," Niki said, trying to put on a brave front. "Surely someone will notice we're unaccounted for in a week or so."

"We have no choice but to wait," Dawn said. "We should get as comfortable as possible."

Niki pulled the four sleeping bags from the corner and unrolled two of them. She used the other two as pillows.

Dawn grabbed two bottles of water from a case and sat down next to Niki.

"May I ask you a question?" Niki said, looking at Dawn through long lashes.

"Sure, you can ask. That doesn't mean I'll answer."

"What's burking?"

Dawn laughed out loud and relaxed on her sleeping bag. "During the early nineteenth century, two fellows named Burke and Hare were grave robbers. They excavated graveyard bodies to sell to medical schools. They decided preying on live alcoholics would make their job easier. So instead of digging up corpses they killed bums. A rather large fellow, Burke sat on the victim's chest, used one hand to cover the victim's nose and mouth and the other hand to close the victim's jaw, resulting in traumatic asphyxia.

"This allowed them to provide a body without digging. It's an example of homicidal traumatic asphyxia in combination with smothering, now called burking. There have been reports of police custody deaths attributed to this action.

"If we get out of this, I'm certain the autopsy will confirm my diagnosis."

"That's horrible," Niki said, sucking air through her teeth. "That's what they were trying to do to me the night you saved my life. When you started screaming, they stabbed me instead. I know who did it. I was afraid to identify them because I knew they would kill me."

They sat in silence, each wrestling with their own demons.

"I heard you say it was the warden's fault you're in prison," Niki said a few minutes later. "Could you elaborate?"

"Why not," Dawn said, sighing. "We know each other's secrets."

Dawn related her story and watched as anger flashed in Niki's eyes. "Does she know she lied?" Niki asked. "I mean, in her pain and the wreck and all maybe she did think it was you who crawled out of the driver's side."

"I don't know." Dawn considered Niki's suggestion. "Maybe she does feel she told the truth.

"Anyhow, I wish I knew what's going on," Dawn said, eager to change the subject. "This waiting is miserable."

"Thank you for having your folks request a visit with me today," Niki said as she played with the paper on her water bottle. "That's the first time anyone has visited me since I arrived in this place."

"They were glad to do it," Dawn assured her. "I bet you'll see a lot more of Flint. He was taken with you."

"He won't be when he learns about the horrible things I've done," Niki whispered.

"You've had some bad breaks." Dawn traced the back of Niki's hand with her finger. "That doesn't make you a bad person."

Niki smiled. "You've made me a better person. Your faith in me and your help have made the difference. I've never had anyone believe in me.

"Growing up, I was never good enough for my mother. She always found fault. Father doted on me, but he died when I was young, and Mother seemed to hate me even more."

"If not for you . . ." Dawn shuddered. "I'd be . . . I hate to think what I'd be. What really matters is that we're best friends. We have each other's back."

"Yeah, that's what really matters." Niki leaned her head on Dawn's shoulder and feigned sleep. *Except that I'm falling in love with you*, Niki thought.

##

"We need at least two more guns," Flo said. "Even one more person could help us lure them into the office and lock them in the safe room until your guards arrive."

Val bit her bottom lip. She didn't want to place Dawn in harm's way but knew no other way to get the drop on the marauders.

"Watch them," she commanded Flo as she keyed in the code to open the safe room door. "We need to move quickly to be ready for them."

Val stopped suddenly when she saw Niki asleep on Dawn's shoulder and the blonde curled around her. She moved to them and kicked Niki harder than necessary to wake her.

The little spitfire sprang to her feet, fists clenched and feet spread apart, ready to throw a punch.

"Easy, killer," Val barked. "We don't have time for this. I need your help."

Dawn wiped the sleep from her eyes and got to her feet. "What can we do?"

67

Val led them to the gun safe and handed each of them a Glock. "Do either of you know how to use a gun?"

"I do," Niki said.

Dawn frowned. "I've never touched a gun."

"Okay, then that makes you the bait," Val growled. "Sit at my desk. Lucky will lead a gang through the door any minute. Draw them as far into the room as possible. Niki, Flo, and I will be hiding behind the doors and filing cabinets. We must get the drop on them."

Loud brawling outside Val's door made everyone jump into their places. Dawn ran behind Val's desk, desperately wanting to keep something between her and the women about to enter the office. She fought the urge to crawl under the desk.

"The doc is mine," Lucky yelled over the din in the hallway. "I called dibs on her the first time I saw her."

"The warden's mine," a male voice hollered. "She's always chewing on my ass. I'll give her a taste of her own medicine, only more physical."

The door swung open. Lucky stuck her head in and then cautiously stepped into the room. She looked Dawn up and down and licked her lips. "Well, well, look who's holed up in the warden's office," she said, sneering.

Dawn backed up as far as possible, until her back pressed against the window ledge. She tried to speak but couldn't make her mouth work.

"You're scared, aren't you?" Lucky drawled. "You shouldn't be. I told you the first day I saw you that you were going to be my woman."

"You didn't tell me you would need a crowd to help you," Dawn taunted her. "I always thought you'd be woman enough to take care of me alone."

Lucky glanced around the room. "Where's the warden?"

"She and her bodyguards are patrolling the prison."
Dawn shrugged. "She didn't know anyone was on the
loose. She thinks you're all on lockdown."

Lucky turned to face the criminals behind her. "Go
find them. My ex is with them. She's a hell of a good-
looking woman now. You can have her, Lefty."

Mumbling and grousing came from the group.

"Go on," Lucky commanded. "You can have the doc
when I finish with her. You know I always share."

Dawn could hear the complaining and groaning as the
five shuffled down the hallway.

"You're gonna wish you'd been nicer to me." Lucky
leered at Dawn as she stepped closer. Suddenly, the door
slammed closed behind her. "What the hell?" She spun
around.

The butt of Flo's gun split Lucky's forehead open as
she slammed the gun as hard as she could into Lucky's
face.

Lucky hit the floor with a loud thud. Val and Flo
grabbed the trustee's arms and dragged the woman into the
safe room.

Dawn watched as blood pooled around Lucky's head.
"She'll bleed to death."

"Nah," Flo said, closing the door. "We won't be that
lucky."

Niki was still crouched behind a filing cabinet. The
thought of confronting Lucky had immobilized her.

Dawn took Niki's hand and pulled her from her hiding
place. "We're okay."

"One down," Val said, "five to go. She grabbed
handcuffs from the gun safe pitching three pair to Flo and
sticking a couple in her pocket."

"We have all the firepower," Flo said. "Let's just mow
them down."

"How would that look on my record?" Val's voice reached an octave it'd never heard before. She inhaled deeply as she tried to calm her nerves.

"Do you have Tasers?" Flo asked.

"Yes, there in the chargers." Val pointed toward a bank of electronic weapons. "And tear gas. Pepper spray."

"I can use pepper spray," Dawn volunteered. "It's saved me on more than one occasion."

All four women grabbed Tasers and pepper spray. "Let's go get us some white trash," Flo said, grinning gleefully.

It didn't take them long to catch up with the noisy hooligans. Flo and Val ducked into a doorway and motioned for Dawn and Niki to do the same. Flo nodded, and Val stepped into the hallway and backed past the three women lying in wait.

"You take that corridor," Val yelled so the criminals could hear her. "I'll go down this one."

The renegade guards and inmates turned and sprinted in the direction of Val's voice, confident they could overpower her.

When the thugs turned the corner, they met a shocked Val, who suddenly seemed disoriented. "Lefty?" she said to the guard. "What's going on here?"

"We're taking over this dump." Lefty's demented laughter curdled Val's blood. She continued to back away from the group until they were between her and the other three women.

"Now!" Val yelled as she sprayed Lefty and the lead inmate with a hefty dose of pepper spray. Dawn and Niki did the same to the ruffians closest to them. Flo's weapon of choice was the Taser. She jabbed it into the necks of the flailing hoodlums.

The criminals clawed at their eyes as they gasped for breath. Despite all the clawing and twitching, Flo and Val managed to handcuff all five lawbreakers.

"Damn you, Flo," one of the guards screamed. "You'll pay for this, you traitor. I'll kill you."

Flo responded by increasing the voltage on her Taser and shoving it between his legs.

Dawn cringed at the smell of burning hair and flesh. Suddenly, a team of guards filled the corridor, their weapons drawn.

Niki sprang in front of Dawn as the guards raised their weapons. "It's the warden," the leader yelled, holding up her hand. "Stand down."

"Thank God you're here," Val gasped. "Put these five in solitary confinement, and I have another one in my office."

##

After the six rebels had been locked up safely, Val pushed the button that returned control of the cellblocks to the guards. Life went on as usual. No one was aware of the life-and-death battle the warden and her friends had fought during the night.

Val turned the two crooked guards over to the local authorities for indictment. Lucky and the three inmates involved were serving life sentences. She initiated the paperwork to transfer them to Huntsville, a high-security prison where they'd have no chance to intimidate and molest other inmates.

Val ordered lie detector tests for all guards and civil personnel at the prison. Flo had given her a list of guards and inmates she had seen abusing other women in the prison. Val was determined that no inmate would suffer at the hands of her employees.

She called Dr. Reynolds to inform him that Dr. Fairchild and Niki Sears would not be reporting for duty. "They'll be back as usual tomorrow," she said. "Oh, and Lance, I'm sending you Flo Menton. Nothing is wrong with her but exhaustion. Please see that she gets three good meals and a lot of rest. I'll check on her tomorrow."

Val rested her head on the back of her chair. The adrenaline was finally draining from her body. She closed her eyes and let images of Dawn Fairchild play across her mind in slow motion. She knew she should get Dawn out of her prison, but she couldn't bear the thought of letting her go, not seeing her every day.

Dawn woke from a deep sleep. She looked at the clock: 7:15. She didn't know if it was morning or night.

She tried to recall the day's events but only had memories of the horrific night she had spent with Niki, Val, and Flo. Had they really saved the prison from an inmate takeover? She turned her head to the left to locate Niki. Her bed was empty. For a moment she panicked; then she heard the sound of running water.

Niki's safe. She's in the shower. Dawn slipped back into sleep.

"Wake up, sleepy head," Niki said as she bounced on Dawn's bed. "We've slept all day and I'm starving."

Dawn stretched, and Niki fought the desire to straddle the gorgeous blonde's waist and kiss her into tomorrow. Niki tried to tamp down the flame that was spreading up her throat and onto her face.

Dawn scrutinized her friend. "Are you running fever?"

"No, I'm starving." Niki darted to her closet and pulled out a T-shirt and jeans. "Let's go see if we can scrounge up something in the hospital kitchen."

Dawn laughed at Niki's exuberance. "Have I ever told you how much you light up my life?" she said, heading for the shower.

"No, you never have." Niki beamed. *Maybe, just maybe,* she thought.

72

Niki and Dawn talked quietly as they walked down the corridor to the hospital cafeteria. "It looks like the kitchen is still serving," Niki noted.

Dawn looked around the lunchroom. "There are a lot of new faces in here. Most of them are armed personnel and younger than usual."

"Val didn't waste any time getting rid of the problem guards," Niki added. "I wonder if she's been able to clean out the high-security cellblocks too."

They selected their food from the buffet and found a table away from the others. "The food looks delicious," Niki said as she placed her tray on the table.

Less than a minute later, two attractive female guards walked toward their table. "Mind if we join you?" one of them said.

"Actually, you aren't allowed to fraternize with us," Niki informed them.

The other guard laughed. "Other than being too beautiful, what's so special about you?"

"We're inmates," Niki said.

"Right." The guard laughed as she continued to place her tray on the table.

Dawn looked up. "You really can't sit with us. We're prisoners here."

The guard picked up her tray and backed away from the table. "Why are you allowed in the hospital cafeteria?"

"I'm a doctor and she's a nurse," Dawn explained. "We live in the doctors' quarters. We're not dangerous."

"Our apologies." The young guard's half smile didn't hide her uneasiness as they backed away.

"I feel like a pariah," Niki grumbled.

"We're living between two worlds," Dawn said, her brow furrowed. "It's good we have each other to lean on."

They ate their dinner, chatting about the events of the last twenty-four hours. Then they returned to their room.

"Want to watch TV?" Dawn asked as they changed into the T-shirts that doubled as their pajamas.

"Sure. Let's see if the warden made the news." Niki pulled on one of Dawn's T-shirts before searching for the remote. She bent over to look for it under a chair.

Dawn was surprised and frightened by the feeling that closed her throat, tightened her chest, and spread into her lower abdomen. It took her several seconds to identify the emotion as desire. She couldn't pull her eyes away from Niki, who looked so damn cute in her oversized T-shirt.

Dawn imagined sliding her hands up Niki's firm legs, over her hips, caressing her back, and tangling her fingers in Niki's luxurious auburn hair.

"Here it is," Niki said as she turned around, the remote in her hand. Dawn let her gaze drift from Niki's legs to her eyes. Niki blushed.

"I didn't . . . I'm so sorry. I . . . ." Dawn dashed into the bathroom and locked the door behind her.

What is wrong with me? Dawn chastised herself. *Have I been in prison that long? I've never been drawn to a woman. Niki's my best friend. She's had enough women looking at her like that to last her a lifetime. I'm no better than Lucky.*

Although she had showered earlier, Dawn turned on the cold water and stepped under it. *God, this is cold coat, but how could I letch after Niki like that? I don't think I can face her. She knew exactly what I was thinking. I could see it in her eyes.*

Dawn took her time blow-drying her hair and slipped her T-shirt back on. She sat on the commode lid, trying to think of the right words to say to Niki. She looked at the time. She had been in the bathroom over an hour. She had to face Niki sooner or later.

Dawn mustered all her courage, closed her eyes against her shame, and opened the door. The room was dark except for the nightlight on her bedside table. Niki was asleep.

It would be just like Niki to make things as easy as possible for me, Dawn thought as she tiptoed across the room and slipped into her bed.

Dawn lay awake, trying to push the thoughts of Niki from her mind. "I'm not a lesbian," she mumbled as she drifted off to sleep.

Chapter 13

Dawn awoke early the next morning, pulled on her scrubs, and picked up her shoes. She locked the door behind her, making certain Niki was safe. She sat on the floor while putting on her shoes and then headed for the infirmary.

"Warden Davis would like to see you in her office," Dr. Reynolds informed her when she entered the room.

Dawn checked the computer charts of a few patients and then headed for Val's office.

Val was on the phone and motioned for Dawn to sit in the chair across from her. Dawn looked around the room as Val continued talking. She caught her breath when she saw Niki's case file lying in the center of Val's desk. A hundred terrifying thoughts ran through Dawn's mind. The scariest one was, *Is Val transferring Niki to another prison?*

"Thank you, Director. I appreciate your continued faith in me." Val hung up the phone and smiled at Dawn.

"I wanted to personally thank you for your help in securing the prison and preventing a possible riot." Val looked down at her hands and opened Niki's file. "I know I could not have accomplished that without the help of you and Niki.

"Since your arrival here, Niki Sears has made a miraculous turnaround. She has taken advantage of the educational programs the prison offers and has completed a semester toward her nursing degree.

"The fact that she already had a BS in biology certainly helped. She's at the top of her class here.

"I've made arrangements for Niki to continue her education at the Harris College of Nursing at Texas Christian University. She'll have a full ride—books and tuition. She'll also receive a small stipend each month for her personal use.

"I've also arranged for the best rhinoplasty surgeon in the Dallas-Fort Worth area to fix Niki's nose. By the time she walks out of here, she'll be as beautiful as any woman you'll ever meet," Val continued.

"It's just my way of apologizing and saying thank you to her. Flo tells me Niki would have died in here if not for you."

"Have you told Niki?" Dawn asked.

"No, I wanted you to know. She seems to have developed a dependency on you, and I'm not sure it's healthy."

I'm the one with the unhealthy attachment, Dawn thought.

"She'll complete her sentence on the thirty-first of next month," Val added. "She will walk out of here a free woman, pending a psych evaluation. I need you to talk to Niki and prepare her for her psych interview."

"Who will do the review?"

"Dr. Merrick. He has Niki scheduled for three o'clock Friday afternoon."

Dawn grimaced. "Merrick? I've heard bad things about him."

"Such as?"

"He's quick to prescribe drugs to patients and has actually caused addiction in a few of them. He mustn't prescribe drugs to Niki."

"I think those stories are exaggerations from malcontent inmates," Val said, throwing back her shoulders. "I've found his work to be exemplary."

77

"Inmates have told me he was sexually inappropriate with them. May I attend the session with Niki?"

"No, it's not allowed. Doctor-patient privilege and all that."

Dawn shrugged. "I'm certain Niki will be thrilled with your arrangements. In many ways it seems only a few months have flown by since I was incarcerated. In other ways it seems like a lifetime ago."

Val walked around her desk and placed a comforting hand on Dawn's shoulder. "I'm so sorry," she whispered.

"But not sorry enough to tell the truth." Dawn stood and left the room.

##

"Hey, you sneaked out of our room this morning." Niki bumped Dawn's shoulder, letting the doctor know that things were good between them. "Everything's copasetic."

"Look at you, using fifty-cent words," Dawn teased. "Want to get breakfast?"

"Of course. You know me, I'm starving." Niki linked her arm through the blonde's and started chattering about a patient with an organism in her eye. "It's repulsive. She told me she had an orgasm in her eye." Niki giggled. "I had to leave the room to keep from laughing in her face.

"I cleaned it but turned her over to Dr. Reynolds. I thought it was Staphylococcus aureus, but after I cleaned it, I saw a parasite in her eye A tiny worm was swimming around in there."

"Now you're just showing off," Dawn said, her eyes twinkling. "Staph infection is so much easier to say."

"Yeah." Niki grinned. "I just threw that in to impress you."

Dawn smiled as they entered the cafeteria. "You've always impressed me."

##

"Dr. Fairchild, report to the emergency room." The public address system blared throughout the hospital.

"We're up." Dawn drained the last drop of coffee from her cup, and they headed for the emergency room.

Dr. Reynolds looked up as Dawn entered the operating chambers. "I need your help. First birth and it's a breech baby. I need you to reach in and turn it. Your hands are smaller than mine."

"Are you insane?" Dawn whispered. "That's too dangerous. Breech babies are always delivered by Caesarean."

"I've never performed a Caesarean," Reynolds said under his breath.

"I'm a surgeon," Dawn declared. "That's what I do. Unless you have a problem assisting me."

"I'd be proud to assist you, Dr. Fairchild." His sheepish smile made it clear he was happy to give up his spot as lead physician.

"Put her under just like you would for any other surgery," Dawn instructed the anesthesiologist. "This is a simple procedure."

Niki arranged Dawn's operating utensils and stood by to assist the doctor.

Dawn prepared to make the incision.

"She's hemorrhaging!" Niki gasped. "Dawn, she's hemorrhaging badly."

"Her vitals are dropping," the anesthesiologist said, his calm announcement alerting Dawn to the dangers of moving slowly

Without hesitating, Dawn made the abdominal incision and prepared to make the incision into the uterus. "Did you try to turn the baby yourself?" she asked Reynolds.

"I might have."

"Might have? Dammit, did you or not?"

"I did," Reynolds mumbled.

"You ruptured the umbilical cord," Dawn said. "We must get the baby out quickly, or it'll drown in the blood."

Moving with the confidence of an experienced surgeon, Dawn clamped off the umbilical cord to prevent additional blood from flooding the mother's uterus. She carefully lifted the newborn from the cavity and handed it to Niki.

"Vitals are returning to normal," the anesthesiologist informed the team.

Niki cleared the baby's mouth and washed its face. Within seconds, the infant's cries filled the operating room. Niki passed the crying baby to a nurse and resumed her position beside Dawn.

Dawn suctioned the blood from the patient's uterus and abdominal area, removed the placenta, clipped off the umbilical cord, and double-checked to make certain everything was cleaned properly. She sutured the uterus, the umbilical cord connection, and the abdomen. "All done," she said, breathing an exhausted sigh.

From the observation room, Val watched the scene below her. She was aware that Dawn's swift action had saved the new mother. If Dawn hadn't been there, the mother probably would have died. Not that Dr. Reynolds was inept; he was just in over his head.

Dr. Dawn Fairchild had nerves of steel. Nothing rattled her in the operating room. Val admired the doctor's self-confidence and her ability. "What will I do without you?" she mumbled.

Chapter 14

Dawn stripped off her blood-covered scrubs and stood under the hot water. She hurriedly shampooed her hair and soaped and rinsed her body. She wanted to leave plenty of hot water for Niki.

"Your turn, Nik," she called out, towel-drying her hair as she walked from the bathroom.

Niki's broad grin greeted her. "I like it when you call me Nik. It's like a term of endearment."

"It is." Dawn beamed. "You're the best surgical nurse I've ever had."

Dawn had mixed emotions about Niki's release. She was afraid the petite woman would backslide. She was aware of how difficult—sometimes impossible—it was to overcome drug addiction. She worried that others would take advantage of Niki, even break her heart.

Dawn worried her bottom lip as she tried to overcome her fears for Niki.

"It's so damn sexy when you do that thing with your lip," Niki murmured standing in front of Dawn. She tilted her head back to look into Dawn's face.

One movement. A few inches and I'll know how her lips taste. Dawn choked. She stepped back as a coughing spasm shook her body. "I . . . excuse me. Water. I need water."

"Are you okay?" Niki asked from the bathroom doorway.

"I'm fine. I just got choked." Dawn sat down in a straight-backed chair and pulled the room's only other chair in front of her. "We need to talk."

"We need to talk," Niki huffed. "The beginning of the death of any relationship." Niki didn't sit but turned her back on Dawn and walked a few feet away.

Dawn tried to lighten the mood. "No, silly. It's about your release."

"My release?" Niki whirled around. "I've been so happy working with you that I'd forgotten about getting out of this place. What will you do? Who will protect you?"

Dawn chuckled. "I'm sure the warden will take care of me."

"I'm sure she will."

Niki's sullen attitude shocked Dawn. "I thought you'd be happy." Dawn frowned, and when Niki opened her mouth to reply, Dawn held up her hand to stop her.

"Listen. Warden Davis has arranged a scholarship for you to the Harris College of Nursing at Texas Christian University. It's a full ride. Tuition, books, and a stipend for spending money."

Niki glared at her. "Who do I have to do for that?"

"What? No, Niki, it's not like that. Val is doing this to thank you for helping prevent the prison riot. This is a good thing."

Dawn stood and caught Niki by the shoulders, forcing her to look into her eyes. "I would never be involved in anything that wasn't in your best interest. You know that. I . . . I care for you."

Dawn dropped her hands to her side. She didn't trust herself to continuing holding Niki.

"She's arranged for the best rhinoplasty surgeon in the Dallas-Fort Worth area to fix your nose. You'll be even more beautiful than you are now."

Niki's hand went to her cheek. "What about the scar? I don't think I need surgery on my face. The scar is almost gone."

Dawn's fingertips gently traced the small scar that ran from Niki's ear to her cheek. "It's barely noticeable. I think it adds character to your beautiful face. Like a tiny butterfly on a rose."

Niki pressed Dawn's hand against her cheek and turned her head to kiss the palm. "I love you," she whispered.

"Not here," Dawn breathed, trying to ignore the fire burning its way through her body. "Not in prison."

Niki blinked back tears and backed away slowly, releasing the soft hand that had made her feel more loved than anything in her life.

Chapter 15

Val reread the reports she was receiving from various departments. She almost gagged when she realized that prisoners in Texas were being fed a product similar to dog food.

VitaMaxPro was a soybean-based powder that all Texas prisons were using as a meat substitute for chicken and beef. Four real-meat hamburger patties became eight patties with half the nutrition when VitaMaxPro was added. She buzzed her secretary.

"I want to speak with Sue Creighton now!"

The prison dietician was in Val's office within ten minutes.

"You wanted to see me?" Sue steeled herself for the tongue-lashing she knew was coming.

"Sue, please tell me if I'm wrong. I have received information from several departments and supporting entities within the prison system, and it appears we are feeding all Texas prisoners dog food three times a day."

Sue studied the warden before responding. "Yes, ma'am."

"Yes, ma'am?" Val gasped. "Is that all you have to say?"

"I'm only following orders," Sue said with a shrug. "When the edict came down—before you came—I fought it, but the TDCJ director ordered me to be a team player."

"What is that supposed to mean?" Val demanded.

"Do as I'm told and keep my mouth shut."

"Why didn't you go to the FBI or someone?" Val croaked. "This borders on criminal."

"And then stand in the unemployment line?" Sue smirked. "No thank you."

"I promise you protection," Val said. "Tell me what you know about this."

"Director Craft signed a big contract with VitaMaxPro and took delivery of enough of the stuff to feed the Texas prison system inmates for a year. It's stored in a humongous warehouse in Paducah. We receive a monthly shipment of it.

"Craft ordered all prison dieticians to rewrite prison menus to incorporate VitaMaxPro as a meat substitute three times a day on a daily basis."

"Is that healthy?"

Sue snorted. "Not at all. Even the owner of the company called it overuse and didn't condone it."

"Thank you, Sue." Val raked her fingers through her hair and sighed. "As I said, I'll protect you."

Sue nodded and walked to the door. She turned before opening it. "Warden, if you pursue this, who's going to protect you?"

Is the entire system riddled with criminals? Val thought as she looked at the $41.6 million contract signed at the beginning of the year by Buddy Craft, director of the Texas Department of Criminal Justice. Documents showed at least six politicians had pushed the purchase of VitaMaxPro.

Buddy Craft is so entrenched in the Criminal Justice department that a Texas tornado couldn't unseat him. The only one who will lose their job is me.

Val wrestled with her conscience. Did she keep her mouth shut and keep her lucrative position or report what appeared to be illegal activities to the authorities?

Can I really make a difference when the TDCJ is a quagmire of crooked politicians and officials?

The criminal activity went far beyond the walls of her own prison. It was entrenched in every Texas prison, affecting every prisoner.

She spent the night researching the possible side effects of consuming to much VitaMaxPro. *Miscarriage!* The word was in every report. Ingesting large amounts of VitaMaxPro could result in a pregnant woman miscarrying.

She pulled up studies that had been conducted on women inmates in Texas. Their miscarriage rate was double that of other states. *How had Craft and his cronies kept this quiet?*

Val knew that if she opened this can of worms her career would be over. If she remained silent she became complicit in one of the biggest Texas scandals since the Sharpstown scandal thirty years ago.

One document made up her mind for her. It was Craft's directive pressuring his subordinates to market the new soy-based chicken and beef supplement to Texas school children.

Why is Craft pushing VitaMaxPro? she wondered.

Chapter 16

Following their usual routine, Dawn and Niki entered the cafeteria at 7:00 a.m. The room was filled with new guards who were wolfing down their food. "The warden said eight o'clock sharp," a stout-looking woman shouted over the din.

"What's going on?" Dawn asked the guard in line in front of her.

"We're having orientation, and the warden is addressing us this morning," the woman answered. "All personnel are supposed to attend. I think you're included."

"I doubt that," Dawn replied.

"I would love for both of you to attend." Val's sultry voice made the fine hair stand up on the back of Dawn's neck. "I'd like to get your feedback on my talk. After you finish breakfast, please join us in the auditorium."

Niki looked around at the room full of new guards. She hoped they were better than the old regime. She turned her attention to Val as she ascended the platform at the front of the room.

"How many of you know why we had job openings?" Val surveyed the group, looking for a raised hand.

A black female guard stood up. "Because a third of your workforce was charged with sexual assault or sexual contact with inmates."

"That is correct," Val said, frowning. "In Texas, sexual contact between staff and inmates is a felony punishable by up to two years in prison. Consent is not a defense. Any guard who participates in sexual contact with an inmate will be fired and prosecuted to the fullest extent of the law. I will not tolerate prisoner abuse or harassment.

"If you feel that you will be tempted to abuse the prisoners under my protection, you need to resign today. If you ever feel that you can't treat the prisoners humanely, please let me know. This is a tough job, and occasionally you will need to get away from it to feel human.

"Some of our inmates are criminally insane. They are dangerous and will kill you, so pay attention during your training," Val continued. "You must deal with them without abusing them. You will be taught to diffuse dangerous situations while protecting yourself.

"Some of our inmates suffer from nymphomania. They will make advances and try to touch you. They will try to seduce you in every way possible. Do not let them. We now have one officer for every ten prisoners. You will work two to a team and will rotate partners every thirty days.

"You will be required to take a lie detector test every sixty days." Val paused, scanning the audience as she let her words sink in.

"Does anyone have any questions?"

Dawn listened as the new hires asked questions. Val was patient and answered all their inquiries—even the difficult ones. Dawn was lost in thought when Niki nudged her in the ribs.

"Yes, we did identify the two guards responsible for the death of Terry Shipman. The cause of death was burking," Val said.

A murmur ran through the room, and the same black female guard got to her feet again. "Ma'am, some of us don't know what burking is."

"I'll let Dr. Fairchild explain the mechanics of burking." Val motioned for Dawn to come to the podium.

Niki listened with pride as Dawn related the information about burking. She was poised and comfortable speaking in front of the new officers. "Unfortunately, this cause of death is most often identified in prisoners or police detainees. It is the first thing we look for in asphyxiation deaths."

The new guards talked among themselves as Dawn returned to her seat. Val waited until they quieted and then continued. "Are there any more questions?"

Again, the same woman spoke for the entire group. "Warden, what do you classify as sexual contact with an inmate?"

Val frowned. "Anything sexual. Kissing, touching their private areas, oral sex, fondling. You get the picture. If you must ask, it is probably wrong. When in doubt, don't.

"Any other questions? If not, you are dismissed."

As Niki and Dawn waited for the new employees to leave the room, Val approached them, a warm smile on her face. "I've arranged for the two of you to have lunch with me," she said. "I'd like to get any feedback you might have for me."

"I have moved quickly to implement security changes to protect the inmates," Val informed them as she poured tea into their ice-filled glasses and offered them their choice of sweeteners. "I've got to find a way to encourage the guards to police themselves. That's why I'm rotating their partners every thirty days. I don't want anyone to get too comfortable with their fellow officer."

"What happened to Lucky?" Niki asked. "Is she somewhere she can't escape?"

"Yes." Val nodded knowingly. "Lucky will never hurt you again."

"Did you have an opportunity to discuss the rhino surgery?" Val asked. "I feel so guilty that you suffered so much in this prison. You and I arrived here about the same

89

time. I was trying to make gradual changes, but I was wrong. I should have made sweeping changes like the ones I'm implementing now."

"Things have worked out for the best," Niki said, casting a shy glance at Dawn.

Val didn't miss the exchange between the two inmates.

"I think you did an outstanding job in the meeting," Dawn said. "You left no doubt in anyone's mind about the consequences of prisoner brutality."

"Thank you," Val half smiled and passed the basket of bread.

Chapter 17

"Dawn Fairchild, Lindsey Lucas, Brenda Lewis, Niki Sears . . ." The PA system blared the names of those who had visitors.

"My name! They called my name." An excited Niki caught Dawn's hand and pulled her toward the door. "Thank you for getting me visitors. Do I look too awful?"

Dawn examined the single bandage that remained across the bridge of Niki's nose following the rhinoplasty. "No, you're gorgeous. A few more days and the bandage can come off, but that's a call your surgeon needs to make."

They entered the visitor's area and waited for the guard to tell them their table number. Ruth Fairchild was already waving at her daughter.

"Number 18," the guard barked.

Niki had to concentrate to keep from running to the Fairchilds. *Dawn is lucky to have such a loving family.*

"Niki, darling." Ruth Fairchild held Niki at arm's length. "What happened to your nose?"

Niki beamed. "The warden had it fixed. She said it was broken under her watch, so she arranged for a top rhinoplasty surgeon to fix it. It will look much better in a couple of weeks when the swelling is gone."

Flint pulled out Niki's chair. "I thought it looked great as it was," he said.

"Thank you." Niki blushed and sat down.

They spent the next hour telling the Fairchilds about Niki's scholarship to TCU and discussing her release.

"We'll pick you up," Flint volunteered.

"You can stay with us until school starts," Ruth added.

"That is so sweet of you." Niki blinked away the hot tears that pooled in her eyes. "I can't tell you how wonderful it feels to know I have friends on the outside."

"You can count on us." Flint covered Niki's small hand with his large, well-manicured one.

Niki smiled hesitantly. *Until you know all there is to know about me*, she thought.

Niki and Dawn sat on the bed, leaning against the headboard as they chatted about the day.

"Your mom and brother are nice," Niki said.

"I'm fortunate."

"My psych evaluation is tomorrow," Niki reminded her.

"I know."

"I wish you could go with me. I've had problems with Merrick before."

"What kind of problems?"

"He always offered me drugs in exchange for favors. On two occasions he gave me drugs that he said would help me relax. I woke hours later on his couch in a disheveled state. I have no idea what transpired."

"I tried to talk with the warden about him," Dawn said, "but she insisted he's one of the good guys."

"I can give you the names of three women he raped after drugging them," Niki muttered.

"Were the incidences reported?"

"Yes, but nothing ever came of it. I reported him too. Maybe he won't remember me. I look a lot different now."

"Let's go talk to the warden." Dawn insisted.

##

Val's secretary informed them the warden was out of the office all day.

"I don't know what to do," Niki said. "If I don't get a good psych evaluation it will hold up my release. I have to go. I'll just take my chances with Dr. Merrick. Until then, I'll stay busy to keep my mind off things. I need to restock the infirmary anyway."

"I'm going to make my rounds," Dawn said as she picked up her hospital laptop. "I'll meet you in the room at two thirty."

As soon as Dawn was out of Niki's sight, she turned and headed for Dr. Merrick's office. She introduced herself as Dr. Fairchild, not bothering to add that she was an inmate.

"I've seen you in the doctor's lounge," the girl at the desk acknowledged. "I'm Justine, Dr. Merrick's secretary." Justine was amiable but explained that the doctor was in a meeting in the assistant warden's office.

Dawn wrote a message on a sticky note she grabbed from the receptionist's desk. "May I put this note on his desk?" she asked.

"I really should put it—"

"Please." Dawn flashed her sweetest smile. "It concerns a patient, and the information is meant for Dr. Merrick's eyes only. I'm sure he shares everything with you, but that's his prerogative, not mine. I'm sure you understand."

"Sure. You doctors have to stick together," Justine said, her head bobbing. "Obviously his office is the one with his name on the door. You can slip in there and put the note on his desk."

Dawn thanked her and headed for Merrick's office. She was pleased that the door had no lock. The windowless room was tiny and poorly furnished, lacking the professional feel of most doctors' offices. A long sofa backed up to the wall shared with the waiting room. Two straight-backed chairs were in front of the desk. An overstuffed armchair faced the sofa. Dawn shuddered at the thought of Merrick trapping Niki on the couch.

Dawn stuck the note to the center of Merrick's desk. It said, "Dr. Fairchild @ 4."

That should keep Merrick wondering, Dawn thought as she left his office, nodding to the ever-present guard at the psychiatrist's waiting room door.

"Ready for your meeting with the shrink?" Dawn tried to put Niki at ease, but she was also concerned about Niki being alone with the doctor.

"I'll walk with you to his office and sit in his waiting room," Dawn reassured her. "Just knock on the wall behind the sofa if you need me."

Niki nodded but remained silent.

Dawn sat in a chair against the wall of Merrick's office as Justine announced Niki to the psychiatrist. "Your three o'clock is here, sir."

"Miss Sears, how delightful to see you again." His voice disappeared as Justine closed his door.

"Please have a seat." Merrick gestured toward the chair across the desk from him. "So, you're leaving us." He thumbed through the forms on his desk. "And you need a clean bill of mental health from me."

Dawn strained to hear any sounds of distress coming from Merrick's office, but all she heard was a barely audible hum of voices. Dawn touched the syringe in her pocket, drawing comfort from its presence. Her mind went to the future.

Next week Niki would be released from prison. She would be safe with Dawn's family and out of harm's way. That was the good part. The bad part was that Niki would be gone from her life.

The silence caught her attention. There was no sound coming from Merrick's office. Dawn sprung from her chair and reached the psychiatrist's door in seconds. She turned the knob and charged into the office.

Niki was knocked out on the sofa. Merrick was standing over her, his belt unbuckled, slacks unzipped, and his appendage sticking out.

Justine looked over Dawn's shoulder. "What the hell?" she whispered in Dawn's ear.

"It looks like your boss was about to rape Miss Sears," Dawn charged. "Or do you have some other excuse for your dilly wacker hanging out, Dr. Merrick?"

A startled Merrick turned to face the two women and the guard who had rushed in to see what the commotion was about.

"Please take Dr. Merrick to the holding room and keep him there until the warden returns," Dawn insisted, giving orders as if she oversaw the prison. The guard obeyed her.

Justine held out her cell phone toward Dawn. "You might want this."

"Why?" Dawn asked.

"I just recorded the entire incident," Justine explained.

"Thank you," Dawn whispered.

Dawn knelt beside the sofa and shook Niki by the shoulders. "Niki, baby, wake up. Niki, it's me, Dawn. She patted Niki's cheek, but the young woman was out cold.

Dawn asked Justine to call Dr. Reynolds and request a gurney. "Assure him it isn't an emergency."

Within minutes a nurse arrived to transport Niki to the infirmary. Dawn walked beside her, dabbing the drainage from Niki's nose. She prayed Merrick hadn't damaged the rhinoplasty surgery. She'd know more when she got Niki into the infirmary and could examine her.

##

A thorough exam convinced Dawn that Niki was okay. Her nose was perfect, and whatever drug Merrick had given her would wear off.

"Hey, how's your patient?" Val asked as she pulled back the drapes around Niki's bed.

"She'll be okay," Dawn muttered, still seething. "No thanks to your Dr. Merrick. If I hadn't been there he would have raped her."

"You don't know that," Val barked.

Dawn pulled out Justine's cell phone and played the video for Val. "I'm pretty sure he wasn't trying to sell her Tupperware."

Val fought to control the anger the video invoked. "I'll take care of him," she promised. "He'll spend the rest of his life behind bars."

"If you're really serious, I have the names of three other inmates he has raped."

Val scowled. "Why haven't I been given this information sooner?"

"I tried to tell you, and all three women filed complaints with your office."

"I never saw them," Val said. "I've never had a complaint about Dr. Merrick cross my desk."

"Your staff really does keep you in the dark," Dawn snapped. "How convenient."

"Look, I didn't come to fight with you." Val bowed her head. "I came to check on Niki and apologize for not listening to you.

"And yes, my staff was keeping me in the dark, but that has changed. When you have time, I'd like to see you in my office. No rush. I just need to talk with someone who isn't afraid to give me honest feedback."

"When Niki comes to, I'll stick my head in," Dawn promised.

Chapter 18

Niki brushed her long auburn hair and watched Dawn as she sat on the bed reading a patient's file on her iPad. "I leave in the morning," she said.

Dawn turned off the device and looked up at her roommate. "I know. I've tried not to think about it."

"Can we at least talk about us?" Niki said.

Dawn's stomach did a summersault. "Us?"

"Dawn Fairchild, sometimes you can be so damn infuriating that I could choke you." Niki slung her hairbrush across the room.

"Oh, I knew it. You do have a temper," Dawn teased. "I've never been involved with a redhead, but I've heard they have awful tempers."

"Don't!" Niki huffed. "Don't tease when I'm trying to ask you about the rest of my life."

"The rest of your life?" Dawn closed her eyes. "I can't have this discussion with you. I fight every day to keep my hands off you. I've never wanted anyone so badly in my life. I only need to be strong one more day."

"Why? You know I love you."

"And right now, I love you," Dawn admitted. "But I don't know if that's because you're the best thing that has ever happened to me or the best thing in this place.

"Being here, locked away from the rest of the world, skews one's ability to discern what's real. Will we still feel the same two years or ten years from now? Do you really feel love for me, or is it gratitude?

"I don't make commitments lightly," Dawn concluded.

"I've never made a commitment in my life," Niki said. "I've never loved anyone before. But I'm telling you right now, whether you want me or not, I'm waiting for you. I'm going to nursing school, and I plan to graduate at the top of my class. I'm going to be the best, so you'll be proud of me. I'm going to be the one waiting for you when you walk out of this place. I love you now, and I'll love you when I draw my last breath."

Dawn dragged her hands down her face. "I can't," she whispered. "I can't take advantage of you. I can't be the one to hurt you if things don't work out."

Niki nodded. "I understand. You're so damn noble. That's why I've fallen in love with you."

Dawn appraised Niki as she slipped on her shoes. "You look gorgeous. That dress brings out the green of your eyes."

"Thank you." Niki sulked as she looked around the room one last time.

"Aren't you taking anything with you?"

"What would I take? Prison issued soap and toothpaste are all I own, and I hope I never see that again."

"Mom and Flint will be here in a few minutes," Dawn said. "They'll call you over the PA when they arrive."

"I know."

"I can walk to the front of the hospital with you."

"I'd like that." Niki moved to stand in front of Dawn.

Neither moved their hands from their side. Dawn leaned down and kissed her. Niki's lips were even softer than Dawn had imagined. They were sweet and warm. The feeling that ricocheted through her body was indescribable. Dawn didn't know how long the kiss lasted. She only knew she never wanted it to end. "I do love you," she murmured. "Please wait for me."

Niki gasped for air and backed away from Dawn. "You know I will. I had no idea you could kiss like that."

Dawn smiled. "Then both of us had the same experience." She leaned down and placed a soft kiss on the scar on Niki's cheek. "I've always wanted to do that. To kiss away the hurt and make it better."

"Niki Sears," the PA system blared. "Report to the front desk."

"I'll see you next week during visitation," Niki promised as she opened the door and stepped from the room. "God, I miss you already."

##

After waving goodbye to Niki, Dawn returned to her room. For the first time, she realized how cold and empty it was without her roommate. With Niki in the room it had been filled with joy and laughter, a lot of teasing, and a sense of being with someone who really cared. She had been with Niki every day of her incarceration. Now she was alone, completely alone.

Chapter 19

"You sent for me?" Dawn said as she walked into Val's office.

"Yes. I'm working with the district attorney's office to file charges against the two guards involved in Terry Shipman's death." Val looked up from the file she was perusing. "I want to make certain I get all the medical details correct.

"The district attorney is always hesitant to prosecute prison murder or assault cases, because in the past the prison system hasn't been very cooperative with them. I want to provide every shred of evidence we can to make certain everyone involved in this case and Merrick's case is punished for the awful crimes they have committed.

"I want to make an example of the guards and Merrick to let the world know things like this will not be tolerated in the federal prison system."

"May I see what you've compiled so far?" Dawn asked.

"Yes." Val pushed the file toward her as Dawn pulled her chair closer to the desk. She spent several minutes reading the reports in Terry Shipman's file. "I see you found the complaints Terry filed."

"Yes." Val looked away from the accusations in Dawn's eyes.

Dawn hissed under her breath as she read the reports. "She claimed she was raped repeatedly." Dawn grimaced. "Was it the two guards?"

"We think so, but I can't find anyone who actually witnessed the abuse. At least no one willing to talk about it."

Dawn nodded. "It'll take a lot to make these women trust the system." She continued to read the file. "This went on a long time, before you came."

Dawn gasped when she saw the photo in Terry's file. "This is grotesque! The rapist? Is that written in her own blood?"

"Yes," Val murmured, looking away. She couldn't stand the look of disgust on Dawn's face.

Dawn studied the photos. "Was she a drug addict?"

"Yes."

"Was she seeing Merrick on a regular basis?"

"Yes, why?"

"The rapist. It seems strange that she would write that instead of the name of her abuser," Dawn said. "Everyone is assuming it's two words: the rapist. What if it's one word? Therapist.

"I think she was trying to identify her therapist as the one responsible for her death."

"Oh my God," Val exclaimed. "You're right. She wasn't very literate and probably had no idea how to spell Merrick's name, so she wrote therapist."

"I'd bet a month's pay your Dr. Merrick was trading drugs for sex," Dawn said.

"A month's pay, eh?" Val smiled.

"Before this place, that would have been a lot of money to bet." Dawn shrugged. "No so much now." *Thanks to you,* she thought as the smile disappeared from Val's face.

"Her family had already hired an attorney to sue Merrick for malpractice," Dawn added. "I'm betting your two guards traded a hit on Terry for drugs. It seems drugs are the top currency in prison."

"I wouldn't take your bet, because I'm sure I would lose, but you have given me an idea to discuss with the DA's office."

They spent the rest of the afternoon writing and rewriting the information for the DA's office to make it as condemning as possible and getting all the facts in order and substantiated. "I'll personally take this to the DA in the morning and reassure him he has my fullest support," Val said as she slipped the information into an oversized envelope.

Dawn stood and stretched. "I can't believe it's so late. My stomach just reminded me that I haven't eaten since breakfast. I'd better run before the cafeteria closes."

"Why don't we get off the grounds and go to a great little Italian restaurant I know?" Val suggested.

"Can we do that? I mean, can you take me outside the prison?" Dawn dared not hope.

"Wardens are autonomous," Val said, laughing. "Our prison is like our own little fiefdom. I think that's part of the problem. When the government gives one person that much power, they must make certain they can be trusted not to abuse that power. What's the old idiom? Absolute power corrupts absolutely."

"I'd love to eat something besides prison food," Dawn admitted. "May I run upstairs and change out of these scrubs?"

"Of course. I'll come get you in thirty minutes."

Dawn walked to the door and then turned around. "Thank you."

Chapter 20

Dawn changed into the dark blue slacks, white blouse, and dark gray cardigan the prison allowed her to wear in the hospital. As she fixed her hair she thought about her afternoon with Val. The warden had played the devil's advocate on several points Dawn had made in the charges that should be filed against Merrick. "We must be able to prove them beyond the shadow of a doubt," Val had insisted. "Anything less will weaken our case."

Dawn eyed herself in the small mirror over the sink. Even without makeup, she was beautiful. Prison had a way of leveling the playing field for women, but even prison hadn't dimmed the sparkle in the doctor's Caribbean blue eyes.

The knock on her door made her heart skip a beat. *Surely, I'm not excited about dinner with the warden*, she thought.

Dawn couldn't hide her surprise at Val's appearance. She had become accustomed to the warden's severe look, with her hair slicked back in a bun at the nape of her neck. The Val standing in her doorway looked like a runway model for women's casual clothing.

She wore fitted jeans with a tight-fitting pullover that accentuated her flat stomach and ample breasts. A leather vest pretended to hide them but didn't. Her thick, dark hair swirled around her shoulders. She was breathtaking.

"You . . . you're gorgeous," Dawn stammered.

"Thank you." Val's shy grin made her even more appealing.

Val stopped at the guard desk and signed Dawn out of the hospital. She made no excuses.

"I'm surprised she didn't ask you why you're taking me off premises," Dawn commented as she fastened her seatbelt.

"I don't answer to them." A twisted smile flitted across Val's lips. "They work for me."

The evening was filled with teasing and laughter as Val related stories about growing up with four older brothers. "They made my dating life a zoo," she snickered. "It was always Mary and me against the boys. When I was seventeen, we had a Rottweiler named Max that wouldn't bite a biscuit, but he looked like the devil reincarnated when he snarled and those fangs came out. His bark was bloodcurdling.

"I was dating a nerdy fellow. You know the type—tall, skinny, glasses, harmless, and thrilled to be dating me. Max hated him for some reason and always lunged and snapped at him. My date was determined to make friends with Max and brought him large milk bones.

"One night we came home a little after curfew, and he walked me to the door. He pulled a handful of milk bones from his jacket pocket and said, 'I brought these in case Max is out.'

"We stood on the front porch, him trying to decide if he could kiss me and me trying to decide if I'd let him. My youngest brother let Max out the back door as my date left the porch. He was halfway to his car when Max rounded the corner, growling and snapping like the hounds from hell. My date screamed like a girl, threw the milk bones into the air, and flew to his car. He laid rubber all the way down the block.

"My brothers laughed until they cried at how shrill my date's scream sounded."

Dawn laughed. "You had to be tough, growing up with four older brothers."

"You think I'm tough?" Val tilted her head, and the candlelight danced in her eyes.

"I'm beginning to change my mind," Dawn mumbled.

"I'm not really." Val frowned. "Sometimes I think I'm in way over my head."

"Would you like dessert?" the waitress said, sliding a small menu in front of them.

Dawn shook her head. "I couldn't possibly eat another bite. We really should get back."

"I have something for you," Val said when the waitress left to get the check. She pulled her purse into her lap, reached inside, and placed a plain, white, rectangular box in front of Dawn.

"You shouldn't give me things," Dawn said as she lifted the lid from the box. "It's a cell phone. Am I even allowed to have a cell phone?"

"You are if I approve it," Val said, smiling. "And I approve it. I'll feel better about your safety if you have it, and it will save you thousands of steps a day. Best of all, I won't have to run all over the prison looking for you. I'll simply call you."

I can call Niki, Dawn thought. "Yes, I suppose it will make it easier on both of us."

Val lowered her voice. "This is also a weapon. When you push this button, these two prongs pop out. It becomes a taser. Simply push it against the skin of an assailant and push the same button, and you'll deliver a shock that will disable any one."

As soon as she entered her room, Dawn plugged in the cell phone and started charging it. She walked to the infirmary and checked on her patients before going to the nurses' station to check everyone's charts.

Even though it was late, she sneaked a call to her mother. "Mom, is Niki around?"

"She's been in bed for hours, dear. Why are you still up? Are you okay?"

"I had to check on a patient."

"We got Niki a cell phone," Ruth said. "Would you like her number?"

"Oh yes, please." Dawn tried to hide her excitement. She wrote down the number and stuffed it into her sweater pocket. "Thanks, Mom. I love you."

She typed her initials onto the last patient's chart and logged out of the computer. She refrained from running as she hurried back to her room.

Deciding to shower in the morning, Dawn slipped into bed and made her first call on her cell phone.

"Hello?" Niki's sleepy voice sounded like music to Dawn.

"Niki, baby, it's me, Dawn."

"Dawn! Oh my God, Dawn." Niki squealed into the phone. "I miss you so much. I can't wait to see you tomorrow."

"I know. I miss you too." Dawn sighed. "I miss you more than I ever imagined I would."

"How are you calling me?"

Dawn told Niki about her outing with the warden.

"And she gave you a cell phone?" Niki said, a hint of distrust in her voice. "What did she want from you?"

"Nothing, silly. She gave me the phone for safety and so the hospital personnel could easily contact me. Tell me what you've been doing."

"Flint drove me to TCU, and I got registered for all my classes. I lucked out and got every course I needed."

"That's great. Niki, I . . . uh—"

"What?"

"I can't stop thinking about how wonderful it felt to kiss you."

"I know," Niki said. "That's all I can think about."

"If you were here I'd kiss you again," Dawn said, snickering at her own audacity.

"Oh, I'd do more than kiss you," Niki whispered into the phone. "I'd touch you and . . ."

Dawn held her breath as she listened to the things Niki had planned for when they were alone together.

"I'd better go," Dawn said when Niki stopped to take a deep breath. "You're killing me."

Niki giggled. "I can't wait to get my hands on you, Dawn Fairchild."

"I'm afraid the feeling is mutual," Dawn said with a sigh. "I love you."

"Love you too. See you tomorrow."

Chapter 21

Dawn showered and dressed. She picked up her new cell phone. It represented a tiny bit of freedom—the ability to reach out to those outside the prison walls. She almost dropped it when it shrilled in her hand. It took her a minute to realize she could answer it.

"Good morning, Dawn." The warden's warm voice filled her ear. "Did you sleep well last night?"

"I did." Dawn sighed, thinking about her conversation with Niki.

"Have you had breakfast yet?" Val inquired. "If not, you're welcome to eat with me in my office."

"I'd like that."

"Twenty minutes," Val twittered. "Breakfast will be served in twenty minutes."

Dawn shoved aside the thought of calling Niki—but not for long. "What can it hurt?" she muttered as she punched in the number.

"Hello, my love," Niki said after just one ring.

"You already have my number programed into your new phone." Dawn approved.

"It's the only number in my phone." Niki giggled. "The only number I need."

"You're so sweet," Dawn said. "How did I get so lucky?"

"I can't wait to visit you," Niki said.

Dawn could almost feel her excitement through the phone.

"I know. I'm excited too," Dawn gushed. "But I have to go. I'm having breakfast with the warden."

"Why?" Niki snapped.

"Because she told me to," Dawn said. "I'll see you in a few hours. I love you."

Four hours and thirty-nine minutes, to be exact, Niki thought as the line went dead.

##

Val looked at her watch as Dawn walked through the door. "Right on time," she said, flashing Dawn a brilliant smile.

"Only a fool would keep the warden waiting," Dawn jested.

"The warden . . . is that how you think of me?"

Dawn cocked her head, confused. "How else would I think of you?"

Val shrugged. "As Val, a friend."

"There's a little matter of being wrongly accused that stops me from thinking of you as a friend."

"Fair enough." Val knew she was fighting a losing battle. *You're so damn stubborn*, she thought.

"I've been going through the records of all the women who were treated by Merrick who are still here," Val informed Dawn as she poured their coffee. "I want to interview all of them. He probably treated them all the same."

"That's a wonderful idea," Dawn said. "If the DA can build a case with multiple witnesses, we can put Merrick away until the second coming."

Val laughed. "The second coming, huh?"

"You know what I mean."

"I do," she said with a chuckle. "I currently have forty-nine of his former patients in the medium-security housing. I'm scheduling them to come in—one every hour. I'd like you to sit in on the interviews."

109

"I'd love to," Dawn said. "I'm curious to know if he manipulated them the way I suspect."

"I know it's asking a lot of you, but if we work ten hours a day we can finish in a week." Val nibbled her bottom lip as she waited for Dawn's response.

"I can do that," Dawn said. "Unless we have an emergency situation in the hospital."

"Perfect." Val beamed.

"I must see my visitors today." Dawn wrinkled her forehead. "Other than that, I'm good for the entire time."

"Oh." Val's flat exclamation left no doubt that she expected Dawn to cancel her visitors. "I could let your visitors come three days next week."

"They're already on their way," Dawn said. "I really need to see them today. They're the bright spot in my day."

"Of course," Val snorted. *Someday I'll be the bright spot in your day.*

They finished breakfast as they discussed the first interviewee of the day. Val asked her secretary to have a guard bring in Madonna Prater.

##

Madonna Prater wasn't the typical inmate. At five foot eight, she was the same height as Val and a little taller than Dawn. Her thick black hair was cut in a stylish bob—as stylish as one could get in prison. Her wry grin was indicative of her distrust of the system—any system. She hesitated when Val offered her a seat but then cautiously lowered her muscular frame into the chair. Her eyes constantly moved from the doctor to the warden.

"You must take advantage of the gym here," Dawn noted. "You look very fit."

Madonna nodded.

"Have you ever done drugs?" Val asked.

"No. I wouldn't do that to my body."

"You're our guest because you were convicted of aggravated assault," Val said.

"Yeah, an off-duty cop ran his hand up my girlfriend's skirt. I beat the hell out of him. I had no way of knowing he was a cop. He was in plain clothes."

Dawn gasped. "Seriously? You're in prison for defending your girlfriend? That's not right. If anything, the cop should be in jail."

Madonna snorted. "My thoughts exactly."

"We're not here to retry Madonna's case," Val said, redirecting the conversation. "We're here to discuss your sessions with Dr. Merrick."

"Merrick?" Madonna gagged in disgust. "What a pig. I heard you had him arrested. Good for you, Warden."

"Tell me about your experiences with him," Val insisted.

"I only had one."

"Hmm. He billed us for eleven sessions." Val shuffled through Madonna's file and produced an invoice for the sessions.

"Slimy bastard. I'm not surprised." Madonna snickered. "I was sent to him because I supposedly had anger issues. The first thing he told me was that I had no right to almost kill a cop because he stuck his hand up my girl's dress. He sat down beside me on the sofa and proceeded to fondle my breasts. He was right. I did have anger issues. I beat the crap out of him. The next thing I knew, I was in solitary confinement where two guards showed up nightly and beat the hell out of me.

"That went on for ten days. I guess the beatings were the sessions you were billed for."

"Did you report it?" Val asked, her face twisted in anger.

"To who?"

"We have protocols in place for inmates to file complaints," Val said.

"That would only have resulted in another beating," Madonna grumbled. "Do you ever check up on your so-called protocols, Warden?"

"Will you testify to the statement you just gave me?" Val asked.

"If it will help put Merrick behind bars, you bet."

"We're interviewing everyone who had sessions with Merrick," Dawn said. "If you know of anyone, please encourage them to cooperate with us."

"I'll give it a few days." Madonna hesitated and then added, "If I don't receive visitors in the middle of the night, I'll trust you, Warden. If I do, I won't help at all. I'll figure I was duped, and you're as bad as all the other bastards."

"Fair enough," Val said.

Madonna looked from Val to Dawn. "Tell me the truth, Warden. Wouldn't you beat the hell out of anyone who snaked their hand up Dr. Fairchild's skirt? She's your woman, isn't she?"

"What? No!" Dawn jumped up. "I'm not a lesbian."

"Oh, I just assumed . . . My bad." Madonna flashed them a look of disbelief.

They interviewed three more women and were discussing the stories they'd heard when the PA system began trumpeting inmates' names to meet their visitors.

"I have to go," Dawn said, beaming. "See you in an hour."

Chapter 22

Dawn saw Niki the minute she entered the visitors' room. *Who could miss that glorious red hair hair?*

She tried to wipe the elated smile from her face and failed. By the time she reached Niki, she was certain her smile had brightened the entire room.

She slid into her chair and grasped Niki's hands across the table. "You look . . . magnificent. Are you trying to kill me?"

"I just wanted you to know what was waiting for you," Niki teased. "I mean, with the warden taking you to dinner and giving you cell phones, a girl has to bring her A-game to hold your attention."

Dawn moaned as she scanned the low-cut dress Niki was wearing. Full breasts rose and fell seductively as Niki breathed. She knew how beautiful Niki's breasts were, but she had never touched them. *My stupidity.*

Niki leaned forward, giving Dawn a better look. "You like?"

Dawn licked her lips and nodded. Her mouth was too dry to talk. She tore her eyes away from Niki's exposed skin and looked into her eyes. "God, I've missed you."

Niki squeezed Dawn's hands tighter. "I want to kiss you, but I know they will throw me out if I do, so tell me about your day. How did the interviews go?"

Dawn told her the sad stories they had listened to all morning. "He molested so many of these women," she said.

"But let's talk about something happy. Let's talk about you."

"I wanted to ask you what you thought about me getting an apartment," Niki said. "Nothing fancy, just a small one-bedroom apartment close to the school."

"Is it crowded living with my family?"

"No. They, uh, just keeping asking me about my relationship with you. I think they know we're a couple."

"We *are* a couple," Dawn said as the realization finally hit her. "I can't keep this stupid grin off my face. I'm just so happy to see you."

"I know," Niki murmured. "Believe me, I know."

"Niki, a friend is living in my home. She's basically house-sitting for me until I get out of this place. You can live there if you'd like. There's plenty of room, and it would make me happy knowing you were there. My folks can be a bit inquisitive. I understand you wanting to live where no one is constantly questioning you. Jacey works nights, so you'll probably only see her on weekends.

"I have . . . *had* a new car in the garage. You can use it. The keys are . . . I'm not sure where the keys are. Ask my mom if the police returned my belongings to her. They took my purse and briefcase the night they arrested me. The keys to the house and car were in my purse."

"Thank you," Niki whispered. "I just wish you could walk through the door with me the first time I enter."

"I could carry you over the threshold," Dawn said breathlessly, her eyes locked on Niki's.

They were interrupted by the squawking buzzer, signaling their time was over.

"No," Niki whimpered. "I just got here."

Dawn took one last look at Niki's cleavage and moaned. "I'll see if I can get some kind of pass. The way I feel, I should surely qualify for a hardship pass or something."

Niki giggled and refrained from tiptoeing to kiss her love. "Call me tonight," she whispered.

##

Dawn returned to Val's office as another inmate was brought in to talk with them. At the end of the day, they had worked through seven of Dr. Merrick's victims.

Val kicked off her heels, leaned her head back against her chair, and closed her eyes. "He definitely had a mode of operation," she mumbled. "Every story is the same. The acts he forced them to do varied, but everything else is by the script."

"You look tired," Dawn observed.

"This stuff gets to you after a while," Val muttered. "But you've been unusually chipper this afternoon. I guess a visit with your family does put you in a better mood."

For the thousandth time, the vision of Niki floated across Dawn's mind, forcing her to smile. "Yes, it does help me, knowing that my life outside prison still exists."

"What will you do when you get out?" Val asked, keeping her eyes closed against the memories of the pitiful women they had talked with today.

"I don't know. I was on track to become the chief surgeon in my hospital before the accident. Now I don't even know if I'll be able to get a job in any hospital."

"Reynolds wants to retire," Val volunteered. "You could have his job if you want it."

Dawn cocked her head and studied the woman who had destroyed her life. "I think not."

Val opened her eyes and raised her head to look at Dawn. She hoped the hurt she felt didn't show in her eyes. "Let's go get some dinner. We both skipped lunch, and I'm starving."

##

"You drink a lot of coffee," Val noted as Dawn ordered the caffeinated brew with her dinner.

115

"A habit I formed in med school," Dawn said. "I love a good cup of coffee—something that is missing at your establishment."

"I have it every time you work with me, but you don't consume much of it."

"As I said, a good cup of coffee is missing at your establishment."

Dawn's emphasis on the word "good" wasn't missed by Val. "Coffee is coffee to me. Do you have a favorite brand?"

"I love Italian coffee. Segafredo is my favorite."

"Hmmm. I'll have to try it." Val cocked a brow and smiled.

Chapter 23

They worked ten-hour days, interviewing women and studying reports and complaints. Dawn was pleasantly surprised to find a fresh pot of Segafredo coffee waiting for her every morning. Val showed her appreciation in little ways, like serving the coffee and Dawn's favorite Danish with breakfast every morning.

"When this project is over I'm going to miss our breakfast together," Dawn said as she refilled their cups.

"There's no reason for that to change," Val said with a smile. "It would be a good idea for you to give me a report on the hospital activities at the beginning of each day. If you'd like to."

"I'd love to." Dawn grinned as she settled onto the sofa in Val's office. "How many more do we have to interview?"

"If we work ten-hour days for the next three days, we'll be finished by Friday. I can put my report together over the weekend and have it ready for my meeting with the DA on Monday."

"I . . . uh . . . don't forget my Wednesday visitor's meeting."

"Surely you can miss one visitor's meeting," Val snapped. The look of disbelief on Dawn's face made her realize how important seeing her family was to her.

Val moved quickly to repair the damage she had done. "Look, if you'll work through Wednesday visitation, I'll arrange a weekend pass for you."

"You can do that?" Dawn's excitement was contagious.

Val grinned. "Of course! I'm the warden."

They shared a laugh. Dawn was learning that Val was indeed autonomous in running the prison.

"I'd like that very much," Dawn said.

Dawn stood in the shower, letting the hot water run down her body. Without Niki there she could stand under the soothing stream and enjoy the warmth of the water longer. She smiled as she thought of telling Niki about her weekend release from the prison. Suddenly she couldn't wait to tell the beautiful redhead they'd have the weekend together.

She towel-dried her hair, slipped on her T-shirt, and climbed into bed. She held the cell phone in her hand, prolonging the anticipation of hearing Niki's voice. She touched the screen, bringing Niki into her life.

"Hi, honey," Niki cooed into the phone. "I thought you'd never call. Long day?"

"Yes. We're still interviewing Merrick's victims, and I wanted to wash this place off me before I called you."

"I can't wait to see you tomorrow." Niki's sultry voice made heat run through Dawn's body.

"Umm, about tomorrow—"

"Don't you dare tell me I can't see you tomorrow because the warden needs you."

Dawn tried again to tell her about the arrangements she had made. "Baby, I can't see you tomorrow because—"

"Dammit, Dawn Fairchild, I live from Wednesday to Wednesday. I—"

"Because I traded it for a weekend pass," Dawn blurted.

"That upsets me so . . . what did you say?"

"I said I traded our one hour on Wednesday for the entire weekend. I can leave at five Friday night and return by six Sunday evening."

"You're not teasing me? You shouldn't tease about something as wonderful as that."

"No, baby, I'm not teasing," Dawn murmured.

"Oh Dawn!" Niki sighed. "I can't believe Old Ironsides is letting you do that. How did you pull that off?"

"She's like a dog with a bone, Niki," Dawn said. "She's a woman on a mission. She's determined to see that Merrick gets the needle for Terry Shipman's death.

"She said if I'd work through Wednesday so we could wrap up the interviews by Friday afternoon, she would give me a weekend pass."

Niki was silent for several seconds. "Does she know about us?"

"Right now, there isn't anything to know," Dawn countered. "We're no more than the best of friends."

"I plan to change that this weekend."

Niki's provocative voice filled Dawn's mind with arousing images. "I plan to let you," she whispered.

After a long silence, Niki spoke. "Your mom said she never received your belongings from the police. Do you want me to see if I can get them?"

"That would be wonderful. I'm not sure they'll give them to someone unrelated to me."

"Oh." Disappointment filled Niki's voice.

"I'll speak to the warden and see if you can pick up my things. I bet she can arrange that."

"I bet she can," Niki grumbled, fighting to keep her dislike of Val from showing. She was afraid Dawn would think her ungrateful.

"What time do you get out of class tomorrow?" Dawn asked.

"One."

"I'll call you and let you know what to do."

"I'll do whatever you want," Niki whispered seductively.

"Are we still talking about picking up my things?" Dawn teased.

"What do you think?"

Dawn closed the file on another case and shook her head in disgust. "How could this go on so long and with so many women?"

Val shrugged. She felt like a fool. She watched Dawn as the blonde relaxed against the back of the sofa and rested her coffee cup on her leg. She looked like she was sharing afternoon coffee with a friend. One would never know she was an inmate in a women's federal prison. She looked like a pampered socialite—a gorgeous pampered socialite.

"I honestly thought I was doing a good job," Val said, cringing. "I was only fooling myself."

"You have to move among them," Dawn noted. "You must listen to them."

"I know that now—now that you were almost raped and a woman has died. That pitiful little excuse for a woman was more effective at keeping you safe than I was."

"Pitiful . . . I don't know who—"

"Niki," Val rasped "Her name was Niki. I released her last month."

"Oh," Dawn exclaimed. "Niki. I forget that she was such a waif when I first came here. She looks so different now."

"Yes, I suppose she does look different now," Val muttered. "I give her a year and she'll be back in here."

Dawn shot an angry glance toward Val. "You truly don't know people at all, do you?"

"I know drug addicts," Val huffed. "They always go back to the stuff."

Chapter 24

"I'll give Bobby a call and let him know someone will drop by his office tomorrow to pick up your things," Val said as they wrapped up Wednesday's marathon interviewing of molested women.

"I'd appreciate that." Dawn's amiable smile was the bright spot of Val's day.

Val called Bobby and explained what she needed.

"He's up to his neck in a multiple murder, but he'll call your mother next week and get your things to her."

Dawn nodded. "Thank you. Is it okay if I call my mom to let her know Detective Jones will be calling her?"

"Sure." Val grinned as Dawn pushed a button on her cell phone.

"Hello, darling," Niki drawled, stretching out the two words as seductively as possible.

Dawn struggled to keep the excitement out of her voice and the pleasure from her face. "Mom, Warden Davis has arranged for you to pick up my belongings from the police. Detective Bobby Joe Jones will call you next week. They still have my purse with all my keys, cell phone, and wallet. They want you to bring my attorney, Libby, with you so she can sign the receipt."

"Oh my God," Niki said breathlessly. "This is really going to happen. I'll have you all weekend."

"Yes, ma'am. I'll see you this weekend. I love you too, Mom."

"Want to get out of this place for dinner?" Val asked as Dawn ended her call.

"Do I ever say no to that?"

"I have a new place for us to try," Val said.

Val had always considered herself asexual. Neither sex had ever appealed to her enough to sidetrack her ambitions. Then she met Dr. Dawn Fairchild. The gorgeous blonde had destroyed every barrier Val had built. Not only was she beautiful, Dawn was genuinely nice—a good, caring person.

Val had been amazed at the transformation of Niki Sears, and it was all because Dawn had taken an interest in the poor pathetic creature. Val had to admit that Niki was now one of the most breathtaking women she had ever met. If she were truthful, she'd admit that she'd been delighted to release Niki just to get her away from Dawn.

She had no reason to believe that Dawn might be a lesbian. Dawn had been engaged to a male doctor before the accident and had vehemently protested when Madonna had assumed she was Val's lover.

Val looked forward to every day, because at some point during the day she would talk with Dawn Fairchild. She searched for unique dining spots the two of them could share. She trusted Dawn's judgment and often had her sit in on an inmate's interview. Dawn had become the bright spot in her day. Val knew she was falling in love with the beautiful doctor. She turned out her night-light and let dreams of Dawn fill her head.

Chapter 25

"That's the last one." Val stretched as Dawn carried her coffee cup to the sideboard. "How can you drink that much coffee?"

"A bad habit I developed during my residency," Dawn chuckled. "We worked horrendous hours. Twenty-four-hour shifts were the norm, not the exception."

"I never did my residency," Val volunteered. "I have degrees in law and medicine from Harvard, but law is my passion."

"I can tell." Dawn smiled. "Just as medicine is mine."

"I thought I'd find you two here," Lance Reynolds said as he entered the office. "Are you finished with your witch hunt?"

Val frowned at his choice of words. "It's not a witch hunt, Lance. It's an honest effort to end the crime in our own prison."

"Whoa," Lance said as he held his hands up in front of him. "I was just kidding, Warden. I'm behind you every step of the way. What Merrick was doing is unconscionable."

"I'm sorry," Val said, shrugging. "The things Merrick got away with gall me. I blame myself as much as my predecessors. He committed appalling crimes and dealt drugs right under my nose.

"He had guards working with him. Relatives of prisoners would pay Merrick to get drugs to inmates. Merrick would give the drugs to the guards, who would deliver them to the inmates—for a cut, of course. I can't believe the corruption going on with my closest staff members."

"What alerted you to his operation?" Lance asked as he settled on the sofa beside Dawn who was still making notes on her pad.

"Dr. Fairchild and Niki Sears. Merrick tried to rape Niki during her exit interview session. Dawn caught him."

"Good Lord," Lance groused. "Are you going to testify against him, Dawn?"

"Of course," Dawn said.

"Her testimony is a vital part of our case," Val added.

"Back to my original question," Lance said as he got to his feet. "Are you finished?"

"We'll wrap it all up Friday," Val replied. "Why?"

"We have a patient who needs heart surgery." Lance looked at Dawn. "I'd like to schedule it for next week, if that is agreeable with you."

"Let's set her up for an evaluation," Dawn said. "I'll need time to interview her and look over her records to make certain it's an operation I feel qualified to do. In the meantime, I'll need some tests completed and the results." Dawn jotted several lines on her notepad, tore of the sheet, and handed it to Lance.

"Works for me." Lance gave a Boy Scout salute. "You ladies have a nice evening."

"Dinner?" Val raised a questioning brow once the door closed behind Lance.

"Always," Dawn said, laughing.

##

"I want to run an idea by you," Val said as the waitress walked away with their order.

"Go for it." Dawn was euphoric. Her good mood extended to the warden. After all, Val was giving her a weekend pass.

124

"I love your enthusiasm." Val laughed. "I . . . I'm thinking about setting up a self-defense school for some of the inmates. The sane ones who are in here for nonviolent crimes like fraud, theft, drug use, that sort of thing.

"If they learn to defend themselves, they'll be less likely to become victims of prison bullies. What do you think?"

Dawn applauded. "Where do I sign up? That is a great idea. How soon can you make it happen?"

"I have two women who have been at Carswell almost a year. They are model prisoners and former owners of a self-defense training center for women."

"What's their crime?"

"Income tax evasion," Val said with a snicker.

"That's about as nonviolent as you can get," Dawn noted. "If Niki had received some self-defense training it might have saved her a lot of agony."

"You do know she has some mental problems?" Val's expression became serious. "Just because she's every woman's walking wet dream right now doesn't mean she's *compos mentis.*"

"Of sound mind," Dawn translated. "Look at you, using medical terms, Warden."

Val chortled then added, "I just want you to know what you're dealing with. I saw her name on your visitors log."

"She's a friend," Dawn said. "She saved me from being raped my second night here. I owe her."

"Then you owe her tremendous gratitude," Val reluctantly agreed. "But once a drug addict, always a drug addict."

Dawn was furious. "You have no idea the hell she has gone through the last two years, Warden. How many times she was raped and beaten. How she was . . . . And all under your watch."

Disgust wrenched Val's face. "I had no idea. I—"

125

"We should go," Dawn muttered as she signaled the waitress.

##

Dawn tried to forget Val's words. Tried to tell herself that Niki was perfect. She tried to revive the elation she had felt at the prospect of spending a weekend with the redhead. But that niggling little sentence kept haunting her. *You know she has some mental problems.* Warden Davis could certainly suck the joy out of one's life.

Chapter 26

Niki glared at her bedside clock, daring it to flip past midnight. Like most things in her life, she didn't intimidate it. It flipped to 12:01 a.m. then 12:02, and Dawn didn't call.

Maybe the call this afternoon was the only one she could get away with today. Maybe she had an emergency in the hospital.

Dear God, please let Dawn call me, Niki prayed.

As if answering her prayers, the phone rang.

"Dawn! Oh God, Dawn. I was so afraid you wouldn't call me tonight. I was—"

"I love you," Dawn blurted. "I love you, Niki Sears."

"Thank God," Niki sobbed. "I love you so much, Dawn. You have no idea how much I love you." Niki couldn't stop the tears running down her cheeks.

"Are you crying, baby?"

"Maybe." Niki sniffed. "I miss you so much."

"I miss you too, honey. Listen, I'm going to catch a cab from the prison to my home. I'll call you when I'm on my way, so you can meet me at the house. We can go in together."

"I'll call Jacey and have her leave the door between the garage and the house unlocked. There's a keypad to open the garage so we can get in."

"I'm dying to see you." Niki giggled around a sniffle.

"I know. I feel the same way. Is there anything you'd like to do while I'm out? A movie or a musical or—"

"I don't want to leave the house," Niki said. "I'll buy groceries so we can cook at home."

"At home." Dawn sighed. "I like the sound of that."

##

Val had their coffee waiting when Dawn entered her office. "I'm sorry I'm a few minutes late. I ran by the hospital to check on our heart patient. She's doing well."

"It's okay," Val said, passing her the cream. "I asked the two women who ran the self-defense school to meet with us this morning. The guards are on their way up with them."

Two women tall muscular women entered the office. Val offered them coffee. The two exchanged glances and then eagerly reached for the cups.

"Oh my, Warden, this is definitely the nectar of the gods," the brunette said after her first sip of coffee. "I'm Gloria, and this is Lynn."

"Have we done something wrong?" Lynn said.

Val tried to put them at ease. "No, not at all. You're model inmates. Dr. Fairchild and I have invited you here today to discuss a project we want to undertake."

As Val talked, the women became more excited. "Well, what do you think?" she concluded.

"We'd love to do it," they chorused.

"It's desperately needed," Gloria enthused. "You know criminals with guns don't go after others with guns. They go after the ones who are unarmed. It's the same with bullies. They don't attack those who can defend themselves."

Val pushed a pen and pad toward them. "Give me a list of what you need, and I mean everything. Spare nothing. I want a state-of-the-art training center. I'll have it all delivered and set up next week."

Before the two inmates could get started, Val's intercom buzzed, and Lillian announced that their appointment was waiting. "Why don't you sit in the waiting room and make your list. Take your time," Val added.

The morning flew by and lunch was delivered to Val's office. Lillian brought in a twelve-page list of equipment and paraphernalia needed for the self-defense center. Val perused the list and passed it to Dawn.

"This is exciting." Val hugged herself. "I feel that I'm finally accomplishing something."

"You are," Dawn said proudly.

##

Val heaved a sigh of relief. "That's the last one. Now all I have to do is compile the information and present it to the DA Monday morning. Let's go somewhere nice for dinner and celebrate."

Dawn tamped down the rising fear that tightened her chest. Surely Val hadn't forgotten her promise of a weekend pass.

"I'll have to take a raincheck," she said, trying to smile nonchalantly. "My mother has invited the entire family for dinner tonight. Everyone is excited that I have a weekend pass."

"Oh, yes. I . . . I'll drive you to your mother's home," Val said. "I'd like to meet your family."

Dawn scowled. "You've met them. All of them were at my trial. You remember, the one where you condemned me to this place?"

A tinge of regret stabbed Val in the chest. She'd forgotten that Dawn's incarceration was her fault. She'd forgotten Dawn was a prisoner.

"I have a ride," Dawn continued. "You can get started on your report."

"I'll need to sign you out," Val said, trying her best not to pout. "I'm not going to put a tracking device on you. I trust you'll return Sunday by six."

"I will," Dawn promised, trying to hide her desire to leave. "I'm ready to go if you'll sign me out now. My ride will be here any minute."

Val signed an official-looking document and handed it to Dawn. "Keep this with you at all times. It's your weekend pass. You'll need to show it at the gate to leave and return."

Dawn folded the paper and slipped it into the cup of her bra. "Lucky paper," Val mumbled under her breath.

Chapter 27

Niki was sitting on the porch swing with her overnight bag and a sack of groceries when the taxi pulled up in front of Dawn's home. She flew down the sidewalk and hugged the blonde from behind as Dawn paid the cab driver.

Dawn turned in Niki's arms and hugged her tightly. "No kissing until we get inside," she warned. Niki giggled and snuggled closer.

The garage keypad worked perfectly. They stepped into the garage and closed the door. Niki slid her arms around Dawn's neck and pulled her head down until their lips met.

Nothing in the world compared to holding Niki in her arms. Dawn reveled in the softness of the other woman. Niki nipped Dawn's bottom lip with her teeth and then pressed her firm, sweet mouth against Dawn's. "Oh dear Lord," Dawn whispered before pulling Niki's lips against hers again.

Niki tentatively slipped the tip of her tongue between Dawn's lips and ran it along Dawn's top teeth before slipping farther into her mouth. She waited for a response, and Dawn didn't disappoint. Her tongue engaged Niki's in the sweetest caresses Niki had ever known. Dawn's hand caught Niki's hair and pulled her closer, as their kiss swept both into an endless tide of passion.

"I should show you the house," Dawn mumbled against swollen lips.

"Yes," Niki whispered before losing herself in another kiss. "But we need to get the groceries and my weekender from the porch swing."

##

Dawn carried the groceries and held Niki's hand as she led her from the garage into the kitchen. "What a perfect kitchen," Niki squealed. "This is a chef's kitchen." She set her weekender on the floor.

"Did I mention I love to cook?" Dawn pulled the redhead into her arms and hugged her tightly. "I can't get over how good you feel."

"It only gets better," Niki said. "Let me put a few things in the fridge, and then you can show me the rest of the house." They walked through the living room, breakfast room, and dining room.

"What's down that hall?"

"My bedroom," Dawn whispered, as if the room might disappear any minute. "Do you want to . . ." Dawn gulped. "Are you ready to—?"

"Yes." Niki laced her fingers through Dawn's. "Yes, darling."

##

"I want to shower," Dawn said as she looked around the room she had sorely missed. "I want to wash that place off me before I touch you."

Niki nodded. "I still take several showers a day," she confided. "I can't get the grime of prison off my skin. It's getting better though."

Niki followed Dawn into the bathroom. "I don't want to let you out of my sight," she confessed. "I just want to look at you."

"Why don't you get ready for bed while I shower?" Dawn said, still shy about undressing in front of Niki.

"Okay, but hurry."

132

Although Dawn wanted to linger under the hot water, basking in the scent of her favorite shampoo and soap, she was anxious to hold Niki.

After her shower, Dawn slipped into her terry cloth robe and opened the door. The only light in the bedroom was a small night-light on her bedside table. She quietly walked to her side of the bed. "Are you awake?"

"Yes." Niki lifted the covers so Dawn could drop her robe and slide into bed. "Oh God, you smell divine." She snuggled into Dawn.

Dawn inhaled deeply. "As do you. I love that fragrance." The scent of Niki, her warm softness, the sweet sounds she made—all combined to set Dawn on fire.

Niki raised on her elbow and studied the face of the woman she'd loved from the moment she saw her. She leaned down and pressed her lips gently against Dawn's. She moved her free hand up Dawn's side and caressed her full, firm breast.

Dawn gasped when Niki touched her nipple. Niki deepened their kiss as she moved to straddle the blonde. "Is this okay?"

"Yes," Dawn whispered. "Yes."

Niki paid homage to Dawn's perfect body, touching her, kissing her, holding her. She caressed Dawn's left breast as she lavished attention on the right breast with her tongue and lips.

"Oh dear God," Dawn moaned. "Do something for heaven's sake. Do something."

"What do you want me to do?" Niki whispered in her ear, aware that her hot breath on Dawn's ear was another stimulant.

"Whatever you want," Dawn begged. "Please. Do whatever you want."

##

Niki fell onto the bed, breathing heavily. "Let me catch my breath," she gasped as Dawn rolled onto her side and pulled the smaller woman in her arms.

"I just want to hold you." Dawn kissed her cheek and neck. "Just hold you."

Niki pushed further into Dawn's arms, touching every inch of skin she could. Dawn felt even better than Niki had imagined. She was a goddess. "I don't know why God decided to have mercy on me and send you to me, but I will live my life being worthy of his gift," Niki murmured to her sleeping lover.

Chapter 28

Dawn was certain she was dreaming. She was in her comfortable bed with sheets and a cloud-like duvet. Best of all, Niki was snuggled into her arms, her head nestled on Dawn's shoulder and her arm across Dawn's waist. Dawn moved slightly and realized Niki's leg was also thrown across her.

She froze when she realized how satiated she felt, how good Niki felt in her arms. She was in bed with Niki.

"Please don't tell me you're having morning-after regrets," Niki mumbled.

"Heavens no." Dawn giggled. "I was just thinking that no one has ever made love to me like that. You're incredible, Niki Sears."

"Umm, I'm glad you enjoyed it as much as I did."

"I think I left you hanging," Dawn whispered. "I fell asleep. The best sleep I've had in . . . ever!"

"My greatest joy is to please you," Niki whispered into her ear.

"Then you must be ecstatic," Dawn teased as she trailed her fingers down Niki's back. She slipped her arm further under Niki and pulled the smaller woman on top of her.

"My favorite place in the world," Niki said as she kissed the lips that had haunted her dreams.

Dawn gripped Niki firmly as she ran her hands down her back to her buttocks and cupped her cheeks. Niki began to grind against her. "I'm not sure what to do," Dawn confessed. "I've never been with a woman before."

"Did you like the things I did to you?" Niki asked.

Dawn couldn't stop the heatwave that ran from her core to her face. "More than anything," she whispered.

"Then do that to me."

The afternoon sun was peeking through the curtains when the two untangled themselves from the sheets. Dawn reclined against the headboard. "Is this the point where we smoke a cigarette?" she said, grinning.

"Umm . . . or make sandwiches." Niki laughed as she stretched. "Must we put clothes on to go into the kitchen?"

"Jacey might wander through," Dawn tittered. "It would be best if we weren't naked."

"Lay with me a few minutes longer." Niki lay across the bed and put her head in Dawn's lap.

"Always," Dawn promised.

"I thought I knew all there was to know about sex," Niki said softly, "but I knew nothing about love. No one has ever touched me like you do or held me like I might break. No one has ever been gentle with me. No one in my entire life has every made me feel loved the way you do."

Dawn traced the scar on Niki's cheek. "No one could possibly love you as I do." Dawn leaned down and tasted the sweetest lips in the world.

"It feels so good to put on my own clothes," Dawn said as she pulled up a pair of jeans and fastened them. "I've lost weight as the fed's guest."

"You look great. You looked soft the first time I saw you. Now you're more toned." Niki ran her hands from Dawn's shoulders down her firm back muscles. "Umm, woman, you are really buff."

Dawn laughed out loud. "I am a lot stronger. You are too."

"I joined a fitness club and go to karate once a week, Niki admitted. "I never again want to be that weakling you first met in prison."

Dawn turned and slowly pulled Niki into her arms. "You're nothing like you were when we met. You've come a long way, honey, and I'm so proud of you."

"Yes, I remember you wouldn't even shake hands with me." Niki pretended to pout. "You were afraid to touch me."

"That has certainly changed," Dawn said, hugging her tighter. "Now I can't keep my hands off you."

"We've both come a long way." Niki tiptoed to kiss her.

Suddenly, a beeping sound filled the room. "What's that?" Niki jerked around to face the bedroom door.

"Relax, baby, it's just the alarm. It'll stop when disarmed. Jacey's home. Come on, I want her to meet you."

##

"Jacey," Dawn called out as they walked down the hallway. "I'm home. I want to let you know I'm here so I don't scare you." She continued in a loud voice as they entered the kitchen.

"Dawn! Girl, when did you get out?" Jacey grabbed her best friend in a bear hug. Her eyes opened wide when she saw Niki over Dawn's shoulder. "Wow! You must be Niki. You never said she was a knockout!"

Niki smiled and nodded at the warm reception from Dawn's best friend.

"Is she?" Dawn teased. "I hadn't noticed."

She pulled Niki closer and made the formal introductions. "Niki Sears meet Jacey Talland.

"I'm not out," Dawn explained. "I'm on a weekend pass. I wanted to introduce you and Niki and help her get settled in."

"I won't get in your way," Niki explained. "I'm finishing nursing school, so I'm in classes all day, and Dawn said you work nights."

"Yeah. I have Wednesday and Thursday off, so we'll rarely see each other. I will be nice to have someone else in this big house even if I don't see you everyday."

"We're making sandwiches for dinner," Niki said. "Would you like one?"

Jacey nodded. "You talked me into it. This calls for a celebration. I'll uncork a bottle of wine."

"I brought cold drinks," Niki noted. "I honestly prefer Dr. Pepper."

"Same here," Dawn said, smiling at Niki.

"Who am I to spoil a party?" Jacey crowed. "Dr. Pepper for everyone. I don't like wine anyway."

The three women visited over their sandwiches and chips. Niki learned that Jacey was the head nurse over the night shift at Dawn's old hospital.

"Do you remember Gloria Putter?" Jacey asked.

Dawn shook her head.

"The tall bleached blonde," Jacey said. "Everyone called her Gloria Puts-out-a-lot."

A light came on in Dawn's eyes. "I do remember her. I'm surprised some doctor's wife hasn't killed her."

"Are you ready for this?" Jacey howled with laughter. "Richard married her."

"Richard? My Richard?" Dawn gasped.

"Yeah, the jerk that sent you to prison." Jacey sobered. "You'll be free in six months, and that stupid bastard will live in hell for the rest of his life."

Niki watched Dawn to see if she was upset. When the blonde caught her eye and smiled, Niki knew everything was okay.

"I know this is going to sound weird, with you being in prison and all," Jacey said, studying Dawn, "but you've never looked better. You're so . . . so luminescent. I've never seen you look so happy. You look like you just got laid."

Dawn couldn't stop the blush that raced from her chest to the top of her head nor the grin that spread across her lips.

Jacey broke the silence. "My God! I don't believe it. You two. You're—"

"Together." Dawn smiled as she reached for Niki's hand.

Chapter 29

Niki moaned in her sleep and snuggled closer to her lover. Dawn hugged her tighter, never wanting to let her go. She dreaded tomorrow when she would return to the prison and a cold, empty bed.

Dawn suppressed the desire to take Niki and run away to some tropical island, Mexico, or even Canada. Any place where no one could find them. *Six more months. You can do six more months alone*, she told herself.

Niki stirred in her sleep and undulated against Dawn. "Are you awake?" she asked.

"I am now," Dawn murmured.

"Good. I want to make the most of the time we have left together."

##

Dawn awoke to the smell of coffee and bacon, two of the things she liked most in life—right after Niki, of course. She opened her armoire and pulled out her favorite T-shirt and a pair of sweatpants. She was delighted to find everything just as she'd left it. It was as if she hadn't been gone at all.

Dawn stopped in the kitchen doorway as a surge of desire drenched her body. Niki's back was to her, and she was wearing one of Dawn's old T-shirts. The shirt reached Niki's thigh, and she was barefoot. Dawn wanted to run her hands up Niki's legs and underneath the T-shirt and . . . .

A startled Niki turned to face Dawn. "Oh, I'm glad you're up. I almost have breakfast ready."

Dawn moved to the redhead and lifted her onto the island in the center of the kitchen. "I know that look," Niki whispered as they kissed. "You should turn off the cooktop first."

Later, Niki rested her cheek against Dawn's chest. "That was a first for me," she said, giggling, "but I trust it won't be the last."

"Um, I'm sorry," Dawn murmured into her ear as she stroked her back. "I didn't mean to act like a caveman, but I can't even begin to describe the feelings that swept over me at the sight of you in my T-shirt."

Niki pulled a serious face. "Note to self—always wear Dawn's T-shirts." She pressed her lips to Dawn's.

"You're much stronger than you look," Dawn said. "The strength in your legs is incredible."

"I'm pretty tough for a little gal," Niki bantered. "Do you think you could take me?"

Dawn laughed. "I just did."

"You sure did," Niki said, sighing.

Dawn showered and slipped back into the clothes she had worn from prison. She didn't mind wearing the same clothes every day or eating the prison food. She didn't mind working in the prison hospital. She did mind being away from Niki. The thought almost paralyzed her. How could two days and two nights make such a difference?

I've got to find a way to get another weekend pass, she thought as she pulled on her shoes. *I've got to be with Niki.*

"I can't stand this," Niki sobbed. "I think I'm going to hyperventilate." She threw herself into Dawn's arms and clung to the blonde.

"I know, honey. I feel the same way. I'll call you tonight. I'll find some way to see you more. I promise."

Niki tried to be brave. "I'll see you Wednesday. We have that to look forward to."

Chapter 30

Monday Niki missed her first two classes. She attended them, but she never heard a word the instructors said. Her mind was filled with Dawn—the way Dawn looked when she slept, the way her eyes gleamed when she looked at Niki. And she would never forget the way Dawn had looked at her Sunday morning in the kitchen. A shiver ran through her body at the thought of what had transpired in the kitchen. She almost jumped for joy to find a note on her professor's classroom door stating class was cancelled for the day.

Niki stood in the shade of the building and watched the two men who were leaning against her car. Her heart was in her throat as she tried to pull their faces from her memories. There had been so many men in her life: Johns, dealers, pimps. Their faces were a blur.

"You okay?"

She jumped as a security guard touched her elbow.

"Oh, yes," she said. "I just . . . there are two men leaning on my car. I don't know them, and it made me nervous."

"I'll find out who they are," the guard volunteered. He talked to the two men and then led them back to where Niki was standing.

"Niki?" The younger of the two men leaned down so his face was level with hers. "It's us, Willard and Renfro."

"She hasn't seen us in several years," Renfro explained to the guard, "but we're her brothers."

"Do you know them, Miss?" the guard asked.

"Yes," Niki said. "Thank you for your help."

"Anytime, Miss. A pretty lady like you can't be too careful."

Niki scowled as the security guard walked away. "How did you find me? What do you want?"

"It's good to see you too, little sister," Renfro huffed. "We're here because Mother wants to see you."

"The warden at your prison is so proud of you," Willard added. "She gladly gave us the name of the university you're attending. The rest was easy."

"I like your Lexus," Renfro said with a smirk. "Which pimp is providing that?"

"I want nothing to do with either of you or Mother," Niki insisted. "Stay away from me."

"Niki, wait." Willard caught her by the arm and instantly found himself lying on the ground flat on his back.

Niki spun around to face Renfro who was backing away from her. "I won't touch you," he grumbled, holding out a hand to Willard who was still trying to recapture the breath that had been knocked out of him.

"Damn, where did you learn to do that?" Willard gasped as Renfro pulled him to his feet.

"Prison, no doubt," Renfro said, raising a judgmental eyebrow. "Anyhow, Mother's dying. She asked us to find you. Here's my business card. All my numbers are on there. Call any time, day or night." Willard followed him to a BMW parked nearby, and they drove away.

Niki got into her car and drove around the campus. When she noticed her brothers following her, she pulled into the parking lot at one of the dorms and walked inside. She watched as her brothers drove by. *Hopefully they'll think I live on campus.*

Niki gave her brothers plenty of time to get out of sight and then walked back to the Lexus. She would stay as far away from them as possible. They were the ones who had gotten her hooked on drugs her last semester of college. They had also convinced their mother to disown her because she was an addict. *So much for brotherly love.*

##

Val sauntered into the diagnostic room where Dawn was looking at sonograms and an MRI. X-rays were clipped to the lightboard above them. "How was your weekend?"

"Good." Dawn tried to suppress the smile that threatened to take over her lips at the thought of her weekend.

"I bet everyone was thrilled to see you." Val toyed with a stethoscope lying on the table.

"Yes, they were delighted." Dawn gently took the stethoscope from Val's hands. "Not a toy." She let the smile take over.

"You certainly are in high spirits. Perhaps I should give you more weekend passes."

"Perhaps you should," Dawn said. "How did your meeting with the DA go?"

"Excellent," Val said, beaming. "They're throwing the book at Merrick and the uncooperative guard. He's asking for the death penalty for both. Lucky's a lifer anyway, but they're fixing it so she will never be eligible for parole."

"That's wonderful news."

"He's holding a press conference this afternoon at three," Val added, "and has asked me to be a part of it to show the cooperation the federal prison system is giving law enforcement."

"Kudos to you," Dawn said. "They rarely share the limelight."

Val agreed. "I think it's a first. I'd like you to attend. You know, for moral support."

"That's very nice of you, but I have a conference call with some top heart specialists at three thirty. We're

Facetiming because I want to discuss an anomaly I've discovered in our heart patient. I've already emailed them the x-rays along with the MRI and sonogram. See here?"

Val studied the x-ray. "It looks like she has two hearts."

"Excellent diagnosis, Dr. Davis." Dawn laughed. "You were paying attention in med school."

"Well, at least enough to recognize two hearts when I see them." Val flashed a pleased smile. "What's her story?"

"She developed heart problems after she was incarcerated. She was sent to us two months ago when she almost died and they defibbed her back to life.

"I've read everything I can find and talked to specialists all morning. It appears to be some underdeveloped form of conjoined twins, and one of the hearts is failing. The other is healthy, so I see no reason why we can't remove the ailing one and let the healthy heart take over.

"She isn't overweight and appears to have no other health issues. But I want to run this by my colleagues to get their thoughts."

"Dawn, I want you to perform the surgery. It would be an incredible coup for the prison to have a doctor on staff capable of performing a procedure like this one. The press coverage would be invaluable."

Dawn tilted her head and stared at Val. "If I feel I'm the best surgeon for the job I'll do it, but if I feel she has a better chance with another physician, I'll turn it over to him. I won't jeopardize a patient's life so your prison can incur glory from the press."

Val's mouth dropped open as she gazed into the stormiest blue eyes she had ever seen. "I . . . I didn't mean for it to come out that way."

"But that *is* what you meant," Dawn hissed, spinning on her heel and fleeing the room.

##

Dawn turned on the TV in the doctors' lounge to see if any of the local stations picked up the DA's news conference. To her surprise, all the local stations and one highly rated cable news station were carrying the briefing.

The DA introduced Warden Valerie Davis and praised her for working closely with law enforcement officers to bring Merrick and the guards to justice. Val maintained a stoic expression, but Dawn knew she was bursting with pride.

Dawn's phone rang, and she opened her iPad to have a larger screen. She spent the next hour discussing her patient with the surgeons who had joined in the conference call.

"I operated on a girl with two hearts," one of the surgeons informed the group. "She wasn't born with it. She had a transplant when she was two. We placed the heart of a nine-month-old in line with her own heart whose muscles hadn't fully developed. It worked great until she was ten. Then the new heart began to fail.

"We removed the transplant and let her own heart take over. That was five years ago, and she is thriving. Just to be safe, clamp off the heart you're going to remove and let the remaining one take over. Watch it until you feel confident the remaining heart can handle the workload alone."

"Judging from your experience and how thoroughly you have delved into this," the senior surgeon on the call said, "I think you may be the best surgeon to perform this surgery."

The others agreed. Dawn thanked them and disconnected the call.

Chapter 31

"Lance said you were in here," Val said, entering the diagnostic room for the second time that day.

"I watched your press conference. It was very impressive, Warden," Dawn said.

"Thank you. How was your conference call?"

"Good."

"Are you going to do the surgery?" Val asked.

"I'm considering it. I'm not certain I'm the surgeon for the job."

"I have faith in you," Val insisted. "How about this? You do the surgery, and I'll give you a weekend pass every weekend for the duration of your sentence."

Dawn shoved her hands into her pockets to keep from doing cartwheels. She knew Val wouldn't be pleased to learn she'd spent her weekend with Niki.

"What if something goes wrong and the surgery is a failure?" Dawn said. "What then?"

"You'd still get the passes. Of course, we'd all be sad to lose an inmate during surgery."

Val looked at her watch. "Let's go out for dinner. I want to get away from this place for a few hours."

"That's supposed to be my line, Warden."

"Tell me about your weekend," Val inquired. "What did you do? I know you had a big family dinner Friday night. What else did you do?"

"Bought groceries. Changed the oil in my car." Dawn tried to remember all the things Niki had done in preparation for their weekend. "Wore my own clothes. Showered with my own shampoo and good-smelling soap. We talked about going to a movie but decided to just hang around the house. It was nice to be home.

"What about you? Did you celebrate with friends after your successful meeting with the DA?"

"No. Like you, I just wanted to relax and spend a nice quiet weekend at home.

"The self-defense equipment was delivered today," Val added. "We should have that up and running by the end of the week. I'm so excited, Dawn. Before you came I felt like I was spinning my wheels. Now, suddenly, things are falling into place."

Val reached across the table and placed her hand on top of Dawn's. "You're my muse."

"You underestimate yourself." Dawn smiled as she withdrew her hand to pick up her drink.

##

"Dawn, you called early tonight," Niki said into the phone.

"I got away from the hospital early and wanted to call you so you could get a good night's rest. I'm exhausted after this weekend. We didn't sleep much."

Niki giggled. "I loved every minute of it. I wish every weekend could be like that."

Dawn thought about telling her about Val offering to allow her to leave the prison every weekend but refrained. She wanted to wait until she was certain it would happen.

"I saw your keeper on TV," Niki said. "She looked marvelous, and it sounded like Merrick will either get the needle or die in prison. I'm good either way."

"Yes, she compiled one hell of a case against him," Dawn said, unable to hide her admiration for the warden.

148

"You helped her," Niki pointed out. "I noticed she gave you no credit."

Dawn shrugged. "I didn't want any. The less my name is associated with that prison, the happier I'll be.

"On a good note, the ladies started setting up the new self-defense center today. Lots of new equipment and state-of-the-art machinery. What about you? How was your day?"

"I received a visit from my brothers today," Niki said, her voice flat.

"Brothers? I didn't know you had brothers."

"Two," Niki croaked. "Two brothers and no sisters. I'm the baby."

"You don't sound very happy," Dawn noted.

"I'm not. I don't want them around me."

"Honey, they're your brothers."

"They got me hooked on drugs," Niki said. "My last semester of college they said I should loosen up. Then when I couldn't kick the habit they washed their hands of me. The big brothers of every girl's dreams."

"I'm so sorry, baby." Dawn fought down the rising sense of doom that invaded her thoughts. "Do they know where you live? How'd they find you?"

"I don't think they know where I live. Val told them where I went to college. They traced me down that way. I made it clear I wanted nothing to do with them. I think I'm through with them."

"I must share something with you," Dawn said, eager to change the subject. "I'm doing the prison's first open-heart surgery Wednesday."

"Oh honey!" Niki gasped, not knowing whether to be pleased or worried.

"It's okay." Dawn chuckled. "I feel confident about it. I've run every test imaginable and have looked at it from all sides. It should be a long but successful surgery."

"Call me as soon as it's over," Niki insisted. "Call me tomorrow night, but then call me Wednesday as soon as it's over. Okay?"

"Of course I will."

##

Tuesday was filled with visits from prison dignitaries and a female reporter. Dawn received rave reviews on the cleanliness of the hospital and the cure rate of patients.

Val led a tour of the prison facilities, sharing how proud she was of the self-defense center they were setting up. "We want to empower our inmates, not leave them helpless prey for prison bullies," Val explained as the VIPs followed her through the prison and into the cafeteria.

"You should dine with us," one of the inmates called out to the group. "The food here is great."

Questioning eyes turned to Val. She shrugged and motioned for the visitors to pick up a tray and get in line for the buffet.

The visitors left at the end of the day with only praise for the prison and its warden. "I'd like to do a piece on you," the reporter said.

"Call me. We'll set up an appointment," Val said. "I'm certain we can coordinate something."

After everyone left, Val sought out Dawn in the infirmary. "Today was perfect," she said, grinning from ear to ear. "Just perfect."

"I'm glad," Dawn said, looking up from her paperwork. "It's about time you started to receive some recognition for the hours you put in here and the innovations you've introduced."

Val laughed out loud. "Let's talk about how great I am over dinner."

"I can't. I have the heart surgery at ten in the morning. I want to get there early to make certain everything is in order and our patient is properly prepped. I need to go to bed early."

"Of course." Although Val admired Dawn's dedication, she couldn't keep the disappointment from her voice. "I'll see you in the morning."

Chapter 32

Dawn drained her coffee cup and headed toward the hospital. She couldn't remember the last time she'd felt so alone. Niki had always been with her during her difficult surgeries. Niki always had the instruments lined up perfectly. She smiled as she briefly let herself think about waking up next to Niki. Then she forced her mind back to the task at hand.

She perused Clarissa Mears's reports on the computer and then walked to the sterilization room. She scrubbed and stood still while an equally sterile nurse pulled Dawn's gloves on.

"Showtime!" She smiled at her surgical team, and they followed her into the operating room.

Val watched from the observation deck. The patient was already anesthetized, and sheets had been taped so the only area exposed was around the heart. Lance had placed Clarissa on the heart-lung machine to keep the blood circulating while Dawn performed the surgery.

Dawn bowed her head and said a prayer for her patient, her team, and herself. Then she went to work.

Val watched the operation through the close-up camera that fed information to her monitor as it recorded the operation. She could see every blood vessel, every artery, and two hearts. One heart was pink and obviously quite healthy. The other heart was darker and struggled to pump. There was more blood than Val had expected. The hearts weren't side by side; instead, the healthy heart lay on top of the weaker heart.

Dawn deftly clamped off the struggling heart, forcing its blood into the healthy heart. She moved methodically, checking her work and traumatizing the good heart as little as possible.

Without warning, Dawn's hands stopped moving. A nurse wiped the sweat from her brow. "Something isn't right," Dawn said. "There's too much blood. The machine should be handling this. How are her vitals?"

"Vitals are holding," the anesthesiologist reported.

"Dear God," Val prayed out loud, "please help her."

Dawn carefully picked up the pink heart and turned it over. "There's a hole. It was hidden from the MRI by the other heart."

Dawn hesitated slightly and then unclamped the weaker heart, letting blood rush into it. It began pumping normally. She picked it up and inspected it. It had no physical flaws, only a lack of arteries feeding it.

Then Dawn made one of those life-changing decisions. She detached the right pulmonary artery from the pink heart and attached it to the dark heart. She did the same with the left pulmonary artery. Then she methodically moved all the arteries and veins from the pink heart to the weaker one. Instead of the simple removal of a bad heart, Dawn knew she was basically performing a heart transplant. The pink heart stopped beating.

"Vitals?" Dawn barked.

"Holding, Doc."

Dawn closed the old arteries and veins that had fed the dark heart, so all the blood flow from the pink heart was directed into it. The dark heart fluttered.

"Vitals dropping, Doc."

Dawn didn't panic. She gently massaged the dark heart and watched as it pulled in the blood from the newly attached arteries. She almost cried when the blood flowed from the veins back to the heart.

Everyone prayed as the heartbeat grew stronger and the heart's color began to improve. Dawn lifted the extra heart from the body, making room for the single heart to expand and contract. Blood flowed from the arteries and returned through the veins.

"Vitals are stable."

The dark heart took on a healthy hue as it assumed the entire job of moving blood through Clarissa's body. "Look at that little sucker go," the nurse squealed.

Everyone laughed softly as Dawn began to close the patient's chest. The surgery had taken six hours, and Dawn was exhausted.

Val said one last, "Thank you, God," and sprinted down the stairs to the hallway outside the operating room. Lance and the surgical team were in the hall, congratulating each other on their success. Dawn wasn't with them.

Val raised a questioning eyebrow at Lance.

"She went to her room," he said. "She's exhausted."

"I want to congratulate you all on a job well done," Val said, smiling. "I am so proud of all of you."

"It was Dr. Fairchild," a nurse said. "She has nerves of steel."

The anesthesiologist echoed the nurse's sentiment. "I've never worked with a finer surgeon. When I saw the size of that hole in Clarissa's heart, I thought she was a goner. But Dr. Fairchild took it all in stride and made the right call. She's amazing."

"Yes! Yes, she is." Val thanked them all again and headed for Dawn's room.

Chapter 33

Dawn stripped off her scrubs and stepped into the shower. When the hot water hit her back, she breathed deeply for the first time in what seemed like a lifetime. She knew how close she had come to losing Clarissa, and the thought still horrified her.

She towel-dried her hair and pulled on the T-shirt Niki always wore. She inhaled the natural scent that was Niki. *God, I need her right now.* She looked around for her cell phone. She needed to call Niki.

A knock on her door preceded, "Dawn? It's me, Val."

She knows I'm in here. I have to let her in, Dawn thought as she reluctantly forced her feet to move toward the door.

Val burst into the room. "I'm so proud of you," she gushed. "I've never observed anything so unnerving and exciting in my life. Clarissa is one lucky patient to have you as her surgeon."

"I had a lot of help from the man upstairs," Dawn mumbled as her knees gave out and she plopped down on the bed. "I'm sorry. I am so tired."

Val looked around the sparse room. "I'll let you rest. I just wanted to thank you and congratulate you. I'll lock the door behind me. You get some sleep."

Dawn nodded and fell backward across the bed.

Val walked closer to look down at the sleeping woman. "Lord, you're beautiful," she whispered.

Dawn waited until she heard the lock snap into place then she opened her eyes.

##

Dawn lay still, unable to make her legs move. She dozed and roused several times before mustering the strength to stand and locate her cell phone. She found it in the bathroom. She double-checked the door lock, climbed between the sheets, and called Niki.

"Dawn, is everything okay?" Niki asked.

"The surgery was a success," Dawn whispered. "It took a lot out of me, Nik. I'm so tired. I wish you were here to hold me."

"As do I, honey. Go to sleep. I won't have class until ten in the morning. If you want to call me, I'll be here. I love you."

"Love you too," Dawn mumbled before drifting into a deep sleep.

Niki wondered if Dawn even remembered they'd missed their regular visitation today.

##

Dawn jerked awake before sunup. *Clarissa. I must check on Clarissa.* She dressed and took the stairs two at a time in her haste to get to ICU.

The hospital lights were still dimmed, and three nurses were at the nurses' station. They all gave her a hero's welcome.

"Your patient is doing exceptionally well," the head night nurse informed Dawn as she handed her a cup of coffee.

Dawn glanced at the coffee. "It's good," the nurse said with a chuckle. "It's not the cafeteria swill. It's fresh, and I even put cream in it for you."

Dawn sipped it. "Mmm, it *is* good. Now I know where to come for a good cup of coffee." Dawn knew the nurses were thinking of her as a real doctor now, not some hack

156

inmate the warden had drafted to fill the void. "Thank you."

Dawn walked into Clarissa's room and was surprised to find her patient awake. "How are you feeling?"

"Honestly, Doc, I never thought I'd see your face again, but you did it. You pulled me through."

"It was an easy operation," Dawn reassured her. "And you're an excellent patient.

"Do you mind if I sit here and drink my coffee with you?" Dawn knew the presence of a physician reassured a patient.

"I'd love it. It's not every day I get to spend time with the gatekeeper."

"Gatekeeper?"

"Yeah, you're the gatekeeper. You decided whether I stayed in this life or passed over."

"No," Dawn said, "that's God. I promise you, Clarissa, I'm no god, but I did call on Him more than once during your surgery."

"That's what's so nice about you," Clarissa said. "You don't have the god syndrome."

"You're very sweet," Dawn said, pausing to sip her coffee. "Do you have any questions for me?"

"I'd like to know what to expect. Will I be able to live a full life, or will I always have heart problems?"

"We'll keep you on a strict drug regimen for thirty days to prevent any infection and give your heart all the help it needs to succeed. I see no reason why you can't live a good long life without any problems from your heart.

"You'll be on a soft diet for twenty-four hours. Then you may have whatever you'd like to eat."

"Steak?" Clarissa's eyes sparkled at the thought of something she hadn't had in several years.

Dawn laughed. "Even steak. I'm sure Warden Davis will make that happen."

"Make what happen?" Val said as she entered the ICU unit and stood at the foot of Clarissa's bed.

"Steak," Dawn said, grinning. "Clarissa would like a steak next Friday."

Val laughed. "How do you want it cooked?"

"Medium rare."

Val pretended to make a note in the palm of her hand. "Medium rare next Friday."

Dawn stood. "You need to rest now. I'll drop in on you throughout the day."

Val wished the patient well and followed Dawn into the hallway. "Mind if I make your rounds with you?"

"I'd welcome the company," Dawn admitted. "I need to return this empty cup to the nurses' station first."

"I have your favorite brewing in my office." Val glanced sideways to see if her revelation pleased the doctor.

"Sounds good," Dawn said.

As they walked, the two discussed the activities going on in the prison. Val had hired an activities director who had set up a softball program, allowing the nonviolent inmates to form teams. Each dorm had selected a team and would compete.

"I have to come up with a trophy or reward for the winning team," Val said.

"They're nonviolent," Dawn thought out loud. "Give the winning team members a weekend pass. It does wonders for the soul."

"I'll look into that," Val promised.

"I think I've earned the weekend passes you promised," Dawn pointed out. "Every weekend until I complete my sentence."

"Yes. I suppose you want to begin with this weekend?"

"I did give up visitation Wednesday to perform Clarissa's surgery," Dawn pointed out. "So . . . yes, I'd love to begin with this weekend."

158

"I'll make the arrangements," Val said, but her heart wasn't in it.

Chapter 34

Clarissa continued to improve during the day, and Val called Dawn to her office to give her the standing weekend pass. Dawn was euphoric when she called Niki later than usual.

"Darling," Niki whispered into the phone. "I was afraid you weren't going to call tonight."

Dawn laughed. "Wild horses couldn't keep me from calling you. This is the highlight of my day. I'm sorry I'm so late. We moved Clarissa out of ICU tonight, and I sat with her until I was positive she was okay."

"I'm glad she's still doing well. Anything else happen today?"

"The entire week has been wonderful," Dawn said. "Spending the weekend with you made the entire week perfect."

"I know. But we missed visitation this week."

"Yes, Val said she felt bad about that." Dawn hesitated, drawing out her announcement. "So, she gave me a weekend pass."

Niki squealed. "You're serious? That's tomorrow. You wouldn't tease me?"

"Serious and excited," Dawn said, her voice thick with emotion. "I can't wait to see you. All I can think about is my weekend with you. I want a lifetime with you, Niki."

"I'll be with you as long as you want me," Niki promised. "Oh, I'm so excited. How soon can you get away Friday?"

"I'm not sure. I'll call you when I leave the prison. I'll take a cab like last time."

The weeks passed, with Niki and Dawn living from one weekend to the next. They settled into a routine: classes for Niki, more patients for Dawn, and two days of heaven on the weekend.

The success of Clarissa's surgery spread throughout the prison system, and more inmates filed requests for treatment by the beautiful blonde doctor. Clarissa's nickname for Dawn became a synonym for the doctor. Everyone wanted the Gatekeeper.

Gloria and Lynn's self-defense training had accomplished what Val wanted. As inmates became more capable of defending themselves, prison crime had dropped.

Dawn showed up at six every morning to take advantage of the training offered by the two experts. She was amazed at how empowered she felt, and her fear of the other inmates diminished as she became more proficient in the skill of self-defense.

Val watched from the doorway as Dawn sparred with another inmate. The blonde was trim and toned. She looked incredible in gym shorts and a workout shirt that crisscrossed her back. Val found herself wanting to touch Dawn's back, to run her hands down the muscular shoulders to encircle her tiny waist.

Dawn's sparring partner lunged at her, and the blonde deftly sidestepped the charge, catching her opponent's arm and twisting it behind her back. "Uncle!" cried the subdued woman.

Dawn laughed and released her. Val applauded.

Dawn walked toward Val, wiping the perspiration from her body with a gym towel. "Warden, are you joining us?"

"I've been taking the training from the beginning," Val informed her. "I manage to work it in every day.

"You handled that attack beautifully. Think you could take me?"

Dawn couldn't stop the smile that covered her face as she flashed back to her first weekend with Niki and making love to the redhead on the kitchen island.

"I . . . um. . . don't know."

"Want to spar with me?" Val asked.

"Sure. First takedown wins."

Val nodded and moved to the closest mat. The other inmates stopped their workouts and gathered to watch the two.

"Don't go easy on me," Val warned. "I intend to beat you."

Dawn nodded and moved so the kickboxing bag was directly behind her. She faked a lunge at Val and then stepped back. She knew patience was the key to sparring with the aggressive warden.

Dawn pretended to look away, giving Val the opportunity she'd waited for. Like a big cat, Val sprang at her prey. Dawn faked a move and sidestepped Val's lunge. She stepped forward, caught Val's arm, and slammed the warden face-first into the kickboxing bag.

Val bounced off the bag and landed flat on her back. She lay still, trying to catch the breath that had been knocked from her. Dawn stood over her, offering her hand to pull Val to her feet. Val's eyes traveled up the long, muscular legs to the flat stomach and the firm breasts straining against the tank top.

"Are you okay?" Dawn asked as she moved her hand closer.

"I'm fine." Val accepted the extended hand and was surprised at how easily Dawn pulled her to her feet. The woman was strong.

The women watching the two applauded as Val and Dawn gave good-natured bows.

"I'm going to my room to shower," Dawn said as they walked from the gym. "I don't suppose you have any of that great coffee brewing in your office, do you?"

"I will by the time you get there." A pleased smile crossed Val's face.

"You look all fresh and ready to face the day," Val said as Dawn entered her office.

"Any workout gets the endorphins going." Dawn poured cream into her coffee. "It's better than any drug on the market."

"I agree." Val settled behind her desk, and Dawn knew they would discuss business. "I have something I want you to watch. Don't say a word until the end."

For the next thirty minutes, Dawn watched a beautifully produced documentary on Clarissa's heart surgery. The video began with Dawn and her team praying. As Dawn made the first incision, the narrator quickly explained Clarissa's medical condition. There was a snippet of the two hearts, followed by the dramatic realization that the good heart had a hole in it.

Dawn's uneasiness upon discovering the hole and her quick action to change directions were both showcased.

The documentary was sprinkled with shots of Dawn interacting with her patients, laughing, explaining, praying. It was a tremendous promotion piece for the prison. The title of the documentary was "The Gatekeeper."

The video ended, and Dawn sat in silence.

"Well?" Val held her breath.

"I don't know what to say." Dawn took a deep breath and fought back the tears that threatened to spill down her cheeks. "It's beautiful."

Val exhaled the breath she was holding. "You're okay with it? You'll sign off on it, giving us permission to use it?"

"Do I have a choice?"

"You always have a choice with me, Dawn."

"How could I refuse? It's a perfect piece to reflect the changes you've made here."

Val clapped her hands. "Wonderful! It's set to air in prime time Friday night. The highest-rated cable news station is doing an interview with me and televising the documentary in its entirety.

"I have a three-day training session in Dallas, but I'll be back Friday in time for the live telecast. This will make us both famous."

Chapter 35

Val had agonized over making the call to the FBI, but the decision was made easily when she met an undercover agent at the three-day seminar on habitual criminals. Java Jarvis had a firm handshake and deep blue eyes. The tall blonde was easy to talk to and had seen it all. By the end of the seminar, Val trusted Java completely.

"Would you like to go out for drinks after this is over?" Val asked as they walked to the elevator.

"That's the best suggestion I've heard all day." Java grinned at her. "The only thing better would be drinks with dinner. Are you up for that?"

"Absolutely!"

"Meet in the lobby at six?" Java suggested.

"That's perfect."

Val showered and put on the only dress she had brought for the seminar. She was pleased with her reflection in the mirror. She was looking forward to dinner with Java. She liked the straightforward woman.

Java was waiting for her in the lobby and rushed to meet her when the elevator doors opened. "I made reservations at a really nice restaurant I'd like to share with you. I hope you don't mind. Everyone from the seminar is dining in this hotel's restaurants."

"I think that's perfect," Val said, smiling. "I'm sure it will be quieter, and we'll be less likely to be interrupted."

"I had the valet pull my car around," Java said as they exited the hotel and headed toward a powder-blue Maserati GranTurismo.

"Whoa!" Val started to have second thoughts. If Java could afford a car like that, she was getting money from somewhere other than her law enforcement paycheck.

"All part of my mystique." Java laughed as she fastened her seatbelt and patted the car's leather dashboard. "Posing as an undercover drug dealer does have some perks."

Val forced herself to relax and thought about the best way to explain her problem to Java. She decided to wait until they had ordered dinner and could talk without being interrupted.

Over a pleasant meal Val told Java everything she had uncovered on VitaMaxPro. "In short, US prisoners are being fed dog food to cut costs so greedy politicians and plutocrats can line their pockets."

Java scrutinized Val for a minute. "You have proof of everything you just told me?"

"Yes. I wouldn't bring you such a story without proof. I even have photos of the VitaMaxPro being used in the kitchens of several of the area prisons I visited."

"Will you testify against your boss?" Java asked.

Val sighed. "I must. I couldn't live with myself if I didn't. I'll probably lose my job over this."

"Maybe not." Java patted her hand. "I'll run this investigation, and I can be very discreet."

For the first time since Dawn Fairchild had entered her life, Val was drawn to another woman.

"Can you bring all the documents and photos you've collected to my office tomorrow?" Java wrote her personal number on the back of her business card. "I'd like to go over everything with you."

166

Val nodded and scribbled on a cocktail napkin. "This is the date, time, and station of a documentary about my prison. If you have nothing better to do, please watch it."

"I will," Java promised as they paid their checks.

Chapter 36

Dawn fell onto her back. She inhaled deeply, trying to catch her breath and return her heart rate to normal. Niki snuggled further into her and kissed the side of her breast.

"You're the lover I never dreamed of," Niki whispered, "because I never knew such love and gentleness existed."

"Neither did I." Dawn stroked her back. "I never considered a woman. I had decided that sex with a man was something I'd just have to tolerate. It left me cold and unsatisfied. I didn't enjoy it."

"And now?" Niki giggled.

"You know I love it. I can't get enough of you. I—" Soft lips cut off her sentence

"I feel the same way, but right now I'm starving. Take me out to dinner."

"May I take a raincheck for tomorrow night?" Dawn asked. "There's a show I want you to watch at eight. We could order in Chinese."

"You know how I love Chinese takeout," Niki said. "I'll order. You find your TV station."

Dawn set up TV trays and was ready when the deliveryman arrived. Niki carried iced tea to the living room as Dawn served the Chinese food. They settled on the sofa, and Dawn grabbed the remote. "I've been recording it so we didn't miss anything," she said, barely able to contain her excitement.

The show host introduced himself and his guest, Warden Valerie Davis. They talked about FMC Carswell and the changes Val had orchestrated there.

"One of our most exciting accomplishments is our medical facilities," Val said, praising Dr. Lance Reynolds and Dr. Dawn Fairchild.

Niki watched, spellbound, as the documentary played. When the station cut to a commercial, she turned to Dawn. "That was incredible. I cried when you discovered the hole in her heart. Your words stopped my own heart for a few seconds."

Dawn sighed. "I almost cried too."

"Warden Davis, we have a surprise for you tonight," the news personality continued. "Your top boss, the US Attorney General Wendy Day, is here."

Niki laughed out loud. "Seriously? The top lawyer in America is named Wendy Day?"

Dawn put her arm around Niki's shoulders and pulled her close. "This should be interesting. I can tell by the look on Val's face she's surprised."

Standing five feet, three inches tall, Wendy Day gave a whole new meaning to the Napoleon complex. Her short-cropped brown hair and hard-set jaw gave her the appearance of a bulldog.

"Attorney General Day, thank you for taking the time from your busy schedule to make a rare television appearance tonight." The show host's eyes gleamed. He knew he had pulled off a coup.

"Thank you for having me," Day said. "I wanted to congratulate Warden Davis on setting the gold standard for all our prisons and providing an example for all wardens across the nation."

"Thank you," Val said.

Day moved so she was facing directly into the cameras and began delivering her prepared speech in the shotgun staccato voice that made her easy prey for late-night comedians. "The documentary you have just watched exemplifies what can be achieved when a warden takes a hands-on approach to a problem.

"The rehabilitation of a prisoner—from serving time for manslaughter to becoming a dedicated surgeon capable of performing open-heart surgery needed by an inmate—is nothing short of a miracle. Dr. Dawn Fairchild's transformation is one of the shining examples of what the federal prison system is capable of doing."

"What the hell?" Dawn jumped up from the sofa, screeching like a banshee. "Is she as stupid as she looks or just doesn't give a damn?"

Niki quieted her lover. "Shh. I want to hear how your mentor responds to this."

Val cleared her throat twice before her voice cooperated. "Dr. Fairchild was an outstanding surgeon before—"

"It gives me great pleasure to present the US Attorney General's Award of Excellence to Warden Valerie Davis," Day continued to bark. "I'm certain Warden Davis has what it takes to go straight to the top."

"My ability to perform Clarissa's surgery had nothing to do with that crummy prison," Dawn raved to Niki. "If not for you, I would have died my first week there.

"She's ruined my name. No hospital in the world will hire a doctor convicted of manslaughter. She didn't even have the decency to say vehicular manslaughter."

"Listen. Val's talking," Niki pointed out. "Maybe she'll straighten out this fiasco."

"Thank you, Attorney General Day. I'm extremely honored to be selected for this award."

The show cut to a commercial as Day and Val shook hands.

Dawn wanted to scream, to break things, to choke Valerie Davis. "What a lowlife," she growled. "Her lies put me into that hellhole in the first place, and now she takes credit for my skills as a surgeon. Warden Davis is a real piece of work."

"Honey, calm down," Niki said. "Your nightmare is almost over. A few more months and you'll be a free woman. Then we can really start our lives together."

"Doing what?" Dawn demanded. "She ruined my career with her worldwide telecast of *Warden Davis, Wonder Woman*. I won't even be able to practice in a veterinarian's office."

"Honey, anyone watching that documentary will know what a competent surgeon you are," Niki reasoned. "Any hospital would be thrilled to have you on their staff."

Niki turned off the TV and led Dawn to their bedroom. "Why don't we take a nice hot shower and forget about Warden Davis? Don't let her ruin the little bit of time we have together."

Although showering with Niki was nice, Dawn couldn't get her mind off what Val had done to her. *I can't wait to get that woman out of my life*, she thought. She relaxed as Niki lathered her with fragrant bath soap.

"Is that a new brand?" she asked.

"It is." Niki lathered between her breasts. "Vanilla Kisses. Do you like it?"

"Very much." Dawn leaned down for a kiss as she took the soap from Niki's hand. "My turn to do you."

They laughed covering each other with soap foam and rinsing it from their bodies. Dawn dried Niki and Niki returned the favor.

They slipped into bed and snuggled into each other. "Don't forget, it's your turn to do me," Niki said.

##

Val waited until Sunday morning to call Dawn, but she didn't answer the phone. She had to talk to her. She had to explain what had happened. Dawn had to know Val had been blindsided by the appearance of the Attorney General at the showing of the documentary.

171

After they were off the air, Wendy Day had informed Valerie that she was being considered for the position of Regional Director over the South-Central Region, having jurisdiction over Texas, Oklahoma, and Arkansas. The promotion meant more money than Val had ever dreamed of, but she knew she could truly implement more humane treatment of prisoners as the regional director. *Any sacrifices made would be for the greater good,* she told herself.

She tried to call Dawn again but received no answer. *I'll catch her this afternoon when she reports back to the prison. Maybe take her to dinner,* she thought.

Sunday with Niki had been relaxing and sweet. Dawn had helped the redhead study for her first physiology exam. "This stuff is really hard," Niki had whined as she tried to seduce Dawn.

But she hadn't fooled Dawn. The doctor was amazed at the intelligence of the other woman and her grasp of the human anatomy.

Niki faded from Dawn's thoughts as her taxi pulled up to the prison gate. Dawn showed the guard her weekend pass, and he waved them through.

"I saw you on TV Friday night," the cab driver said as they approached the hospital. "You're really impressive."

"Thank you," Dawn mumbled as her anger at Val rushed back.

"I figured you were a civilian working here. I never dreamed a woman like you would be a prisoner."

"Neither did I," Dawn huffed as she paid the driver and got out of the car.

Val was in the hospital lobby waiting for Dawn when she arrived. The look in Dawn's eyes made her cringe. It was the same look Dawn had flashed at her at the end of her trial.

172

"Dawn, I need to explain," Val said as the doctor signed in at the guard desk.

"I can't talk right now." Dawn choked back her anger. "Just let me cool off first and get a good night's sleep. We'll talk in the morning."

Val nodded as she watched Dawn disappear into the elevator.

Chapter 37

Val paced the floor. She knew she had sacrificed Dawn for her career. She'd made a half-hearted attempt to correct the Attorney General but was so busy basking in the limelight that she failed to consider the cost to Dawn.

Beautiful women like Dawn always landed on their feet. She'll be okay, Val reasoned. *I'll only get one shot at the promotion I've dreamed of.*

Besides, the little voice that wasn't a conscience whispered, *she can always work here at the prison hospital and be with you.*

Sometime after two a.m., Val climbed into bed and tried to sleep. *I'll talk to her tomorrow. I'll find a way to make it right.*

##

"Good morning," Lance said, greeting Dawn with a smile. "That was an incredible documentary the warden had on television Friday night."

The icy glare Dawn shot at him silenced any further conversation. She made her morning rounds and was finishing her notes on patients' computer files when the head nurse signaled her for a phone call.

She took the handset from the nurse. "Dr. Fairchild."

"Dawn, may I see you in my office?" Val asked.

"When?"

"Now, if possible."

"Ten minutes. I need to see one more patient."

"Of course."

Ten minutes seemed to take an hour to pass. Then a knock on Val's door made her jump. "Come in."

"You wanted to see me?" Dawn stood in the doorway.

God, she's the original ice queen, Val thought as she motioned for Dawn to sit in the chair across from hers. She poured coffee for them and leaned back in her chair.

"Dawn, I know I messed up." Val bowed her head. "How can I make this up to you?"

Dawn glared at her. "Get me an early release. Get me out of this prison that you have changed single-handedly."

"I . . . I know the hospital has improved solely because of you and Lance. I know it was you who pushed for decent food for the inmates. I know you and Niki were the catalysts for cleaning up the corruption in this prison. I know—"

"In short," Dawn said, "someone else was responsible for most of the things you took credit for on TV Friday night."

"I . . . you don't understand," Val wailed. "The attorney general all but told me I will soon get my dream job. The job I have worked for all my life."

"What about me, Val? Do you know how difficult it is for a woman to make it through med school and work her way up to chief of staff?"

"I have some idea."

"Then you know that you destroyed my reputation and my career when you pretended on national TV to have rehabilitated me. You and the attorney general acted as if you were turning out prize surgeons. This place has nothing to do with my abilities as a surgeon. If anything, this place would destroy me if I'd let it."

"Dawn, please, just complete your sentence and be cooperative. My promotion depends on it."

"It's not like I have a choice." Dawn stormed out of the office.

She didn't touch her coffee, Val thought as she carried their cups to the sideboard. *God, she's hot when she's mad. And dammit, I'm in love with her.*

As usual, they met every morning and Dawn gave Val a report on how the hospital was doing.

"I set two broken arms last week and a broken thumb. Did everything I could for a woman whose eye was gouged out over a pack of cigarettes. All women will leave this place in worse shape than when they arrived here. Your rehabilitation program is on track, Warden."

"Dawn, you know I'm trying. My self-defense program has cut prisoner-on-prisoner crime by a fourth. Eventually I hope to have a prison where violence among inmates is negligible."

Dawn snorted as she stood. "That makes me feel safe outside the hospital. I know I can count on you to have my back. I just have to get your knife out of it first."

Val charged around her desk. "That's not fair. You know I wouldn't let anything happen to you. I . . . I love—"

Before she knew what she was doing, Val grasped Dawn's shoulders and kissed her.

Kissing Dawn wasn't at all like she had dreamed. In her fantasies, Dawn melted into her arms and parted her lips, slowly running her tongue along Val's lip before slipping it into her mouth to engage her tongue. This wasn't at all as she had imagined. Dawn didn't kiss her back. Instead, she stiffened and pulled away.

"I think you just committed a felony, Warden. One that carries an automatic two-year prison sentence."

Val stared in silence as Dawn slammed the door behind her. *Dear God, what have I done?*

Chapter 38

Val's usual calm façade was crumbling. She couldn't sleep or eat. She couldn't stop thinking about Dawn Fairchild—a woman who obviously hated her. Val knew her carefully constructed world was unraveling, and she didn't know how to stop it.

She watched out the window as the taxi picked up the blonde doctor and took her out of Val's world for the weekend. She had her dinner served in her quarters and fretted over resolving her issues with Dawn.

A cold, hard knot formed in the pit of Val's stomach as she realized that Dawn Fairchild wasn't a lesbian. She slammed the palm of her hand against her forehead. *What a fool I am.* Dawn had just broken a two-year engagement with her boyfriend when the accident occurred. No self-respecting lesbian would tolerate a man for two years.

What made me think she was a lesbian? Val wondered. *I never saw any evidence of it. She is just a sweet, girl-next-door, beautiful woman. She never made any inappropriate moves when we were together. Dawn is a regular straight woman. Just because she's in prison doesn't mean she's a lesbian.*

Jesus, she must think I'm an animal. I must make this right.

As always, Niki was waiting on the front porch when Dawn arrived. She was beside Dawn before the cab pulled away from the curb. Dawn slipped her arm around Niki's shoulders, and they walked inside clinging to each other. "I love your jeans," Niki ran her fingers along the waistband.

"The warden is allowing me to wear civilian clothes when I leave the prison," Dawn said. "I'm glad you like them."

Dawn closed the door and locked it. "I've missed you so much," she murmured as she pulled Niki into her arms. Niki tilted her head for Dawn's kiss. It was a sweet, tender kiss, as Dawn moved her soft lips slowly against Niki's. "You taste like honey," she whispered.

"Do you need anything?" Niki asked.

"Just you," Dawn said, her voice breaking. "Just you, Niki."

Asking no questions, Niki led her lover to their bedroom. "Mmm. You smell good," she mumbled as she slipped Dawn's blouse off her shoulders and let it fall to the floor.

Niki unzipped Dawn's jeans as she kissed the valley between her breasts. "You're so beautiful," she murmured as she paid homage to Dawn's perfect breasts. "So soft and smooth." Dawn's jeans pooled around her feet as she pulled Niki's sweater over her head and tangled her hands in the glorious shades of red.

Dawn nuzzled her face in Niki's hair. "I love your hair. I love losing myself in it."

"I love when you grab it and pull me to you," Niki whispered as she slipped her hand between Dawn's legs. "You need me, don't you, baby?"

"So badly." Dawn sat down on the bed, pulling Niki onto her lap. "Oh, how I need you."

They made love and then lay in each other's arms, cooing to one another or kissing just to feel silky, swollen lips.

"You want to talk about your week?" Niki asked as she stroked Dawn's flat, firm stomach. "My, someone has really worked out this week."

178

"Uh-huh. I took my frustrations out on the kickboxing bag. I pretended it was Val."

"I take it your talk with her didn't go well."

"She . . . she kissed me," Dawn blurted. "What kind of person does that? Why in the world would she think I wanted to kiss her?"

Niki stiffened and sat up in the bed. "She kissed you? What do you mean?"

"Where's my cell phone?" Dawn reached for her jeans on the floor. "Here. I had it in my hand with the audio and video on. You can see for yourself."

Niki gasped as Val charged around her desk and grabbed Dawn by the shoulders, forcing her to kiss her. "It's a crime for a prison employee to kiss or fondle an inmate," Niki cried. "You need to file charges against her. Does she know you have this video?"

"No, I knew she would take it away from me." Dawn touched the screen on her phone and sent the video to Niki. Niki's phone dinged as it received the video. "Now you have it, so I won't lose it if she confiscates my phone."

"You should send it to your attorney," Niki advised.

Dawn pulled up Libby's number and forwarded the video with a text to "Hold onto this."

"Let's talk about the warden tomorrow," Niki whispered as she kissed her way down Dawn's stomach. "Right now I want to make you forget everything but my name. And you may scream it frequently."

"I always do." Dawn inhaled deeply, anticipating the pleasure Niki always gave her.

##

Later they lay with their legs and arms tangled. It was impossible to tell where one woman stopped and the other started. Dawn trailed her fingers down Niki's back as the redhead lay on top of her, her cheek resting between Dawn's breasts.

179

"I love to listen to your heartbeat." Niki raised her head and planted a kiss on Dawn's neck. "I have everything we need for sandwiches. Want one?"

"I do." Dawn laughed as she flipped Niki over onto her back and kissed her soundly.

"No, no." Niki giggled. "You must feed me first."

Dawn pretended to pout as she rolled off the smaller woman. "I'm hungry too."

They padded into the kitchen, both wearing only T-shirts. "You are so damn cute in my shirt," Dawn said. "I can't keep my hands off you."

Niki let out a squeal of delight as Dawn lifted her onto the kitchen island. Both quieted when the doorbell rang.

Dawn frowned. "Who would be here this time of night?"

"Probably Jacey. She forgets her key all the time. I'll let her in."

Niki unlocked the door. "Warden, what are you doing here?"

"I, oh, I didn't know you were here," Val blurted out. "I'm looking for Dawn."

"Who is it, honey?" Dawn said as she walked to the front door. "Val, is everything okay at the prison?"

"Yes." Wide-eyed, Val looked from one woman to the other. It was obvious they had been in bed. "You . . . you two are together?"

"Yes," Niki said. "Please, come in."

"No, no. I wanted to talk to Dawn, but it can wait until Monday. I'm sorry I disturbed you." Val backed from the porch and darted to her car.

"What was that all about?" Dawn said, closing the door.

"That was a thwarted booty call, my love." Niki waggled her eyebrows.

"Oh God," Dawn groaned. "Just what I need."

Chapter 39

Monday morning Val waited impatiently for Dawn to keep their usual meeting. She decided Dawn wasn't coming and tried to think about how to approach the blonde and what to say to her.

I'm an even bigger fool than I thought. Dawn is in love with a woman, but that woman isn't me.

Her intercom interrupted her thoughts. "Dr. Fairchild is here to see you."

Val took a deep breath and made a split-second decision. She would send Dawn back to general population and cancel her weekend pass.

Dawn met Val's dark gaze as she entered the room and sat down in front of the warden's desk.

"I'm sorry I'm late," she mumbled. "Emergency appendectomy."

"Is everything okay?"

"Appendix ruptured during the night, but the guards didn't bring her to the infirmary until this morning. It's a miracle she didn't die. But she's going to be okay."

Maybe I should keep her in the hospital quarters, Val thought.

"That's good to know," Val said, her voice cracking.

"Dawn, I need to, um . . . revoke your weekend pass. The prison inspection team will be here for the next ten days checking our operations."

Dawn snorted in disbelief. "You're such a liar. You're revoking my pass because I spend my weekends with Niki. Do you think I'm stupid?"

"How can you fall in love with someone like Niki?" Val screeched. "She's a drug addict and a whore."

Dawn clenched her fist. She knew hitting Val would land her in solitary confinement.

"Before you came, every woman on that ward had her."

"And you knew about it but did nothing to stop what was happening to her," Dawn lashed out. "You're no better than a pimp."

"She was a druggie," Val howled.

"Just because she was serving time for drugs didn't give everyone she met the right to rape her," Dawn said, seething.

"If it hadn't been for Niki, the same fate would have befallen me. You certainly did nothing to protect me.

"Why don't I share this with the inspectors when they're here?" Dawn turned on the video and placed her cell phone on Val's desk.

Val snatched the phone from her desk to get a closer look at what Dawn had recorded. *I am so screwed*, she thought.

"I'm keeping this," she snarled.

"Suit yourself." Dawn shrugged. "I've already sent a copy of it to Niki's phone and my attorney. You didn't think I'd be foolish enough to let you get your hands on the only copy, did you?"

"I should move you back to general population," Val threatened. Fear flashed across Dawn's face. Val knew she had hit a nerve.

"Dawn, I don't want to be at odds with you. I was wrong. I had a bad lapse in judgement and tried to kiss you, but the truth is, you are one of the most desirable women I've ever met. Not just your looks—you know you're beautiful—but your high standards, your kindness, and your devotion to your calling as a doctor. Who wouldn't be drawn to you? Can we call a truce and get along for the next few months?"

"If you'll let me keep my weekend pass." Dawn was adamant.

"Okay, but I must have you here this weekend to show the inspectors around the hospital."

"And my cell phone?" Dawn raised her brows.

"I'll keep that."

Val waited until Dawn had closed the door behind her then replayed the video of the ill-advised kiss. She rubbed her face with both hands, trying to clear away the cobwebs in her mind. It felt as if everything was coming at her at once. She had the recording on Dawn's phone, and Niki had a recording on her phone. *If I can get Niki's phone, it would be Dawn's word against mine,* she mused.

Just like at the trial, the little voice in her head said. But the attorney had a copy too.

Dawn had never felt so alone. She couldn't call Niki and let her know what had transpired with Val. She was cut off from the world. She would see Niki during visitation Wednesday, so she could tell her what was happening. Until then Niki would be frantic. *Maybe Lance will let me use his cell,* she thought.

Chapter 40

Niki stepped into the hot shower. She was anxious about seeing Dawn today. The blonde hadn't called her since their weekend when Val discovered them together. Two days didn't seem like a long time, but it was an eternity when you were away from the one you loved.

Niki heard the sound when she turned off the shower. Someone was walking around in the house. She stepped from the shower and pushed the button locking the bathroom door. The footsteps entered the bedroom and stopped, as if the intruder was trying to decide what to do. Niki held her breath.

The footsteps sounded again, getting louder as they approached the bathroom door. Niki pulled the towel tighter around her. She looked around the bathroom for something to put on, but the towel was her only cover. She knew how fast a towel could be ripped away.

She saw her cell phone light up and prayed it was still on silent from her morning class. She thanked God when it only flashed and didn't make a sound. The intruder was opening and closing her dresser drawers as if in search of something.

She heard a loud clattering and jangling of keys. The prowler was emptying her purse onto the dresser top. "Dammit," a male voice mumbled. "It's not here."

The footsteps approached the bathroom door. Niki desperately sought anything that might serve as a weapon. *A rattail comb.* She clutched the comb, the teeth biting into the palm of her hand. In prison, a rattail comb was considered a lethal weapon.

Out of the blue, Jacey's voice rang out in the house as she slammed the front door. "Niki, are you here?"

The intruder's footsteps moved away from the bathroom. She could tell by the clicking of locks and latches that the man was leaving by the French doors in the bedroom.

"Niki, are—"

Niki ran from the bathroom and threw herself into Jacey's arms.

"Thank God you came home," she sobbed. She locked the French doors as she described her ordeal to Jacey. She looked at her lipstick, house keys, change, and other items that had been dumped from her purse. Some of the dresser drawers were still open, and lingerie was scattered on the floor.

"What was he looking for?" Jacey asked.

"I have no idea," Niki said. "The only thing that wasn't out here was my cell phone. The key fob to Dawn's car is missing."

##

Niki took a taxi to the prison and debated whether to tell Dawn about the break-in. She decided not to worry her lover. She was concerned that Dawn hadn't called her. She prayed everything was okay.

"Dawn Fairchild," the loud speaker bellowed. Niki held her breath as she waited for the blonde to walk into the room. *Where is she? Why isn't she here?* she thought.

Niki's panic was rising when the svelte doctor strode into the room. At the sight of Dawn, all of Niki's fears and anxieties melted away. She had to grip the table to keep from running into Dawn's arms.

"I was getting worried," Niki whispered.

"I'm fine, baby. Are you okay?"

"Yes. Why haven't you called me?" Niki asked.

185

"The warden took away my phone. I'm being punished for falling in love with the wrong woman."

"Oh Dawn, I don't know what to say."

Dawn shrugged. "I'll just keep my head down and stay out of her way. She was going to take away my weekend pass too, but I basically blackmailed her with the video on my phone. Transfer that video to your computer. I wouldn't put it past Val to try to steal your cell to get the video. I do have to stay at the prison this weekend to help her entertain visiting dignitaries, but I'll be home next weekend."

"I love you, darling." Niki swiped away a stray tear with the back of her hand.

"Don't cry, baby. Everything will be okay," Dawn assured her. "How is Jacey?"

"She's wonderful," Niki said between sniffles. "She is so nice and kind—much like you. Oh, which reminds me. I've lost the key fob to your car. How do I get another one?"

"Did you ever pick up my belongings from the police station? There's an extra key in my purse."

"No, but I'll get Jacey to run me by there and take care of it."

"Call Libby. She's my friend and my attorney on record. They won't release my things to you, but they will release them to her. Libby Howe. You can find her on the internet."

Visitation was over too quickly, and Dawn reluctantly returned to the prison hospital.

Chapter 41

Detective Bobby Joe Jones smiled as the two attractive women stood to greet him when he entered the police department's waiting area. "Libby, it's a pleasure to see you." He extended his hand to the woman he had testified before many times.

Libby shook Bobby's hand as she introduced Niki. "This is Niki Sears. She asked me to meet her here to sign the receipt for Dawn Fairchild's belongings."

Bobby Joe acknowledged Niki and then motioned for them to follow him. "Things have been crazy this morning. I haven't been down to evidence storage yet." He held the elevator door open for the two women, and the trio rode down to the basement.

"This won't take but a few minutes. I've already filled out the online request to have Dr. Fairchild's belongings pulled. They should be waiting for us.

"I never felt right about that case." Bobby Joe talked as the elevator lumbered to the basement. "A beautiful woman like that—and a doctor to boot. She should have been given deferred adjudication."

"She would have if she'd only pleaded guilty," Libby said. "I had the judge's assurance that she would be released with deferred adjudication. Dawn refused to plead guilty."

"Because she wasn't guilty," Niki mumbled.

The elevator door slid open, and they entered the cavernous home of all Tarrant County evidence files.

"Hey, Bobby Joe," an officer called out. "I just pulled the evidence you requested." He handed Bobby Joe a clipboard to sign and shoved a clear-plastic tub toward the detective. "You can use any table that's free," he added.

Bobby Joe led them to a table in the corner and pulled the lid from the tub. "Yeah, here's her purse," he pointed out, "and her cell phone. No, this isn't her cell phone. This cell phone is bagged and tagged as belonging to Raymond Scott."

"Who? Why is it in Dawn's evidence file?" Libby said, her brain kicking into high gear. "What case number is written on it? What date was it entered into evidence?"

"It's Dr. Fairchild's case number, but it wasn't entered into evidence. There's no entry date."

"We should call Mr. Scott and let him know we have his cell phone," Libby said.

Bobby Joe nodded and pulled his phone out to make the call. Raymond Scott said he was off work and wanted to run by and pick up the phone. "I can be there in fifteen minutes. I hope it helped prove that doctor was innocent," he said as he hung up.

Libby didn't miss the look of horror that spread across Bobby Joe's face. "What's wrong?"

"We need to get to my office. Come on." Bobby Joe took the evidence tub with him.

The women hurried to keep up with the long strides of the detective as he hurried to the elevator.

##

"I've got a charger here somewhere." Bobby rummaged through his desk drawers and pulled out a fast charger that would fit the iPhone he held. "This baby will charge an iPhone in under fifteen minutes."

"What's going on?" Libby demanded. "Why are you charging that phone?"

Bobby Joe shrugged. "I'm not sure, but I think this phone will prove your client's innocence."

188

Bobby Joe checked the other items in the evidence tub. "Looks like all of Dr. Fairchild's things are here—key fob, several keys on a key ring, wallet, sunshades, lipstick, cell phone, her last paycheck. Whoa!" he said, whistling softly. "She made more in a month than I make in a year." He made a list of the items on his computer and then printed out a receipt for Libby to sign. Libby completed the transaction and handed Dawn's belongings to Niki.

"Detective Jones?" A middle-aged man stuck his head into Bobby Joe's office. "I'm Raymond Scott."

Bobby Joe jumped to his feet. "Come in, Mr. Scott. I appreciate you coming. We're charging your cell phone now. What's on it that will clear Dr. Fairchild?"

Scott seemed puzzled. "The video, of course. I played it for the ADA handling the case. He said it was definitely a game changer. He insisted on confiscating my phone."

Bobby Joe reached for the phone as it lit up signaling a charge. He turned it on.

"It's the last video in my storage," Scott said, keying in his password and handing the phone back to Bobby Joe.

Bobby pulled up the recording and pushed Play. Scott had shot the video from the sidewalk across from the accident, and it clearly showed Richard Wynn exiting the driver's side of his car and running between two buildings. Moments later it showed Dawn getting out of the passenger's side and going to aid the others involved in the accident.

Niki slapped her hand over her mouth. "I knew she was innocent. Dawn wouldn't lie."

"No," Libby hissed, "but Valerie Davis would."

"Come on, Bobby Joe," Libby said as she got to her feet. "All of us are going to see Judge Cranfield. We must get Dawn out of prison before something happens to her."

Chapter 42

Libby was on her cell phone to Judge Cranfield's office as Bobby Joe, Niki, and Raymond Scott followed her from the building.

Bobby Joe pointed to his police cruiser. "Let's take it. It's bigger than your Beemer."

"The judge can see us in forty-five minutes," Libby crowed. "I can type up the plea for release while we wait and print it out on his secretary's printer. I'll have all the paperwork done by the time he meets with us."

Judge Cranfield wrinkled his brow as he listened to Libby and then watched the video. He turned to Raymond. "You say the ADA suppressed this evidence?"

"Yes, sir," Raymond said. "I was transferred out of town before the trial ended, but I left the ADA my phone numbers to reach me in case I needed to testify. He led me to believe that the charges would be dropped based on my evidence."

"They should have been dropped," Judge Cranfield grumbled. "Our court system has failed Dr. Fairchild." He signed the release forms and handed them to Libby.

"Go get your client, Counselor," the judge said with a smile. "My office will call ahead right now and make certain she is released to you."

"May I go too?" Raymond asked. "I want to see this."

Libby grinned. "That'll max out our passenger space, but what the hell. You're the one we owe for this. I'm sure Dawn will want to thank you."

Bobby Joe parked in front of the entrance to the prison hospital and turned to Libby. "Let's do this."

##

The guard looked over the release papers signed by Judge Cranfield. "Let me get the warden."

The four waited as the guard spoke with someone in the warden's office.

"Warden Davis is in a meeting," the guard advised them after hanging up the phone, "but Assistant Warden Ray McDonald is on his way to comply with the judge's orders. In the meantime, I'll call Dr. Fairchild down here."

##

Dawn wondered why the guard was calling her to the front desk. Patients were always brought to her. She stepped from the elevator and was engulfed in a party of hugs, slaps on the back, and mumbled explanations.

Assistant Warden McDonald arrived, signed where required, and presented Dawn's copies of the forms to her. "You're a free woman, Dr. Fairchild. It has been a pleasure to have you in our hospital."

"What's going on?" Dawn stumbled along as the group pushed her outside to the police car. Inside the prison she was afraid to touch Niki or grasp her hand.

Once the car drove through the prison gates to the world outside, Niki brushed Dawn's lips with a quick kiss. "You're free, honey. Judge Cranfield signed your release."

"How? Why?" Dawn was afraid to let loose the yelp of happiness rising inside her. Afraid she was dreaming.

"You explain, Libby," Niki said, deferring to the attorney.

"First, let me introduce you to Raymond Scott," Libby said. "During your trial, Mr. Scott gave the ADA a video he made on his cell phone the night of the accident. It clearly showed Richard exiting the driver's side and running down the alley.

"The ADA suppressed the evidence that would have set you free. Judge Cranfield rectified it immediately, overturning your conviction and issuing a warrant for the arrest of the ADA."

Dawn was stunned. The only thing really registering with her was the soft fragrance of the woman sitting beside her, clutching her hand. She bowed her head and closed her eyes. "Niki," she murmured.

"I'm here, honey." Niki squeezed her hand tighter.

Chapter 43

"We'll talk tomorrow," Libby said as they returned to the police station. "Oh, here's your purse and other belongings. Call me. We have a hell of a lawsuit on our hands. The state owes you a fortune in lost wages, not to mention the false imprisonment by a warden who was the witness that put you in prison in the first place."

"Mr. Scott," Dawn said, turning to Raymond, "I don't know how to thank you. If you ever need a good surgeon, call me."

Scott laughed and hugged her. "I'm just happy to see justice done."

Niki rummaged in Dawn's old purse and pulled out the key fob. "You wanna drive?"

"No, I just want to stare at you." Dawn laughed. "I just want to reach over and touch you and sit beside you. I want to make certain this isn't a wonderful dream that will disappear when I awake."

"It's real, honey." Niki held her hand as they walked to their car.

##

Bobby Joe's cell phone started ringing before he reached his desk. "Detective Jones," he said.

"Bobby Joe, what the hell is going on?" Val yelled into the phone. "Where's my prisoner?"

"She's innocent, Val," Bobby explained. "I found the evidence to free her. The ADA had suppressed a pedestrian's recording of the accident clearly showing

Richard Wynn exiting the driver's side of the vehicle and running down the alley.

"It also showed Dr. Fairchild getting out of the passenger's side and rushing to help you. You convicted the only person who came to your aid."

Val was silent.

"Val, you still there?" Bobby Joe asked.

"Yes, thanks, Bobby. I appreciate your help."

Val hung up the phone. She pictured herself working in some small town as the jail matron. Worse than that, Dawn was gone from her life.

##

Dawn and Niki were giddy on the trip home. "I can't stop holding my breath," Dawn said. "I'm afraid I'll exhale, and everything will go up in smoke."

"You and me together," Niki said with a giggle as she pulled into the driveway. "I can't believe you're going home with me, to my bed."

They showered, made love, dried each other, snuggled beneath the comforter, and made love again.

"I can't believe I'll wake in your arms every morning." Niki kissed Dawn's neck and shoulder. "You're so beautiful . . . and you're all mine."

"I know," Dawn murmured, stroking Niki's silky-smooth back. "For the rest of my life, your face will be the first thing I'll see in the morning and the last thing I'll see at night."

"I have a ten o'clock class in the morning and a one o'clock after that." Niki ran her hand down Dawn's flat stomach. "Do you want to drive me and meet with Libby while I'm in class?"

"Yes. I'm not certain where to start picking up my life. I need to let my family know I'm out of prison and contact the hospital about getting my job back. Right now, all I want to do is hold you until we fall asleep."

##

194

"Um, I could wake up like this every morning," Dawn whispered in Niki's ear as the redhead wiggled her back harder against Dawn's stomach.

"Good, because that's what I have planned for you." Niki turned over to face her lover. "We have just enough time before we have to shower and face the day."

"Enough time for what?" Dawn teased.

"If you don't know, I'm not very good at—"

Dawn pulled Niki beneath her. "You are just perfect at everything."

They made love, showered, dressed, and walked to the garage.

"We need to think about getting you a car," Dawn commented as she steered the Beemer from the garage.

Niki pulled Dawn's hand into her lap. "I rather like you driving me to school."

"I know, but once I go onto hospital rotation I may not be available. We'll need two vehicles. Do you have a preference?"

Niki wrinkled her brow in thought. "Let me check on the internet. I'll narrow it down to two or three, and then we can drive them and select one."

Dawn pulled Niki's hand to her lips and kissed her knuckles. "Works for me, baby."

Dawn dropped Niki at college and headed to her parents' home. Flint was having coffee in their mother's kitchen when Dawn arrived.

"Sis? Oh my gosh! Mom, come here quick!" Flint stopped short of jumping into the air. He hugged Dawn and then looked at her in disbelief. "How? Why? You're out of prison!" he stammered.

"Yes, I am." Dawn couldn't suppress the happiness that filled her heart. "I'm free, Flint. Exonerated."

"You've been cleared?" Tears ran down Ruth Fairchild's face. "You're out of prison for good?"

"Yes, Mom. A Good Samaritan turned in a cell phone before the trial that had a video of Richard exiting the driver's side and slinking down an alley. The ADA prosecuting my case suppressed the evidence that would have cleared me."

"Oh honey, I'm so happy for you." Ruth clutched her daughter to her and cried into Dawn's shoulder. "I have been worried sick every minute you were in that place."

"I know, Mom. I know. Tell Dad I'll return later after he gets off work. I want to hug him too."

"What are your plans?" Flint asked as he placed two coffee cups on the table and filled them.

"I'm heading to Libby's office when I leave here," Dawn said, pausing to take a sip the coffee. "Mmm. This is so good."

"A lot better than prison coffee, I bet." Ruth chuckled.

"Much better, Mom."

"Looks like the state is going to owe you a bundle of money," Flint said. "Lost wages, wrongful imprisonment, and I'm sure Libby has a long list of other things."

"The last time I saw Libby she was sharpening her pencil," Dawn said. "I'll probably have to rein her in. All I want is a front-page apology, so people will know I was wrongly accused."

"I'm betting the warden loses her job over this," Flint added. "She knew she was lying."

"It was pouring down rain," Dawn said. "Her sister was lying in a pool of blood, and she was hysterical. Who knows what she thought she saw?"

Flint scowled. "Don't defend her. She stole two years of your life."

"She's a good warden. She is making a difference in that snake pit. She's dealt with most of the rattlesnakes that were there when I arrived. It would be a shame to lose someone like her—someone who really cares. God knows I wouldn't want to run a women's prison."

"Dawn, you don't have to answer this question," Flint said, "but I'd like to know what prison was like."

Dawn bowed her head and closed her eyes as she searched for words to describe it. "It wasn't so bad for me. I was housed in the hospital, so I wasn't in the general population. But I treated women who suffered every indignity imaginable.

"It's like hell. There are no levels of good, bad, or awful to fit the crime. Whether an inmate was in prison for drunk driving or for brutal murder, they were all thrown into the same cesspool.

"Think of the worst scenario imaginable and multiply it by twenty. That's what prison is like for most inmates."

Dawn finished her coffee and hugged her brother and mother goodbye. Libby was the next name on her list.

"I may be able to purchase my dream home after this settlement," Libby said as she walked around her desk to greet Dawn.

Dawn laughed. "I doubt that. All I want is my lost wages and a lot of advertising on TV and talk shows acknowledging my innocence."

"But we can get lost wages, wrongful imprisonment, mental cruelty." Libby paced the floor. "Were you raped by any chance?"

"No! By the grace of God, Niki saved me from that."

"Oh." Libby was crestfallen. "That would have been good for a few million more. Gorgeous, All-American beauty like you tossed into a viper's nest."

"It wasn't like that for me," Dawn declared. "The warden moved me into the hospital facilities the third day I was there."

"What about your friend?" Libby said. "Uh . . . Nancy?"

"Niki."

"Niki, yeah. Did she do well in prison?"

197

Dawn was reluctant to discuss Niki's treatment in prison. She'd rather put the bad karma behind them. "Look, Libby, all I want is a very public exoneration. Niki and I just want to get on with our life together."

"Together?" Libby said, nearly choking on the word. "You mean . . . as in together, together? Uh, lesbians?"

Dawn frowned. "You can put whatever label you want on our relationship. We love each other and plan to spend our lives together."

"Oh, that's even better," Libby crowed. "I'll charge that the prison system turned you into a lesbian. After all, you were engaged to Richard for two years prior to your incarceration, so you obviously preferred men at the time you were imprisoned."

"Ha!" Dawn snorted. "If anything would turn a straight woman into a lesbian it'd be spending two years with Richard."

Libby laughed. "Yeah, what kind of asshole slinks away from an accident he caused and lets his fiancée of two years take a murder rap?

"I'll set up a meeting with the Texas Department of Criminal Justice attorneys and—"

"Let's start with a discussion with the warden and go from there," Dawn said.

"Okay, but I see my mansion dwindling to a log cabin."

Dawn smiled at her friend's antics. "Right now, I need a copy of the judge's order absolving me of all wrongdoing."

"I have copies for you right here." Libby pulled a file folder from her desk drawer. "You'll find everything you need in here."

As Dawn walked to her car, a text dinged into her phone. "We're doing a lab today. I'll be here til 4. Love u."

I should have time to talk with the hospital personnel office, Dawn thought as she headed her car toward downtown.

Dawn read a magazine as she waited for the personnel director to see her.

A few minutes later, Zeb Lewis stood in the doorway of the waiting room. "Come in, come in. You look great, Dawn." He did an appreciative survey of her.

"Thank you, Zeb. It's good to be back among the living."

"I can't believe how great you look," he said again as he gestured for her to sit down.

"Please don't tell me prison agreed with me."

"Well, something did." Zeb chuckled. "What can I do for you?"

Dawn placed her file on Zeb's desk. "I'd like my old job back."

Zeb tried to hide his shock. "Dawn, I'm not sure . . . I don't know if . . . . Do you still have your license to practice?"

"Yes. I never lost my medical license. In fact, I've been the hospital doctor at the Carswell Women's Prison for the past eighteen months."

"But you're a convicted felon."

"No, I've been exonerated." Dawn flipped open her file. "Here's Judge Cranfield's letter."

Zeb took a minute to read through the paperwork. "This is wonderful." He scowled as he read Libby's letter requesting that the judge overturn the verdict and find Dawn innocent. "Richard? Richard was driving the car?"

"Yes."

"Of course you can have your job back," Zeb said. "But I need your help with something."

"I'll do anything I can to help you," Dawn said. "What is it?"

199

"After you left we put Richard on the chief of staff track. He's not half the surgeon you are, but he's pretty good with paperwork. The problem is . . . we think he's stealing pharmaceuticals from our drug room.

"When you were with Richard, did he have a drug problem?"

"No. Richard would never take drugs," Dawn said. "But I did catch him taking hard drugs from the drug closet on his floor."

"What did he do with them?" Zeb asked.

"I think he sold them. You should get Detective Bobby Joe Jones involved with this case," Dawn recommended.

"Isn't he the one who arrested you?"

"Yes, but he's also the one who found the evidence to free me." Dawn opened her purse. "I have his card."

"I'll call him," Zeb said, glancing at the business card she handed him. "Maybe you and I can meet with him tomorrow. In the meantime, just know you have your job back, and we'll sort things out with Richard."

Dawn left Zeb's office in a cheerful mood and rode the elevator down to the garage level. The farther she got from the prison, the happier she was. It was as if her mind had opened and let in all the light in the universe.

Now to pick up the woman who lights up my world, Dawn thought as she buckled her seatbelt.

Chapter 44

Val clenched her fists as she waited for Dawn and her attorney to enter the room. William Frick, the attorney from the Texas Department of Criminal Justice, continued to squirm in his chair.

"This could be very bad," Frick informed her. "Very bad for the prison system and very bad for your career."

"Just hear them out and keep your mouth shut," Val snapped. "Let me do the talking. You just make certain I don't commit to something we can't do."

"You're not going to cave to their demands?" Frick whined.

"Probably," Val muttered. *I must find a way to save my career.*

##

"Let me do the talking," Libby instructed before entering Val's office. She led Dawn into the room, introduced herself to William Frick, and acknowledged Val.

"Dawn, I want to say how sorry I am about the ordeal you've gone through the past eighteen months. I did everything I could to protect you," Val said as they all took a seat.

Thoughts keep slamming into Val's mind. *She has a video of you forcing a kiss on her. You knew you were lying at her trial. It just seemed like the truth at the time.*

"Val, I—"

"Dawn, please let me do the talking," Libby cautioned. "Warden Davis has her own attorney here."

Val turned her attention to Libby. "Miss Howe, why don't you tell us what you want as compensation for Dr. Fairchild."

"Dawn told me you were very direct," Libby said, raising an eyebrow. "Okay, here's the last paycheck Dr. Fairchild received before she was wrongly imprisoned. She'd like this for each month she was incarcerated."

"This is for $26,892," Val read out loud. "This must be for a quarter?"

"A month." Libby smiled like a Cheshire cat.

Val ran a hand through her hair. "A month? That's over a quarter-million a year."

"We are also filing for two million for wrongful imprisonment and three million for defamation of character."

"I will need to discuss this with my client," Frick asserted. "We will consider your—"

"We'll pay what you're asking," Val declared. "It has to be a closed deal. No information pertaining to this agreement can be leaked to the press. If it is, Dr. Fairchild must return the money."

"More than the money," Libby said, "Dr. Fairchild wants you to go on national TV and declare her innocence. She wants a half page ad on the front page of the major newspapers and—"

"That's not going to happen," Val said, fuming. "I'll agree to your monetary demands, but I'm not admitting to any wrongdoing."

Libby stood. "You and Mr. Frick need to put your heads together. Send me your proposal for handling this situation. It must contain ways to exonerate my client publicly. Frick and I will negotiate in the future. Warden, don't try to contact my client."

Frick and Val stood silently and watched their adversaries leave the office. Val was furious. She was so close to obtaining her goals, and Dawn Fairchild could bring it all tumbling down.

"Fix this," Val growled to Frick. "You're the lawyer. Fix this!"

"Warden, there's a JJ on the phone for you," Val's receptionist called through the open office door.

Val gestured for Frick to leave. "Close the door behind you," she said to him.

She took a deep breath, counted to ten, and picked up the phone. "Java, I wondered when I would hear from you again."

"We need to meet," Java began. "This keg of worms you dropped into my lap has crawled all the way to the governor's office."

"Okay. When and where?"

"Tonight, at the Italian Inn on Camp Bowie. You know, the place where you can slip into a booth and close the door for privacy?"

"Yes, I'm familiar with it. What time?"

"Six okay?" Java asked.

"I'll be there."

Maybe the day wouldn't be a complete waste after all. She had grown fond of the FBI agent as they worked together on the corruption in the TDCJ. Java could almost drive Dawn from her mind.

Chapter 45

Java stood as Val entered the restaurant. The shadowy darkness of the candlelit dining room made it difficult to identify others. She made it easy for Val to find her.

"I ordered your favorite wine," Java said, smiling as she waited for Val to slide into the booth. "If you'd prefer something different—"

"No, this is perfect and thoughtful." Val smoothed the skirt of her dress and settled in the booth. Java followed and pulled the door closed.

"Val, this VitaMaxPro thing is getting scary. I've linked senators, state reps, and more bureaucrats than I can count to this scandal. When we start arresting people, it's going to hit the fan."

"Can you keep my name out of it?" Val asked. "I fear repercussions, and God knows I don't need that in my life right now."

"Yeah, I saw the newspaper article on Dr. Fairchild. That's a shame. She's lucky she survived prison unscathed. She's a looker."

"I did everything I could to keep her out of the general population," Val pointed out. "But the whole thing is coming back to bite me in the butt. Damage to her reputation and all."

"The hospital did reinstate her, and it looks like she'll be their new chief of staff," Java said as she sipped her wine. "That documentary you made on her was a boon to her legend. Rumor has it some big filmmaker is trying to sign her to produce her life story. I don't see how her reputation has been damaged."

Val wanted to tell Java that it was more than that. She wanted to confess that she had tried to kiss Dawn and been rebuffed. That she had committed the cardinal sin for a prison warden: she had made sexual advances to an inmate.

Java pulled a flowchart from the file folder she had placed on the table. "Look at this."

"The problem begins with Buddy Craft then creeps out to the prison board members. It slimes its way to a couple of senators, and its tentacles wrap around at least ten bureaucrats I've identified.

"The owner of VitaMaxPro is clean. He even admits he would never recommend feeding anyone his product three times daily seven days a week under any circumstances. Craft is the sole architect of the scheme. I will need your dietician to testify."

"I have a copy of the letter Craft sent to all the prisons, directing them to incorporate the meat substitute in their meal plans," Val volunteered. "Would that be enough? I promised Sue I'd keep her out of this if possible."

"That should do for now. I just want you to be aware that everyone will be questioned when this lands on my boss's desk and then on the governor's. Your refusal to serve VitaMaxPro to the inmates in your prison was the catalyst that caused Craft's plan to unravel."

Val nodded.

"Are you hungry?" Java asked as she lifted the latch and pushed open the door on their booth. They ordered and Java pulled the booth door closed.

"I've looked into your background." Val blushed as she admitted that she had stalked Java on the internet.

The agent laughed. "Please don't believe everything you read on the internet."

"You don't exist on the internet, but you have quite a dossier in the federal records. You've had a colorful

205

career." Val smiled. "Often decorated and frequently reprimanded."

"Um, my sins have found me," Java said.

"Not sins." Val searched the sky-blue eyes that danced with laughter. "More like, 'Damn them all! Justice will be done.'"

Java snickered. "You can read between the lines. I'm not exactly a rule follower, but I don't break them either.

"I have to admit, I did my background check on you too," Java told her. "You have been quite a supporter of prison reform and have made strides in that direction. I know your self-defense programs are being initiated in other prisons, and your decent food initiatives have been applauded.

"The cleanup sting you ran in your own prison caught everyone off guard. They're still talking about how you kept it quiet and pulled it off without outside help."

Val wanted to tell Java that it wasn't a sting. It was a reaction to an attack from within her prison. That prisoners had helped her gain control of the situation and emerge smelling like a rose.

How many skeletons do I have in my closet? she thought. *How much of my success is based on Dawn Fairchild?*

Chapter 46

Zeb Lewis was excited at the thought of spending the day with Dawn Fairchild. He impatiently thumbed through her file again. *Damn, she's a good-looking woman,* he thought. He was glad Richard Wynn was out of the picture. Wynn had married the hospital trollop. Zeb hadn't bothered to confront Wynn. He knew it was just a matter of time until the police showed up to arrest him for vehicular manslaughter. He silently cursed the man for letting Dawn serve prison time for a crime he committed.

"Good morning, Zeb." Dawn burst into his office like a breath of spring on a cool morning. "I appreciate you taking the time to show me around and introduce me to the new people. A lot has changed in eighteen months."

"I'm delighted to do it." Zeb held out his elbow, and Dawn slipped her arm through his.

"I wanted to give you an opportunity to get settled into your life," Zeb said, "so I put you on rotation beginning next Monday."

"That's perfect." Dawn squeezed Zeb's arm against her body.

They visited the nurses' stations, and Dawn met new and old head nurses. "We opened the new surgical wing while you were in . . . uh, away," Zeb stammered.

"I'd like to see it." Dawn's enthusiasm was contagious.

##

"And last, but not least, this is our new emergency room." Zeb's proud smile pleased Dawn. An administrator should be proud of his facility.

Just then, a slender nurse approached them and smiled at Zeb. "What brings you to our part of the world?"

"Darcus Martin, this is Dr. Dawn Fairchild. She is now on staff here. Darcus is the head nurse over the emergency room."

"You have a marvelous facility," Dawn said to the woman. She chatted with Darcus for several minutes and was pleased to find that the facility was state-of-the-art.

"A doctor could perform surgery in this room," Darcus said proudly. "Of course, it would have to be a last-ditch effort to save the patient, but it would work."

"That's good information to know," Dawn responded. "I rarely work the emergency room, but it helps to know what's available." She thanked Darcus and followed Zeb into the hallway.

After the tour Zeb led her to the new doctors' dining room. "You'll love this," he said with a grin as he led her into the state-of-the-art kitchen. "We even have our own chefs. Open twenty-four hours a day."

"Very nice." Dawn surveyed the stylish dining room and read the daily menu. "This is making me hungry."

"We'll have lunch here today." Zeb beamed. "Give you a chance to try our cuisine. It's delicious."

"I'd love to," Dawn said, "but I have to pick up someone at one. Maybe another day this week?"

"What day?" Zeb asked.

Dawn laughed. "I know this sounds like an excuse, but I'll need to check my calendar."

They turned to leave the dining room and ran into Richard Wynn.

"Dawn?" Richard gasped. "Dawn, what are you doing here? You're supposed to be—"

"Serving time for your crime?" Dawn scoffed. "I've been exonerated, Richard."

"How? When?" Richard ran his finger around his shirt collar as a bead pf sweat trickled down his cheek. "May I buy you a cup of coffee for old times' sake?"

Zeb came to her rescue. "Dr. Fairchild was just leaving. She has another engagement." He took Dawn's arm and steered her toward the elevator.

"Call me and we'll have lunch," Zeb whispered in her ear as he urged her into the elevator. He watched until she disappeared behind the closing doors.

"You've always wanted her," Richard barked behind him. "Were you sleeping with her before she went to prison?"

Zeb clenched his fists. "That's really none of your business, Dr. Wynn."

"I wonder how many people were on her dance card in the pen," Richard snarled.

"Probably not as many as you'll have where you're going." An evil grin twisted Zeb's face. "I understand they love pretty boys like you."

Zeb knew he was being cruel but took joy as he watched the blood drain from Richard's face. "They'll probably have several dance cards for you, buddy."

Chapter 47

Dawn parked her car in front of the building that housed the Harris College of Nursing at Texas Christian University and went inside to meet Niki outside her classroom. She had thought about the pretty redhead all day.

The classroom door burst open, pouring a horde of noisy young women and men into the hallway. Dawn was swimming against the crowd and decided to stand against the wall and catch Niki as she walked by.

The hall quieted as students left the building. Only a few women remained, studying messages posted on the bulletin board. Dawn pushed open the classroom door and walked in.

Niki and her instructor were arguing with two muscular men who were insisting that Niki go with them. The fear in Niki's eyes was unnerving.

"Is there a problem here?" Dawn asked as she moved closer to the group.

"No, we're fine," Niki croaked.

"Are these men bothering you?" Dawn kept her distance from the two men but watched them carefully.

"Yes, they are," the instructor said. "Please call the campus police."

One of the men moved swiftly to block the door. "We're here for our sister," the other man countered.

"She doesn't want to leave with them," the instructor bellowed. "Please call security."

"Do you know these men?" Dawn asked.

"They're my brothers, Renfro and Willard," Niki replied. "But I have no desire to go with them. Frankly, they scare me."

"That's ridiculous," Willard scoffed, continuing to lean against the door.

"Then you won't mind moving and opening the door," Dawn said. "She doesn't want to go with you. She's leaving with me."

The man looked Dawn up and down. "I don't think so," he grumbled.

Dawn moved toward the door and reached for the handle. The man was fast but not fast enough. As he stepped forward to grab her arm, Dawn took one step to the side, leaving her right foot planted solidly in front of him. She grabbed the arm reaching for her and yanked the man forward, tripping him over her foot.

"Bitch," he screamed as he grappled for her legs.

Dawn stomped his outstretched hand and landed a solid kick to the side of his head, rendering him unconscious. She turned to face Renfro who had a choke hold on Niki.

"Just back off," Renfro growled, "and no one gets hurt. We're taking our sister home. She isn't well. She has mental problems, and we need to get help for her."

Dawn pulled her leg back, aiming the toe of her boot at Willard's head. "Release her, or my next kick will turn your brother into a vegetable," she threatened.

Renfro hesitated.

"Now! Or I'll leave you with someone who will really have mental problems, and you can change his diapers for the rest of your life."

Renfro released his grip on Niki, and the redhead ran into Dawn's arms. "Mrs. Prater, come with us," Niki said to the instructor.

The three women backed out of the classroom as Renfro fell to his knees to check on his brother. "Can you lock this door?" Dawn asked.

"Yes," Mrs. Prater said.

"Then lock it and contact security to pick up those two."

The instructor was on the phone with security as Dawn and Niki pulled from the parking lot.

"What's going on, baby?" Dawn caught Niki's hand in hers and kissed her fingers.

"I don't know," Niki said as she fought back tears. "This is the second time they've tried to make me get into their car. They say Mother is dying and wants to see me, but I know that isn't true. She was at a fund-raising dinner two nights ago. I saw the write-up in the newspaper."

"Would they harm you?"

"I think so," Niki whispered.

Dawn pinched the bridge of her nose. "It's been a long day. Can we do something decadent, like order in pizza tonight?"

"I'd love that." Niki brightened. "You can tell me about your day. How did the meeting with Zeb go?"

They discussed their day until Dawn pulled the car into the garage and pushed the button that closed the door. Her seat slid back when she turned off the engine. She caught her breath as Niki scrambled over the console and landed in her lap.

"God, I've missed you," Niki murmured between fervent kisses. "I've wanted you all day."

Niki straddled Dawn, caught her face between her hands, and kissed her as if there would be no tomorrow. Dawn's heart pounded as her lover took her breath away.

"You are so gorgeous," Dawn whispered, kissing the small scar on Niki's cheek.

"You're not just saying that?" Niki whispered. "You think I'm pretty now?"

"More than pretty." Dawn kissed the soft spot in her throat. "You're breathtaking."

Dawn knew Niki was still uncomfortable in her own skin.

She slid her hands beneath Niki's skirt and caressed her firm round buttocks. Niki began to grind into her as she smothered Dawn's moans with soft, sweet kisses.

"Is it wrong that I'm so turned on by the beating you gave Willard?" Niki pressed her lips firmly against Dawn's and wrapped her arms around Dawn's neck. She rose onto her knees and pulled Dawn's head to her breasts. In a frenzy, Dawn released Niki's bra and removed it with her blouse.

"Yes, baby," Niki urged her. "Suck me. Harder!"

The world fell away. Niki was all she was aware of. Niki's scent, her softness, her lips, her heat. "I can't get enough of you," Dawn groaned as she slipped her hand between Niki's legs.

"All of me." Niki moaned loudly. "You own all of me. Do whatever you want to me. I'm your bitc—"

Firm lips silenced her.

"No," Dawn whispered. "You're my woman. Don't ever use that word with me. You're better than that."

"Yes, I'm your woman," Niki said, awed by the very thought of it. "Your woman."

Dawn watched in amazement as Niki threw back her head and arched her body harder against Dawn's hand. She chanted Dawn's name over and over until she couldn't catch her breath and could only make little mewling sounds as Dawn took her higher and higher.

Niki collapsed against Dawn with a whimper. "So good, baby. You're so good."

Dawn caressed Niki's back as the smaller woman rested her cheek against Dawn's chest. "I love you," Dawn whispered as she buried her face in soft red hair. "I love everything about you. Damn, you smell good."

Dawn scooped up Niki's bra and blouse and followed her into the house. "It's hardly fair that I'm half naked and you're fully dressed," Niki said with a wicked grin.

Dawn dropped the things she was carrying on the dresser as Niki wrapped her arms around the blonde from behind. She slid her hands beneath Dawn's pullover and pushed it over her head. "But I can fix that." She kissed down Dawn's back and reached around to unzip her jeans. Dawn pulled Niki around to face her and kissed her.

"Umm, I should beat up men more often." Dawn gasped as Niki wrapped her arms around Dawn's neck and lifted herself to wrap strong legs around Dawn's waist. Dawn slid her hands beneath Niki's hips, providing her a place to rest in her arms.

"Take me to bed," Niki whispered.

"It's almost midnight." Niki wiggled onto Dawn's stomach and ran her hands down Dawn's arms. "You're so strong. Your strength amazes me." She shuddered. "I love it when you make love to me and grip me tight and crush me to you. I love—"

Dawn kissed her. "You do realize you're working yourself into another round of 'Dawn takes it all,' don't you?"

Niki giggled and stretched hard against her lover. "I just love you so much, but I am hungry."

"I'll order that pizza now." Dawn rolled over to locate her cell phone and called the pizza place, as Niki continued to rub against her back and caress her breasts.

Dawn frowned as she ended the call. "They're closed."

Niki groaned. "What time is it?"

Dawn checked the time on her phone. "Five minutes after midnight. You have ravaged me for about six hours."

"I ravaged you?" Niki's indignant question made Dawn laugh.

"I might have been a tiny bit to blame." She caught Niki's hand and kissed the palm. "Let's see what we can scrounge up in the kitchen."

"I really had my mouth set for pizza," Niki whined like a teenager.

"Let me find my clothes, and I'll go get you pizza at that twenty-four-hour drive-through place," Dawn volunteered.

"I'll do it." Niki sprang from the bed and pulled on Dawn's soft Henley and a pair of sweatpants. "You call it in, and I'll pick it up."

"You don't have to do that, baby." Dawn caught her in her arms.

Niki tiptoed to kiss her. "I know, but I like to do things for you."

As Dawn waited on hold to place her order, she thought about the woman who had made her life a living fantasy. Although she had never considered herself a lesbian, she couldn't imagine ever loving anyone the way she loved Niki.

Niki was lightness and happiness. She was laughter and easy loving. She was everything Dawn had ever imagined a loving relationship should be. *God, she's the sexiest woman alive. She drives me wild!*

Niki hummed a love song as she started the car and raised the garage door. She had never been so happy in her life. She pinched herself to make certain she wasn't dreaming. That a woman like Dawn Fairchild could love someone like her. *I am her woman*, she thought. *Even better, she is mine.*

Niki never knew what hit her. She never saw the big Dually truck turn on its lights and start its engine as she pulled out of the garage. Too late, she faced the iron grill of the lethal weapon hurtling toward her.

The truck slammed into the BMW and pushed it a block before dragging the car off its bumper and into a huge oak tree. The vehicle sped away from the scene before anyone could run outside to see what happened.

Chapter 48

Sheer horror wrapped itself around Dawn's body and squeezed until it stopped her heart from beating. The screech of metal slamming into metal was a sound she would never forget. The shrill scraping sound of a vehicle being dragged buried itself in her brain.

She dialed 911 as she ran for the door. At first, she didn't see anything. Then she spotted her car a block away. It looked like someone had crumpled a piece of paper and tossed it against the oak tree. Somewhere in that wreckage was the essence of her soul.

Dawn sprinted to the rubble, knowing what she would find. No one could live through that destruction, but maybe, just maybe, she could hold Niki and comfort her and say, "I love you," one more time.

In the darkness Dawn could see nothing. She flicked on her cell phone light and flashed the beam through the rivulets of metal and fiberglass. Niki's arm hung loosely over a twisted car seat. The rest of her was buried in the demolished car. Dawn inched her way closer and held Niki's hand. She hoped Niki knew she was there. Her heart almost leapt from her body when the hand squeezed hers. *Please God, please let her be alive.*

Everything else was a blur. The ambulance and firetruck arrived, and neighbors gathered around the scene. Dazed, Dawn obeyed reluctantly when a fireman gently pulled her away from the wreck. "She's alive," Dawn sobbed. "Please be careful."

Dawn prayed as she watched the firemen assess the damaged vehicle. "We'll need both of them," a tall husky fireman yelled toward his truck. Within seconds two large power tools that looked like giant pliers appeared. The fireman carefully spread the crushed metal away from Niki. The husky man stepped back, and another fireman moved in with a similar-looking tool and began to cut away the crumpled car frame. Faster than Dawn would have dreamed, the car began to disappear from around Niki.

The men nodded to each other and placed their power tools on the ground. "Easy, Mac," the husky man cautioned his partner. "She's under the seat." Another man joined the two, and they slowly lifted the seat from the debris.

Dawn tried to reach Niki. She wanted to touch her, wipe the blood from her face, hold her. "Ma'am, please step back and let the medics get her into the ambulance."

Dawn clenched her fists as the medics lifted Niki onto the gurney. Her lifeless body reminded Dawn of a rag doll.

"I want to ride to the hospital with her," Dawn declared.

"Ma'am, we can't let—"

"She's my wife," Dawn sobbed. "I need to be with her."

The man nodded as they hurried the gurney toward the ambulance. "Sit right here in this corner and stay out of the way," the medic commanded.

Dawn watched as the medics did all the things she would do to save Niki. Even with the oxygen, Niki's breathing was labored. Dawn knew she had a pulmonary contusion caused by a hard blow to her chest, probably the airbag or steering wheel.

"What hospital are you taking her to?" Dawn asked.

"All Saints," the medic said.

Dawn dug into her pocket for her cell phone and called the hospital where she practiced. She identified herself and told the emergency room nurse Niki's condition. "She is hemorrhaging and has fluid filling her lungs. We need to rush her into surgery to remove the liquid from her lungs before she drowns in her own blood. Then we can take x-rays to determine the extent of her injuries. Have a doctor standing by."

##

Everything was a blur as Dawn stayed beside Niki and entered the hospital. The attendants rolled the gurney into the open space between the machines and paraphernalia that occupied the emergency room. Nurses began taking Niki's blood pressure, while another shoved a clip on her finger to check her heart rate.

An intern placed his stethoscope over her heart and lungs. He inhaled sharply and looked up at Dawn with wide-eyed concern. "She needs . . . she's, er . . ."

"I know what she needs," Dawn barked. "Where's the emergency room doctor?"

"I'm the only one here," the intern replied.

"Have you ever performed a—"

"No," he interrupted Dawn. "I guess there's a first time for everything."

"She won't be your trial run," Dawn growled as Darcus approached them. "Darcus I need an operating room."

"We're fresh out, Dr. Fairchild." Darcus glared at the pulse oximeter that had started beeping spasmodically.

"She needs surgery now," Dawn declared. "Where can I scrub? Get an anesthesiologist in here."

"You can't do that," the intern bellowed.

"She can, and she will." Darcus pushed him aside as she called for the anesthesiologist and began barking orders to two other nurses. "Come on, Doc, I'll scrub you."

##

Dawn stood over Niki, waiting for the go-ahead from the anesthesiologist. She took a deep breath before making the incision to insert the tube to drain fluid from Niki's

219

lungs. Never in her life had she been nervous about performing surgery, but she'd never had so much to lose if she made a mistake. She exhaled and started to work.

Four hours later, Dawn closed the incision she had made to stop Niki's internal hemorrhaging. She set her broken arm and ordered an MRI to check for a concussion.

It was daylight when the exhausted doctor stumbled outside.

"Can I give you a ride home?" a familiar voice asked behind her.

She turned to face Detective Bobby Joe Jones. "Bobby, what are you doing here?"

"I could ask you the same question," he said. "But I already know the answer."

"Surely you aren't working traffic accidents," Dawn said, yawning. "Sorry, I've been up all night."

"I'm not certain Niki's collision was an accident," Bobby Joe informed her. "Get in the car. I'll drive you home. We can talk on the way."

Too tired to argue, Dawn slipped into the car as Bobby Joe held the door open for her.

"Dawn, do you feel like coming to the station with me?"

"Last time I did that, you kept me." Dawn glanced at the detective.

An uncomfortable laugh escaped Bobby's lips. "I need you to look at someone and see if you know them."

"Okay."

Bobby Joe drove through Starbucks. "Maybe this will keep you awake a few hours longer." He handed her a cup of the dark, hot coffee.

The ride to the station was short, and Bobby led her into the viewing side of an interrogation room. "Do you know that man?"

Dawn studied the man carefully. "I've never seen him before in my life," she whispered.

Bobby Joe grinned. "You don't have to whisper. He can't hear you."

"Who is he?"

"We arrested him in Laredo. He was trying to cross into Mexico. He was the driver of the truck that hit Niki."

"How did you ascertain that?"

"He stole the truck off a Walmart parking lot. Thankfully, Walmart has cameras all over the premises, especially in the parking lots.

"We got several excellent face shots of him as he stole the truck. Traffic cameras picked up the truck at the intersection near your home when he stopped at a red light.

"After the wreck, we found the truck abandoned in a Cracker Barrel parking lot. Video from Cracker Barrel showed him getting into a Pontiac Firebird and driving off. We picked up his license plate and issued a BOLO on him.

"The hit on Niki was very carefully planned. He had ten thousand dollars on him, your home address in his wallet, and a photo of your car."

Wide-eyed, Dawn studied the man again. "He's a hit man? He was hired to kill Niki? But why? Niki's never hurt anyone in her life."

"Niki wasn't his only target," Bobby said, lowering his voice. "He was hired to kill you both."

Dawn sat in stunned silence. "Who hired him?"

"He doesn't know. He was hired through the dark web and never met his employer. He doesn't know if it was a man or a woman."

"Why? Who would want us dead?" Dawn's mind raced through the people she knew.

"Let's start with the obvious," Bobby Joe said, pulling out his pen and notepad. "Richard Wynn will surely do jail time if you push it."

Dawn nodded.

"How about prison? Did you make any enemies while you were in there?"

"Edward Merrick, the therapist turned rapist," Dawn said. "And Lucky. I don't even know her real name. You'll have to ask Warden Davis."

Bobby Joe thumbed through his notes. "Uh, you had an altercation with two men at the university yesterday."

"Yesterday?" Dawn tried to focus. Had it only been one day since her life had teetered between heaven and hell? "Oh, yes. Niki's brothers tried to force her into their car."

"You stopped them?" Admiration rang in Bobby Joe's voice.

"No. No, not them," Dawn recalled. "Just one of them. He blocked the door to keep us from leaving."

"Were they mad?"

"Furious." Dawn snickered.

"Mad enough to kill you?"

Dawn shook her head. "Surely not. I didn't hurt them seriously."

"You broke one man's hand."

"I . . . yes, I guess I did," Dawn admitted. "He grabbed for my leg."

"So, we have at least five people who have reason to want you dead: Edward Merrick, Lucky, Niki's two brothers, and Richard Wynn.

"Who has the most to gain if you die?"

"Warden Davis," Dawn whispered.

"Valerie Davis?" Bobby Joe said, astounded that his friend's name might find its way onto his list of murder suspects. "Why would Val want you dead?"

"Libby filed a lawsuit against the State of Texas. Val agreed to the monetary demands but refused to grant my request for a talk show tour to publicly exonerate me."

"Why wouldn't she do that?"

"Because she feels it would discredit her. It would make people question her character if she weren't a credible witness in her own sister's death. And she . . ."

222

"She what?" Bobby Joe prodded her.

"And she forced a kiss on me," Dawn mumbled.

The detective gaped at her. "Wow. I don't know what to say. One word from you and her career would be over. Do you have anything to substantiate your claim? A witness?"

"I have a video," Dawn snapped. "I'm sorry, Bobby Joe. I'm exhausted. Could you take me home?"

"Do you have a place to stay other than your house?"

"I can stay with my parents," Dawn said. "I need to see them anyway. I'll have to borrow a car from them until I can make arrangements to replace mine."

"I'll start interviewing suspects tomorrow," Bobby said as he led her to his car. "I'd like to place a security detail on you until we solve this."

Dawn nodded. She wasn't stupid enough to turn down a bodyguard if someone was trying to kill her and Niki.

Chapter 49

"Dawn! Thank God you're all right," Ruth said, hugging her only daughter tightly. "Jacey's worried sick about you. She saw your car as they were towing it away. What happened?"

Dawn spent the next two hours answering her parents' questions. Flint volunteered to help her procure a car. "Get on the internet, Sis, and order what you want. I'll pick it up and bring it to you to test-drive. I'm sure you have more than enough in savings to pay cash for it. It'll be a simple transaction. You can have it by tomorrow."

I'll take care of getting insurance on it and filing a claim on your old car," her father offered.

Dawn didn't tell her family that the accident was a deliberate attempt on her life. She knew her mother would worry herself into a migraine.

She borrowed her mother's car and drove home. Jacey was sleeping, so she slipped into the shower. In an hour she was dressed and ready to face the situation she was in. She packed clothes for the week. She planned to stay right by Niki's side until she improved.

##

"How is she?" Dawn asked Bill Bartlett, the staff neurosurgeon who was shining a tiny beam of light into Niki's eyes.

"Her MRI looks good. She has a concussion but nothing a lot of bed rest won't cure. She needs to take it easy for a couple of months. She's suffered a lot of trauma."

"I'll see to that," Dawn said, a hint of a smile crossing her face. "Has she regained consciousness since the accident?"

"No, but I'm certain she will. The body has a way of protecting itself." Dr. Bartlett patted Dawn's arm. "Hold her hand and talk to her. Let her know you want her to wake up."

"I will," Dawn promised.

"Aren't you on the hospital rotation now?" Bartlett asked.

"I'm scheduled to start on Monday. That gives me five days to try to reach her."

After Bartlett left, Dawn set up her computer and began searching for a vehicle. She talked continuously as she worked, telling Niki everything she was doing. She settled on a red Lexus RX 350. She knew Niki would like the flashy car. She emailed her selection to Flint and then closed her computer.

She downloaded a book to her Kindle and began reading to Niki.

##

"Hey, how is she doing?" Darcus asked as she poked her head into the room.

Dawn turned off her Kindle and laid it on the table. "She hasn't regained consciousness, but Dr. Bartlett said that was to be expected."

"I heard you're staying right by her side." Darcus looked around the room. "You need another bed in here. There's plenty of room."

"I suppose I should—"

"I'll take care of it," Darcus volunteered. "Meals too?"

Dawn nodded.

"I've heard nothing but good things about you, Doc," Darcus said. "After watching you work, I understand why. I also know you got a crappy break a couple of years ago. I just want to let you know that we're all behind you, so call on us for help, okay?"

"Okay." Dawn fought back tears. "I . . . thank you."

"By the way, did you know there's a uniformed policeman guarding your door?"

Bobby Joe spent the afternoon setting up security for Dawn and Niki and pulling together as much information as he could on the suspects. Niki and Dawn's testimony could put each of them in prison for a long time. He listed his six prime suspects. He would work methodically work through the list.

Lucky was Lucinda Juarez, wife killer.

Edward Merrick the psychiatrist turned rapist.

Richard Wynn, the weasel who had allowed Dawn to rot in prison for a crime he committed.

Niki's two brothers, Willard and Renfro Sears. Their names rang a bell, but Bobby Joe couldn't put his finger on anything.

Last and with the strongest motive, Warden Valerie Davis. Bobby Joe had a hard time believing the law-and-order warden would put a hit on anyone. Especially someone who had helped her as much as Dawn had.

Tomorrow I'll put together mugshots and have the criminal we arrested see if he recognizes anyone, he thought. *Then I'll go visit Val.*

226

Chapter 50

"You're gonna love this, Warden." Val's secretary, Lillian, placed two file folders on her desk. "The new prisoner transfers are arriving today."

Val picked up the two folders. One was labeled Daisy Darling, and the other was labeled Passion Flower. Val slowly raised her eyes to meet Lillian's. "Is this a joke?"

"I wish." Lillian curtailed her smile.

"Dear Lord, give me strength," Val mumbled as she opened the file to see the photos of Daisy and Passion. "They're men!"

"Nooo," Lillian said. "They're transgender. Transitioning from male to female."

"And we get them because?"

"Lawsuits." Lillian couldn't stand it any longer. She burst out laughing. "This just isn't your week, Warden. Read the file."

Passion Flower's given name was Tyler Duncan. Tyler had decided to change his name and referred to himself as a transgender woman. Although Passion had not had sex reassignment surgery, she behaved in a feminine manner and identified as a thirty-year-old black transgender woman. She was slight—five-six—and weighed 125 pounds.

In Texas, transgender prisoners are housed according to their sex at birth. Passion had filed a lawsuit claiming that the State of Texas had failed to protect her from sexual and physical abuse while incarcerating her in all-male prisons.

After she filed charges naming her molesters, she was told to "stop being so swishy and asking for it." She was returned to general population in the same cellblock as the attackers she had identified. She was gang raped and slashed across the face several times with a razor.

According to the lawsuit filed by an action group, Passion had been in general population the fourteen years she had served in prison. Only after the lawsuit was filed did prison authorities move her to secure housing to stop her abuse.

My God, Val thought. *What took them so long?*

Val made notes to discuss with her staff how to handle Passion Flower, who was up for parole and would probably win her multimillion-dollar lawsuit against the state.

Now for Daisy Darling. What's her story?

Val rubbed her eyes as she read Daisy's story. Daisy was a twenty-eight-year-old male who identified as a transgender woman. He'd also had no sex-altering surgery. Because of Passion's lawsuit, the State was rethinking its policy of assigning transgenders to prisons based on their sex at birth and had decided to assign them according to the gender they identified with.

Daisy had been assigned to a women's prison where she had been housed in a pod with three women. The three women had filed a lawsuit claiming that Daisy had raped, or tried to rape, each of them.

And there's the uglier side of this, Val thought. *We're damned if we do and damned if we don't.*

She decided to house each of the transgender women in a private cell until the lawsuits were settled.

She leaned her head back, and visions of Dawn Fairchild flooded her mind. *I'd give anything to share a cup of coffee with her and discuss the madness going on in my life,* she thought. *Maybe Java.* She dialed the blonde FBI agent and left a voicemail.

Chapter 51

Dawn gathered her clean clothes and headed for the shower while the nurse's assistant changed the linens on Niki's bed. She took the fastest shower of her life and returned as the woman finished her task.

Niki's vital signs weren't as good as Dawn wanted, and she hadn't regained consciousness. Her breathing was becoming more labored. Sometimes, Niki would cry out or whimper during the night. Dawn would carefully slide into the redhead's bed and hold her until she slept peacefully.

Dawn hadn't left her side for the past five days except to dash into the bathroom for a quick shower. She read to Niki. Told her about the new car Flint had brought to the hospital for them. Discussed the future they would share.

She stood when Dr. Bartlett entered the room. "How's our patient?" he inquired as he opened the computer to peruse Niki's chart.

"I'm concerned." Dawn frowned. "Her vitals have dropped a little below normal, and she seems to have difficulty breathing."

Bartlett scowled as he read the information on Niki's chart. "You're not going to like this, but I think it's time to put her on life support."

Dawn nodded. She had already arrived at the same conclusion.

"You know she had severe chest trauma," Bartlett continued. "If not for you, she would have died in the emergency room. The pain of breathing is causing her body to take small, shallow breaths. I'd like to put her on a ventilator. That will force her to take deeper breaths. It will be good from the breathing standpoint and to increase the strength of her lung muscles.

"We've been feeding her intravenously, but it's time we stepped up our game. A gastric feeding tube is called for, so I'll order a G-tube for nutrition and hydration.

"I'd suggest a tube directly into her stomach since we're putting her on a ventilator. As you know, it's a minor surgery that takes about twenty minutes."

Dawn stared at the woman who was more important than anything in her life. "Whatever it takes," she mumbled.

"Hmm. She doesn't appear to have insurance," Bartlett said, looking at the computer.

"I'll get with finance and sign whatever is necessary to show that I'm responsible for her hospital bills," Dawn reassured him. "Just do what needs to be done to make certain she walks out of here under her own steam."

Bartlett nodded and began typing instructions into the computer. "Everything should be in place within the hour." He patted her hand. "I'm sorry your friend has to go through this, but we need to give her all the help we can."

"I agree," Dawn said. "I've always hated tubes down patients' throats. It's so uncomfortable. You know the pain from the increased muscle use will cause her body to respond to protect her, so it could extend her coma. We're now calling it a coma, right?"

Bartlett nodded as a team of nurses and specialists rolled machinery into Niki's room.

"You go on rotation tomorrow," he said, his conversation taking Dawn's mind off the intubation process.

"Yes, I have a surgery in the morning."

"Would you like to perform the gastrostomy?"

"Yes, I would," Dawn answered.

In a matter of minutes, the team had connected Niki to a ventilator.

Dawn fought back the thought that Niki was deteriorating.

Bartlett left, and a few minutes later she received her first visit from Father Anton Garza.

Chapter 52

"Good morning," Java Jarvis said as she sauntered into Val's office. "I heard your message this morning and decided a visit would be better than a phone call."

"I'm glad you made that decision." Val beamed. "I was just about to have coffee. Would you like a cup? It's fresh."

Val poured the coffee, and they sat on the sofa to visit. She told Java about the two new inmates.

"Wow! Your job is no float down the river, is it?"

Val laughed at Java's expression. "No, it's not, but I suspect that yours isn't either."

Java set her cup down. "As a matter of fact, our jobs are about to get more difficult. We're serving warrants on forty people involved in the VitaMaxPro scheme."

"I wondered when that would happen," Val said, shrugging. "It was inevitable."

"You and your dietician will have to testify."

"We will," Val promised, reaching for Java's hand. "I know you have our backs. Right now, I desperately need someone I can count on."

"You have nothing to worry about," Java reassured her. "You're squeaky-clean on the VitaMaxPro thing. Do you wear a gun?"

Val grimaced. "No, should I?"

"I think you should. A lot of people will be gunning for you. You're authorized to carry. You should get used to it."

"I will," Val promised.

She continued to hold Java's hand. It was a good, strong hand. The kind of hand that made one feel safe.

"Val," Java said, gently pulling her hand away, "I'm in a very committed relationship."

"Oh, of course." Val looked at the ceiling. "A woman as beautiful as you would be in a relationship."

"I'm sorry if I misled you in any way," Java added.

"You didn't, Java. You've been very kind and helpful. I overstepped the boundaries. I owe you an apology."

"I'd better go," Java said. "I'm serving the warrant on Buddy Craft and some of his staff. My team will be calling any minute."

As if on cue, Java's phone rang. She headed for the door. As she listened, a pink blush colored her cheeks. "Honey, I'm in a meeting with the warden right now." Java waved goodbye to Val as she walked toward the door. "Love you too," Java said into her cell phone.

I've got to get out more, Val thought after Java left.

##

"Your ten o'clock appointment is here," Lillian announced through the intercom.

Val stood to greet her childhood friend Bobby Joe Jones. She hugged him and motioned toward the chair in front of her desk as she settled into her own.

"What a pleasant surprise," Val said with a smile.

"I hope so," Bobby Joe said. "Did you know that someone attempted to kill Dr. Fairchild and Niki Sears?"

Val's lips moved but nothing came out. She finally managed a breathy, "No!"

Bobby shifted in his chair. "They made a mistake and just got Niki. It was a murder for hire. We have the culprit, but he has no idea who hired him. Everything was handled through that damn dark web."

"The dark web?" Val raised a questioning eyebrow. "I don't know anything about a dark web. I'm not very computer literate. You'll have to explain."

"You access it using Tor, a browser favored by the military, journalists, whistleblowers, the government, police, and criminals.

"The Tor browser guarantees anonymity. The dark web is commonly referred to as the secret internet for drug dealers, assassins, and pedophiles. There are a few murder-for-hire sites. Money transactions go through PayPal, usually using Cayman bank accounts that can't be traced to anyone."

"That's interesting," Val said.

"The perp had $10,000 on him when we arrested him. That's the price of a life nowadays."

Val looked down at her hands. "I'm sorry to hear that. Niki was a former inmate here. I believe she lived with Dr. Fairchild."

Bobby Joe slid a photo in front of Val. "Have you ever seen this man before?"

Val studied the picture. "No." She slid it back across the desk.

Then Bobby Joe played his ace. "He was a prison guard here until a few months ago."

Val was appalled. "Bobby Joe, surely you don't think I had anything to do with the murder of Niki Sears?"

"I didn't say—"

"You're questioning me. Isn't that why you're here?"

"He was a guard here when Dawn and Niki were inmates, but you don't know him?"

"Bobby, I don't know half the people who work in this prison. Do you have any idea how many guards we employ? No, I don't know him. I've never seen him."

"What about Lucinda Juarez?"

Val gave Bobby Joe a blank stare and shook her head.

"Lucky. She was one of your trustees until you transferred her to Huntsville."

"Ah, yes. What about her?"

235

"Didn't she blame Dawn and Niki for her problems here?"

"Yes, but she's in violent criminal lockdown."

"Could you make a phone call and verify that?"

"Of course." Val pushed the speed dial on her phone and waited while she was shuffled between departments. She finally spoke with someone who provided the information she needed.

"Lucky escaped six weeks ago," she told Bobby Joe after ending the call. "How is that even possible?"

"Would she go after Dawn?"

"Yes. She blamed Dawn for her takedown, and Dawn took Niki away from her."

"Your therapist, um . . . Edward Merrick, is he incarcerated?"

"Out on bail, awaiting trial. Dawn and Niki will be the state's chief witnesses."

Bobby Joe sighed. "My list just keeps getting longer."

"Surely you marked my name off your list," Val said, scowling at him.

"Of course." Bobby Joe chuckled.

The visits from Java and Bobby Joe made Val uneasy. She pulled her shoulder holster from her gun cabinet and slipped it on. After checking to make certain it was loaded to capacity, she snapped a clip into her Glock. She put the gun into the shoulder holster and pulled on her suit coat. She checked herself in the mirror. The gun and holster were invisible under the jacket.

Chapter 53

Dawn was consulting with Dr. Bartlett when Zeb entered Niki's room. "How's she doing?" he asked.

"She's holding her own," Bartlett said. "For a little thing, she's a fighter. We should start seeing improvement by the weekend."

Dawn asked the question she had been dreading. "If she hasn't improved by Monday, what other course of action can we take?"

Bartlett glanced down at his feet and then looked back at Dawn and shrugged.

"That's what I thought." Dawn turned her back to the men and stared down at Niki. *This can't be happening. God, please don't let this happen*, she prayed silently.

"I'll check on her this afternoon before I leave the hospital," Bartlett said as headed from the room.

"Are you okay?" Zeb touched Dawn's elbow.

She wiped her eyes and turned to face him. "Yes, it's just difficult to see her this way. She looks so frail."

"It's hard when patients don't respond the way we'd like," Zeb said.

"You've been a busy doctor this week. Three surgeries per day, sometimes more. That's pretty impressive."

"I have to work twice as hard," Dawn said, a slight smile softening her face. "I'm a woman."

"I'm sure no one would ever argue that point." Zeb gave her an admiring glance. "The nurses tell me you watch over this patient whenever you aren't on duty. That you haven't left the hospital since she arrived. You even perform the needed physical therapy to keep her limbs from atrophying."

"She's important to me," Dawn admitted.

"I'm sure she is. Your first operation in this hospital and it was pretty dramatic. Isn't this your day off?"

"Yes, but—"

"No buts accepted." Zeb grinned. "I'm taking you to lunch. You need to see some sunshine."

Dawn was tempted. A breath of fresh air sounded good, but a glance at Niki changed her mind.

"I can't," she mumbled. "My brother is bringing me some legal papers I need to sign."

"Oh." Disappointment covered Zeb's face. "How about dinner tonight?"

"Honestly, Zeb, I'm exhausted. I just want to veg out in that recliner and read a good book."

Zeb smiled. "I understand. Can I bring you anything?"

"No, Flint is bringing me lunch, but thank you for your kindness."

"Maybe another time," Zeb said. "Let me know if I can do anything."

##

Dawn rubbed her eyes, opened her Kindle, and began to read. It wasn't long before she dozed off.

"I am her mother!" a high-pitched voice shrieked in the hallway. "I demand that you let me see my daughter."

Dawn jerked awake and rushed to the door. Willard and Renfro were standing in the hallway behind a woman who was an older, harder version of Niki. She was bundled in a fur coat.

"Dr. Fairchild," the police guard said as he rolled his eyes, "she says Miss Sears is her daughter."

Dawn had no doubt the woman who reminded her of a mean Chihuahua wrapped in chinchilla fur was Niki's mother, Sylvia Sears.

"Miss Sears is in a coma," Dawn said. "She can't have visitors. She is also under police security. Someone tried to kill her. I'm her attending physician, Dr. Fairchild. I'll be happy to answer any questions you may have."

Sylvia stood up to Dawn as if she were a foot taller than the blonde instead of three inches shorter. "I have a right to see her. I'm her mother!"

"You may see her," Dawn acquiesced, "but they can't. She informed me she was afraid of them. Willard and I have met before." She smirked as she looked at the cast on Willard's hand.

"You! You were at the university," Willard growled as he backed away from Dawn.

Dawn observed as Sylvia looked at her only daughter. There was no emotion. The woman's hair was an excellent beauty-parlor red with highlights. Not as fine as Niki's or as soft-looking. She had the same beautiful, delicate face as Niki and perfect cupid-bow lips. She had none of Niki's softness or sweetness.

"How's she doing?" Sylvia barked.

"She's responding to treatment. She'll be fine," Dawn said with more confidence than she felt.

"You're keeping her alive through artificial means," Sylvia declared. "A machine is breathing for her, and you're feeding her through a tube."

Dawn fought the anger rising in her. "She was in an automobile accident. She had severe chest trauma. The ventilator helps her breath until she can breathe without pain. Obviously, the feeding tube is needed to provide nourishment and hydration."

"If you took her off the machines, would she die?"

"Possibly," Dawn choked out.

"What is she to you?" Sylvia demanded.

"She's my patient."

"Hmm." Sylvia shook her head. "We'll be back to check on her tomorrow."

"Mrs. Sears, Niki led me to believe that she hasn't seen you in several years. Did you know she was in prison?"

"Of course I knew. That's why she hasn't seen me in several years. Unlike my sons, Niki has never been a child I could be proud of."

Dawn bit her lip to push back her sharp retort. "Why are you here now?"

"That, Dr. Fairness, is none of your business."

Dawn didn't bother correcting the woman's distortion of her name. She wasn't worth the effort. She just wanted Sylvia and her spawns gone.

Flint arrived with lunch and the papers that needed her signature to register the new car in her and Niki's name.

Flint frowned as he looked at Niki. "Is she doing okay? I mean—?"

"No, she isn't," Dawn said, choking back a sob. "She isn't responding to treatment."

Flint glanced sideways at his sister. "Sis, why was Niki driving your car after midnight?"

Dawn had flashes of the last night they'd spent together. She smiled as she recalled their activities "I . . . we, uh—"

"Are the two of you together? I mean like partners or significant others?"

"Yes," Dawn admitted for the first time. "We're a couple."

Flint wrapped his arms around his sister. "Is there anything I can do to help? I can sit with her when you're on duty or—"

"There's a guard here 24-7." Dawn sniffled as she leaned against her brother.

"We'll be okay, Flint. I appreciate you acting as my messenger and taking care of all the legal things I have going on."

"I'm happy to help." He hugged her one more time. "I've got to run by the store for Mom. Do you need anything?"

"No. Just be careful. I don't know what I'd do if anything happened to you."

As Flint was leaving, Father Garza entered the room. He had visited every day since Niki had been placed on the ventilator. Dawn enjoyed his company and their many discussions regarding the existence of God. Father Garza was a comfort to her, and he always prayed over Niki.

At this point we welcome any help we can get, Dawn thought as Garza prayed.

After Father Garza left, Dawn nestled into the recliner and began to read again.

Jacey arrived at the hospital two hours before her shift to relieve Dawn. "How's she doing?"

"She may be turning around," Dawn answered, turning off her Kindle. "Her vitals are better and she is respond well to the physical therapy."

"That's good news. I thought I'd sit with her while you go home and get some clean clothes. I know you need to pick up some long-sleeved shirts. The weather has turned cooler. I didn't know what to bring you, and you need to get some fresh air."

Dawn smiled at her oldest friend. "You are always so thoughtful. I feel safe leaving her in your care, and I'll leave the guard outside her door. I won't be long. There's a book by Sarah Markel on the bedside stand. It's really good. I'd appreciate it if you'd read to her."

"I'd be happy to." Jacey smiled.

##

Dawn inhaled deeply as she waited for the valet to bring her car. She couldn't wait to drive the new vehicle. Couldn't wait to take Niki home in it. She thought about notifying Bobby Joe that she was leaving the hospital but felt safe running home and back.

She tipped the valet and slid into the driver's seat. The car had everything: Wi-Fi, bird's-eye-view cameras, air-conditioned and heated seats, and more. Everything Dawn could imagine was built into the car.

When she reached home, she didn't bother pulling into the garage. She entered through the front door and hurried to their bedroom. Memories overwhelmed her as she entered the room. Niki prancing around in her Henley. Niki leaning above her, long red hair falling around them as she lowered her lips to Dawn's. Niki was everywhere. Even her subtle fragrance filled Dawn's nostrils.

No time to dawdle, Dawn, she told herself as she went to the closet and began pulling out warmer clothes. She put her dirty clothes in the bathroom hamper and packed enough clothes for another week at the hospital.

She looked around to make certain she had gotten everything she needed. Then she locked up and headed back to the car.

Her mind was on Niki as she walked to the car, pushing the fob button to open the rear door. She stumbled and pitched forward when a wheel on her suitcase caught on a sprinkler head at the edge of the driveway. A shot rang out, and a bullet whizzed past her face.

Dawn immediately flattened herself against the ground and scrambled underneath the car. She pulled her phone from her pocket and dialed 911.

"Operator, I'm at 721 Royal Court. Someone is shooting at me. This is Dr. Dawn Fairchild."

"Stay on the phone, Dr. Fairchild."

Dawn listened as the dispatcher directed a nearby police car to her location. "Are you still with me, Dr. Fairchild?"

"Yes," Dawn whispered. She wasn't sure where the shot came from or if the shooter was still close by.

Within minutes a patrol car arrived at the scene with their lights flashing and siren blaring. Two policemen got out of the car. "Dr. Fairchild?" one of them called out.

"I'm under the car," Dawn said as she wiggled out from under the vehicle.

"Don't stand up yet, ma'am. Let us form a shield for you. Do you know the direction the shot came from?"

"The bullet lodged in the column on the left," Dawn answered, rising to her feet.

"You should get back inside the house, Dr. Fairchild."

When Dawn informed them that she needed to get to the hospital, the officers insisted on escorting her.

As she pulled into valet parking, the patrol car pulled alongside her. "Dispatch gave us the rundown on your case," the officer said. "We've been instructed to stay with you until Detective Jones arrives."

Seconds later, Bobby Joe pulled his car behind Dawn's and got out. "I'll take it from here, fellows." He thanked the patrolmen and opened Dawn's door.

"We're going to have to find a better way to meet," he joked as he followed Dawn into the hospital. "You're becoming a full-time job."

A shiver ran through Dawn's body. "I don't know what's going on."

"It's pretty obvious someone wants you dead," Bobby Joe said as they stepped into the garage elevator. He pushed the button and waited until the door closed.

"Did anything else happen today? How did anyone know you were at home? Did anyone follow you from the hospital?"

Dawn dragged her hand across her eyes as if wiping away cobwebs. "Just let me get my bearings," she croaked.

"Niki's family visited her today. They made me very uneasy. Her mother hasn't seen her in years but came today with her two brothers."

Bobby Joe thumbed through his little notebook. "The same two brothers that accosted you at the college?"

"Yes."

Bobby's eyes scanned the page. "You sent one of them to the hospital?"

"Yes."

"You must be a hell of a lot tougher than you look, Dr. Fairchild."

Dawn shrugged. "People tend to underestimate me."

They left the elevator and walked toward Niki's room. Bobby Joe nodded to the policeman standing guard in the hallway. "I'll be here for a while. You can take a thirty-minute break."

The guard thanked him and hurried for the elevator.

"Did anyone follow you from the hospital?"

"I didn't see anyone, and only Jayce knew I was going home. It was a spur-of-the-moment decision."

Dawn introduced Jayce and Bobby Joe. "She's my housemate and watched Niki while I ran home for clean clothes."

"I'm glad to meet you," Jayce said, shaking hands with the detective. "I've got to run. Duty calls."

Bobby Joe followed her into the hallway and watched Jayce get onto the elevator. "She's the only one who knew you'd be at your home?" he said returning to Dawn.

"We've been friends since grade school," Dawn explained. "I'd trust Jayce with my life."

"While I'm here I'll let you know where I am in my investigation." Bobby Joe kept his voice down so Niki wouldn't hear him.

"I've interrogated Warden Davis. Lucky, whose name is Lucinda Juarez, by the way, has managed to escape from prison." Dawn opened her mouth to speak, but Bobby held up his hands. "Don't ask me how.

"Every agency in Texas is looking for her. Edward Merrick's attorney is bringing him in to talk to me tomorrow. I'll catch up with the Sears brothers and your ex-boyfriend tomorrow."

"Basically, what you're telling me is that you have no idea who is trying to kill us."

"Yeah, that about sums it up." Bobby Joe cringed. "Forensics has the bullet that lodged in your column and are running it for a ballistics match. Maybe we can find one that matches it and connect it to a shooter in our database."

Bobby Joe stood when the guard returned. "I'll let you get some rest, Doc. You've had a rough day."

After Bobby Joe left, Dawn pulled her chair closer to Niki's bed. "God, I miss you, baby. I'd give anything to hear your voice."

She reached for her Kindle and noticed someone had slipped an envelope inside the cover. She pulled it out. *A hospital invoice.* She ripped the end from the envelope and pulled out the thick bill. She flipped to the last page and gasped when she saw the cost of the past two weeks. *I'll transfer enough out of savings to cover the bill and take a check to finance tomorrow,* she thought.

She had no idea how long Niki would remain in her present state. *I need to accept more surgeries,* she thought. *At this rate, we'll deplete my savings within a month.*

She hated the thought of spending less time with Niki, but she knew they would need the income. She reached out and gently caressed Niki's cheek, tracing the scar with her fingertips. "I love you so much, little one."

Chapter 54

The next morning Bobby Joe walked through the hospital corridors to the office with Dr. Wynn's name stenciled on the door. He knocked, entering when invited to do so.

"Dr. Richard Wynn," Bobby Joe said without breaking stride, "you are under arrest for the murder of Mary Davis." He read Richard his rights as he fastened the cuffs around the man's wrists.

"Oh, for Christ's sake, get these things off me," Richard wailed. "Dawn did this, didn't she?"

"No one but me." Bobby Joe was clearly enjoying himself as he pulled the man to his feet. "I have video and testimony. It's a sorry man who lets a woman like Dawn Fairchild do his time in prison."

"So, the time has been served for the crime," Wynn whined. "There's no reason to arrest me."

Bobby Joe snorted. "It doesn't work that way. Where were you between seven and nine last night?"

"At home with my wife. Where else would I be?"

"Anyone else see you around that time?"

"No, we were . . . um, you know. My wife requires a lot of attention."

"I'll verify that," Bobby Joe growled as he pushed Richard out the door.

"What's last night got to do with this?" Richard held up his handcuffed arms.

"That's what I plan to find out."

News of Dr. Wynn's arrest flew around the hospital like a bullet on a still day. Everyone was talking about it. Dawn tried to ignore the gossip and concentrate on the task at hand. She had to take Richard's surgery load, but she didn't mind. They needed the money.

She performed four surgeries before noon and was drinking a cup of coffee in her office when Val walked in.

I've missed you, Dawn thought as she silently surveyed the curvy brunette. She was glad to see her. She wanted to run to Val and hug her. In spite of all they had been through, she still respected Val's abilities as a prison administrator.

"I know I'm not supposed to talk to you," Val said. "But I miss you and I wanted to talk to you. Like we used to do."

Dawn poured Val a cup of coffee then returned to her chair across the desk from the warden.

"Aren't you going to say something?" Val blurted. "Hello, Val, or get the hell out of my office, Val, or—"

"It's so good to see you, Val," Dawn muttered. "I've missed you."

"I heard about Niki," Val said still thinking Niki had died. "I'm so sorry, Dawn. I wish I could help—make things easier for you."

"It's hard," Dawn said, faking a thin smile. "I'm managing."

Val changed the subject. "Bobby Joe said he arrested Richard Wynn this morning."

"Yes." Dawn's voice caught in her throat. "He was charged with the crime I served time for."

"Dawn, I want to make it up to you," Val said. "I'll do the television talk shows with you. I'll appear in public and admit I was mistaken. I'll do whatever it takes to make this right.

"I've already signed off on the monetary settlement. Six million. You'll get the check in a few weeks. I should have agreed to do it to begin with. I was so wrong.

"I want us to be friends. I want to talk to you over coffee. I . . . I just miss you.

"I have so much to tell you, to share with you. I want you to know some of it before the news media blows everything out of proportion.

"Maybe we could have dinner tonight," Val concluded.

Dawn wanted to tell her about Niki lying in a coma. That she only wanted to be at Niki's side. But she didn't. She agreed to dinner.

"Why don't we meet at that little Italian place with the privacy booths," Dawn suggested. "I can get away for a couple of hours. I'm carrying Richard's load too until we can hire another surgeon."

"That's fine. Or I could cook, and you could come to my place," Val suggested.

"The Italian place would be closest," Dawn said as her name spilled over the PA system. "I have surgeries to do this afternoon. Is six o'clock okay?"

Val nodded and stood. "Tell Libby to send over whatever you need me to sign. I'll have it done by tomorrow."

Dawn smiled. "See you tonight."

Val was pleased with her meeting with Dawn. She congratulated herself for reaching out to the blonde. *She looks even better than I remembered,* she thought. *With Niki out of the way, maybe we can move toward a more meaningful relationship. If she can ever forgive me for sending her to prison.*

She took her time showering and dressing. She wanted to look just right for Dawn.

##

Dawn finished her last surgery for the day. She had an hour to shower and read to Niki before meeting Val. She wondered if she'd ever get off the endless treadmill.

Six million will certainly help, she thought as she dressed. *I won't have to worry about Niki's hospital bills and can spend more time with her.* A sob caught in her throat. Her heart hurt every time she thought about Niki. *She'll pull through. I know she will. She's a fighter, a scrappy little angel. I can't even think about life without her.*

Dawn finished dressing and then read to Niki for thirty minutes. "I won't be gone long, baby," she murmured. She kissed Niki on the forehead and tiptoed out.

##

Val and Dawn talked as if they'd never had a river of distrust between them. Val explained in detail about the VitaMaxPro scandal that was rocking the Texas government.

"Dog food?" Dawn chuckled in disbelief. "They were feeding the prisoners the same ingredients used to beef up dog food? I'm so glad you put your foot down and stopped it."

"Oh, me too," Val huffed. "But that was all because you told me how awful the cafeteria food was. If you hadn't made me pay attention, I would have been caught up in the scandal. As it is, I'm being considered for Craft's replacement."

"You'd be the director of the Texas Department of Criminal Justice!" Dawn suppressed a squeal. "Oh, Val, you really could make a difference in that position. I'm so proud of you."

Val sat up a little straighter and basked in Dawn's approval. "It just keeps getting better," she said, smirking. "I now have two transgender women in my prison. Wait until you hear their stories. The state is in turmoil over how to handle them."

Val emptied the bottle of wine and opened the booth door to signal the waiter for another one. Then she settled in to tell Dawn about Passion Flower and Daisy Darling.

Dawn laughed until her sides hurt as Val did her impersonations of the two inmates. "I swear, I'm in a quandary about what to do to keep them safe, and they won't tone it down one bit.

"Passion is about to be paroled and has already signed off on the settlement which will make her a millionaire. I just hope she manages to stay out of prison.

"Daisy isn't filing a suit. It's the three women she was housed with that are filing. I have no idea how long that will last."

They finished the second bottle of wine and were giggling like school girls when the waiter knocked on the door of their booth. "Ladies, I need to settle your check," he said with a smile as he opened the door. "We close in ten minutes."

Dawn fought the nausea that welled inside her. She'd been gone for four hours. For four hours she'd forgotten about Niki. *What kind of mate am I?*

She reached inside her purse for her credit card to pay her half of the bill, but Val beat her to it.

"My treat," she insisted. "This is the best time I've had since you left."

"I . . . I really must go," Dawn said as she got to her feet. "Thank you so much for a delightful dinner. I truly enjoyed it."

"Can we do it again soon?" Val asked.

"I'll be in touch," Dawn promised as she walked out the door.

##

Dawn ran to her car. *God, how could I forget Niki? How could I leave her alone for four hours?* She couldn't conjure a hair coat big enough to take away her guilt.

When she reached Niki's room half an hour later, the guard was dozing in the chair outside the door. She slipped inside without waking him, feeling less safe than usual.

Niki's vitals had improved, and she was breathing better, the gasping breaths replaced by slow, steady ones. "Thank you, God." Dawn prayed as she knelt beside Niki's bed. "Thank you."

Chapter 55

True to her word, Sylvia Sears and her sons showed up again the next day. "How's she doing today?" Sylvia asked charging into Niki's room.

"Better." Dawn beamed. "She's doing better."

"Better?" Sylvia barked. "Yesterday I thought she was knocking on death's door."

Dawn frowned. "Yesterday she was. But I think she has turned a corner. I think she's going to make it."

"I want her life support removed," Sylvia demanded. "If we're taking her home, she needs to be breathing on her own."

"Taking her home?" Dawn was dumbfounded. "Who said anything about releasing her? She isn't strong enough to be moved. That could kill her."

"She's my daughter," Sylvia wailed. "I want her at home where we can take care of her."

"No," Dawn growled. "I won't release her."

"Please, Dr. Farnsworth." Sylvia's cunning expression made Dawn sick to her stomach. "You're not her doctor. You're her lover. Does the hospital board know that?"

Dawn felt as if Sylvia had slapped her face. She stepped back. "I thought you'd see it my way," Sylvia sneered as she motioned for Willard and Renfro to enter the room.

"Guard," Dawn yelled. "These people are endangering my patient. Please call security and remove them immediately.

"Mommy Dearest, you need to take the Tweedle boys and leave before I have you all arrested."

Sylvia pulled herself up to her full height.

Dawn leaned into her face. "Don't make me throw you down an elevator shaft!"

Sylvia backed away from the fury she saw in Dawn's eyes. "I'll be back tomorrow, Dr. Frankenstein, and I'll have my attorney. You will release my daughter to me."

"Over my dead body," Dawn shouted.

"That can be arranged," Sylvia hissed through gritted teeth.

As hospital security pushed the Searses from the room, Dawn dialed Libby. "I need you now," she whispered into the phone. Then she called Bobby Joe. She knew she was on shaky ground. She had no legal right to make decisions for Niki, even if they were in her best interest.

Bobby Joe, Libby, Flint, and Dawn huddled outside Niki's room.

"I can hold her in protective custody," Bobby Joe said, pacing the floor outside Niki's room. "Legally I can only hold her for twenty-four hours, but that might give Libby time to get a court order to stop Sylvia from taking her."

"I filed that motion this morning," Libby said. "Even if they go to court, we can prolong the court proceedings for weeks or months. However long it takes for Niki to come around."

Father Garza walked toward the small army of Niki's protectors. "You look like you're planning a revolt," he teased.

Dawn explained the situation.

"Is there any chance you two got married somewhere along the way?" Father Garza asked.

"No, everything happened so fast. We haven't had time."

"That's a shame." Libby sighed. "That would solve all of our problems. As her wife you'd be next of kin and have the right to make her medical decisions."

"You need to get a marriage license," Libby advised. "Apply for one. In Texas you must wait seventy-two hours to use it, but it's good for ninety days. Surely in three months Niki will revive."

"Yes," Father Garza said. "When Niki wakes up, I can perform a marriage ceremony for you, and you'll be legally married."

"Sounds like we have a plan," Bobby Joe said, clapping his hands.

"I'll get the marriage license," Dawn said. "Flint, can you sit with Niki while I take care that?"

"I'll do anything you need, Sis." Flint slipped his arm around her shoulder, and for a minute she let herself relax against him.

"Thank you, Flint. I've always been able to count on you."

"I'll stay too," Libby volunteered. "Just in case the wicked witch and her flying monkeys return before you get back."

##

Dawn checked to make certain she still had Niki's driver's license and birth certificate she'd used to admit her to the hospital. Bobby Joe drove her to the Tarrant County Court House and located the county clerk's office. There was a long line of people waiting to be served. The clerks were obviously overworked and understaffed.

The man in front of Dawn was loud and obnoxious, complaining about the long wait and how he was missing an appointment because the clerks were so slow and stupid.

The clerk gave him the copies he'd requested and informed him the charge would be ten dollars.

"Ten dollars?" the man bellowed. "I've been standing in this line for an hour. Do you have any idea how much I make an hour? You should pay me ninety dollars for wasting my time."

"Sir, please just pay the ten dollars and get out of line so someone else can be served." The clerk gritted her teeth.

Dawn could tell the clerk was about to reach her wit's end. She dug into her purse and pull out a ten. "Here. I've had a wonderful day. Please allow me to pay it forward."

The man looked at her as if she had set the counter on fire. The clerk grabbed the bill and said a thankful, "Bless you," to Dawn.

"I need a marriage license," Dawn said, leaning around the man who still blocked her access to the counter.

The clerk shoved a form to her and glared at the man who still stood there. "I thought your time was too precious to waste," she blurted.

"Yeah, buddy," the man behind Dawn growled. "Why don't you move along? You got what you wanted."

Dawn pulled out her driver's license and showed it to the clerk, who glanced at it while eyeing the two bickering men.

Dawn started to fill out the form.

"Where's your fiancé?" the clerk demanded. "Both of you must sign in my presence."

"He'll come in later," Dawn said.

The man behind Dawn slugged the troublemaker who was still holding up the line, and all hell broke loose. Two deputies handcuffed the men and led them away.

Dawn filled out the form using Niki's name and information. She signed Niki's name and shoved the form to the clerk with the necessary payment.

The clerk gave her a receipt. "Just tell him to ask for the form by your name, Miss Sears. It'll be right here in the pending folder." The woman never noticed that the name on the form was not the same as the name on the driver's license Dawn had presented.

"I'm sorry," the flustered clerk muttered. "It isn't normally this chaotic. Thank you for paying his fee." The clerk placed a tent sign at her station that said, "Next Clerk Please."

"Happy to do it." Dawn smiled and walked away.

She headed to the end of the dimly lit hallway and waited until the clerk went into the ladies room. She returned to the clerk's office and stood in the shortest line, praying she would be waited on before the other woman returned.

"May I help you?" a smiling clerk asked.

"Yes, I'm supposed to come by and sign our marriage license," Dawn said, blushing appropriately. "My partner came in earlier today and signed. The name is Niki Sears."

The woman thumbed through the pending file and pulled out the marriage license. "I'll have to see your driver's license."

Dawn produced the required identification, and the woman checked it thoroughly. Dawn filled out her part of the certificate and signed it.

The clerk studied the license. "Looks like everything is in order." She leaned across the counter toward Dawn. "Are you marrying another woman?"

"Yes. Yes, I am," Dawn said proudly.

"You're so beautiful," the clerk whispered as she pushed the license to Dawn.

"So is she," Dawn whispered back. Just saying the words made her heart ache.

Chapter 56

Flint and Libby were laughing and talking when Dawn entered Niki's room. It was good to have normal activities going on around the patient.

"Did Mrs. Sears come by?" Dawn asked as she looked around the room.

Flint laughed. "Yeah. Bobby Joe arrested Tweedledum and Tweedledee. One of them took a swing at me, and the other joined in. The officer outside the door handcuffed them together and hauled them away with their mother squawking like an injured grackle."

"Be careful," Libby said. "If any of her curses come true, you'll be buried in fire and brimstone by morning."

"Did she bring her attorney?"

"Yes," Libby said, "but my assistant showed up at the same time with the injunction needed to keep them from moving Niki or interfering with her treatment.

"I'm sure he'll counter file just to get the billable hours. But I'll drag this out so long they won't even remember Niki's name."

Dawn shook her head. "I don't know what I'd do without you two."

"We're going to dinner," Libby said with a smile. "Your handsome brother has finally asked me out."

Flint blushed slightly. "Why don't you join us, Sis?"

"No," Dawn said. "I just want to be with Niki, but thank you."

After Flint and Libby left, hospital food service brought dinner. Dawn suddenly realized she was starving. She hadn't eaten all day.

She watched the news as she ate. Just as Val had predicted, the state of Texas was all over the national news with its latest scandal, feeding dog food to prisoners. No one ever explained that VitaMaxPro was a meat substitute with added protein. That it was used to enhance many products, including dog food.

To make the story more sensational, the main news feed was always, "Texas prisoners fed dog food."

She was glad Val had been exonerated and named the interim director of the Texas Department of Criminal Justice. She suddenly had a desire to hear Val's voice. She pressed the button to dial the warden's cell phone.

"Dawn!" Val said, her voice a breathy whisper. "I'm so glad you called."

"I called to congratulate you," Dawn said. "I'm watching the interview you did earlier today. You're so confident, so sure of yourself. You'll make a perfect director."

"Thank you," Val said. "That's sweet of you. Are you home?"

"No, I'm at the hospital. I'm not—"

"It's late," Val interrupted. "You should get some sleep. I'll call you tomorrow."

"Okay, good night," Dawn said.

She pulled her chair closer to Niki's bed, opened her Kindle, and began to read.

Val poured a glass of wine and leaned back in her recliner to watch the replays of the announcement of her promotion. It was only interim director, but she had been promised the job and would drop the interim part as soon as things calmed down. The governor thought it would be good to have a woman at the helm of the Texas prison system to counter the good-old-boy accusations flying around.

She called the Reata, one of Fort Worth's most expensive restaurants, and made reservations for two for the next night. She was certain Dawn would want to celebrate her promotion with her.

Dr. Dawn Fairchild. She let her mind wander as she envisioned pulling the beautiful blonde into her arms and kissing her. A slow, easy kiss that morphed into a smoldering need to touch the woman, to run her hands up her long legs and kiss her flat stomach. She was sorry Niki was dead but glad she now had a chance with Dawn Fairchild.

I won't screw this up, Val thought. *I'll take as long as she needs to fall in love with me.*

I also need to renege on my promise to appear on television with her. I'll contact the controller's office and pick up Dawn's check myself. I'll deliver it to her. Yeah, that'll make her like me more.

##

Libby entered her office to find a busload of lawyers milling around her waiting room. "Who are they?" she asked the receptionist.

"Sylvia Sears's legal team."

Libby's vision of tying up Sylvia in court evaporated. If the woman had this kind of manpower she would overwhelm Libby and her staff.

The yappy Chihuahua appeared as the lawyers around her opened a path to Libby. "Miss Howe, you really should come to work earlier."

"What can I do for you?" Libby asked, trying to be civil.

"Drop this ridiculous injunction so I can take my daughter home."

"I have to wonder why Niki has suddenly become so important to you." Following her hunch, Libby went for the

259

jugular. "A will, perhaps? Does Niki get half the farm or maybe all of it? You'd really rather see her die than recover, am I right?"

Libby knew by the gleam of hatred in Sylvia's eyes that she had nailed her motives.

"Foolish girl, your injunction has already been overturned. In court this morning the judge threw it out since you didn't show up to defend it. Our counter injunction prevailed." Sylvia slapped the folded papers into Libby's hand.

Libby looked at the documents. The judge had granted the Searses an injunction forcing the hospital to remove life support from Niki. Sylvia had also filed a petition to have herself named executor of Niki's estate because her daughter was medically incapacitated and unable to represent herself.

"I wasn't notified of any hearing this morning." Libby scowled. "You've pulled a dirty trick. I'll fight it."

"Miss Howe, it is imperative that I get my daughter out of the hospital immediately and take her home where she belongs. I know that you can slow down that process with your constant court orders and petty legal moves, so tell me how much I need to pay you to make you go away."

Libby seethed. "I'm sure you're used to dealing with unprincipled people who will do anything for a dollar, but I'm not one of them. Take your intimidation team and get out of my office."

Oh Dawn, what have you gotten yourself into? she thought.

Chapter 57

Bobby Joe was no closer to finding the would-be murderer of Dawn and Niki than he had been the day Niki was rushed to the hospital. Forensics on the bullet they'd dug from Dawn's porch column had failed to match anything in the database.

Lucky had been apprehended but had an ironclad alibi. She had been in a lesbian brothel that provided security videos to prove it.

Edward Merrick had no alibi but seemed clueless about the internet. "Besides, I'd have to kill at least four people and destroy a video that even you have a copy of, Detective Jones." Bobby didn't really consider him a suspect.

That left the Sears family and Val.

He could tell by talking to Val that she was in love with Dawn, so that left only Sylvia Sears and her rabid sons.

Yep, Bobby thought. *My killer's last name is Sears. Now to prove it.*

##

Val waited in Dawn's office. The nurse had informed her that the doctor was in surgery but would return to her office as soon as the surgery was complete.

She looked around the neat, organized office. The awards and certificates on Dawn's wall caught her attention. The woman had received every humanitarian award imaginable and had numerous letters of praise from important people, including the US president, two Texas governors, and multiple mayors. For the first time, Val was genuinely ashamed of the part she had played in sending Dawn to prison. *I'll find a way to make it up to her*, she thought.

The door opened, and Val turned to face the woman of her dreams.

"Val, what a nice surprise." Dawn removed her hospital jacket and motioned for Val to sit beside her on the sofa.

"I wanted to hand-deliver this," Val said as she pulled the check from her purse. "I know things have been tough and thought you might need it before the state comptroller got around to putting it in the mail."

Dawn stared at the check. "Thank you. I can't tell you how much this means to me." She exhaled a breath she had been holding for days. The check would more than cover Niki's hospital bills, with extra in case they needed it.

"It's the fair thing for us to do." Val included herself among those who had wronged Dawn. "I've made reservations at the Reata for tonight. I hoped you would help me celebrate my promotion and us settling this suit."

"Oh, I'd love that." Then Dawn sighed, thinking of Niki. "But I'm pulling two shifts with Richard in jail. I must turn down your invitation."

"I understand," Val said as she took Dawn's hand. "Maybe after things settle down."

Dawn nodded and stood as her name was called over the PA system. "My public awaits!" She leaned down and kissed Val on the cheek. "Thank you so much for this." She put the check in her lap drawer. "I'll ask Flint to deposit it for me," she said as she escorted Val from the room.

Val touched her cheek where the softest lips had been only seconds before. *I will make her fall in love with me*, she thought as she headed for her car.

##

Dawn looked around the surgery prep room and found it empty. She walked to the nurses' desk and asked about the page over the PA.

"It was me." Libby grinned as she stepped out from behind the desk. "I stopped by your office and saw Black Heart in there, so I decided to get rid of her."

Dawn chuckled. "She's really a good person. Our entire thing was an awful, painful misunderstanding."

"The only one it was painful for was you," Libby declared. "But that's not why I'm here. The judge granted the Searses' injunction to stop you from keeping Niki on life support."

"What? How can a mother do something she knows will kill her child?" Dawn sobbed.

"Maybe that's what she wants," Libby said. "I'm certain there's a will and huge amounts of money involved. I'm trying to find out, but it's slow progress. Bobby Joe can keep her away from Niki for another day. After that it's just a matter of what the judge decides."

"I need to check on Niki," Dawn said. "Keep me informed."

"I will. Dawn, don't trust the Searses. Don't be alone with them or leave them alone with Niki. We'll fight this."

Dawn headed for Niki's room. Outside the door, she pulled herself to her full height, threw back her shoulders, and put a smile on her face. *Just in case Niki is awake,* she thought.

Niki wasn't awake. She was as still and lifeless as she had been for weeks. Dawn sat down in the chair beside her bed and leaned forward, resting her forehead on Niki's arm. She closed her eyes and prayed.

Chapter 58

Dawn held Niki's hand in hers and traced the angles of Niki's face with her free hand. "You're so beautiful, so small. I want to gather you in my arms and rock you like a baby." She gently pushed a stray strand of red hair away from Niki's face.

"Let's discuss our future. I'm thinking that after you get your nurse practitioner's degree we'll both work in this hospital. You might even want to get your medical degree. We could be Doctors Without Limits, because there is no limit to how much I love you.

"After we're married, what name do you want to use? Niki Fairchild Sears, or Niki Sears Fairchild, or Mrs. Niki Sears, or Mrs. Niki Fairchild, or—"

"Mrs. Niki Fairchild," a faint voice mumbled as Niki squeezed Dawn's hand.

"Niki! Oh my God, Niki! You're awake. Oh baby, I've prayed. I've . . ." Tears ran down Dawn's cheeks, and she struggled to breathe. She pulled Niki's hand to her lips and kissed it. "I've missed you so much, baby."

Niki's smile was weak but genuine. "Mrs. Niki Fairchild caught my attention. I mean, were you proposing or just practicing?" she mumbled.

"Proposing." Dawn leaned down and gently placed her lips on Niki's cheek. "So, will you marry me?"

"Yes," Niki whispered, groaning as she moved. "But not anytime soon. I feel like I've been run over by a truck."

"You were. You've been unconscious for weeks, and a lot has transpired."

Dawn called Father Garza and asked him to grab a witness on the way. She didn't want to take a chance that Niki might slip back into a coma.

"We need to get married right away." Dawn explained the steps Sylvia was taking to gain control of Niki. "If I'm your wife, I'm considered next of kin and the one with the authority to make decisions about your medical care. Libby also drew up a power of attorney giving me the right to act on your behalf."

Niki's eyes glazed over. "Stay with me, baby," Dawn said loudly. "Your life depends on it."

Father Garza and a nurse entered the room. "Is she coherent?"

"Yes." Dawn moved so the priest could stand beside Niki's bed.

"Niki, I'm Father Garza, the hospital chaplain," he explained. "Do you understand me?"

"Yes," Niki croaked.

Dawn picked up a cup of water and held a straw to Niki's lips so she could moisten her mouth and tongue.

"Do you want to marry Dawn Fairchild?" Father Garza asked.

Niki smiled weakly. "More than anything."

"Then I'm going to perform the wedding ceremony," Garza said. He pulled Dawn closer and placed Niki's hand in Dawn's.

"Do you, Nicole Maria Sears, take this woman, Dawn Aden Fairchild, to be your lawfully wedded wife?"

"Yes," Niki said.

"Do you, Dawn Aden Fairchild, take this woman, Nicole Maria Sears, to be your lawfully wedded wife?"

"I do," Dawn said.

"By the powers vested in me, I pronounce you . . . woman and wife." Father Garza beamed, knowing he'd gotten it right.

Dawn, Niki, and Father Garza signed the marriage certificate and power of attorney, and the nurse witnessed them. "I'll file these today and bring back copies," he said as he left the room.

When they were alone, Dawn sat down on the side of Niki's bed. "How do you feel?"

"Married." Niki giggled. "But I've always felt married to you. Now it's legal."

Dawn leaned forward and kissed the scar on her wife's pale cheek. "I love you, Mrs. Niki Fairchild."

Niki's eyes closed as she slipped into a dreamless sleep.

Dawn laid her head on Niki's arm and cried. All the tension, all the fear, all the worry slipped away. She closed her eyes and slept peacefully for the first time in weeks.

Chapter 59

"Hey, sleepyhead." A gentle hand played with Dawn's hair. "Do you think you could get this tube out of my nose? It's uncomfortable as hell."

"Oh God, yes!" Dawn almost jumped for joy. "Let me check all your vitals and make certain you can eat."

"I promise I could eat a horse right now." Niki chuckled. "I'm starving."

"I'm afraid you'll be confined to Jell-O until your stomach adapts to food again."

Dawn scrambled for her stethoscope and held it against her breast to warm it.

"Do you do that for every patient?" Niki's eyes gleamed as she watched.

"Only the ones I plan to seduce at a later date," Dawn teased back, placing the chestpiece over Niki's lungs. "Take a deep breath."

Niki did as instructed.

"Did that hurt?"

"No, it felt good," Niki replied. "I was waiting for pain to hit but it didn't."

"That's good. Let me get a nurse, and we'll get these tubes out."

"Dawn, wait!" Niki touched her own face with her fingers. "Is my face okay? Am I still beautiful for you?"

"You'd be beautiful to me no matter what," Dawn said softly. "Your face is perfect, and so is your beautiful soul."

267

Dawn placed the feeding tube and other paraphernalia on the rolling cart as the nurse pushed the ventilator from the room. Dawn wet a washcloth and washed Niki's face. "You're so beautiful," she whispered.

"Uh-huh," Niki said, mocking her.

"I've ordered you some strawberry Jell-O. I remembered it's your favorite."

Niki frowned. "Only because BD I had no teeth."

"BD?" A quizzical expression crossed Dawn's face.

"Before Dawn," Niki murmured. "Before Dawn I was a lost cause. I doubt I'd be alive today if you hadn't taken an interest in me."

"Neither would I if you hadn't sacrificed your safety for me." Dawn shrugged. "But enough reminiscing about awful times. We have nothing but sunshine and rainbows ahead of us."

Scuffling in the hallway drew their attention toward the door. "I have a court order to remove my daughter from life support," Sylvia Sears shrieked as she burst through the door with hospital administrators and attorneys behind her.

"I've already complied with your court order," Dawn said, stopping Sylvia before she could reach Niki.

Sylvia glared at her daughter. "You're better?"

Niki nodded. Her eyes darted to Dawn.

"What do you want?" Dawn asked. "We've complied with your order. I believe your business here is finished."

"I want to speak with my daughter alone," Sylvia demanded.

"There's no way I would leave you alone with Niki," Dawn said as she moved to her wife's side. "Anything you have to say to her you can say to me. She is much improved but not completely out of the woods yet. I won't allow you to cause her to relapse."

"Dr. Fairway, you are a pain in the ass," Sylvia cackled. "My daughter can speak for herself."

"Dawn's right. I don't want to be in a room alone with you," Niki said. "I haven't seen you since I graduated college. Why your sudden interest in me now?" Niki slumped back against her pillows. It was obvious she was exhausted.

"Look here, you ungrateful little—"

Dawn caught Sylvia by the shoulders, whirled her around, and shoved her out the door. "Officer, please have security escort Mrs. Sears from the hospital and tell them she isn't allowed in Niki Sears's room again under any circumstances."

"You can't do that!" Sylvia bellowed. "You have no right to interfere."

"As her doctor I have every right," Dawn said, seething. "I don't ever want to see you again."

When Dawn returned to the room, Niki was sleeping. Dawn slipped into bed with her, and for the first time in weeks, leaned down to kiss her lips. She slid her arm under Niki's neck, and Niki snuggled into her side. "I love you," she whispered to Dawn.

"I've been on this case hard for the past three months," Bobby Joe informed Niki. The redhead sat on the sofa in Dawn's office. "I've narrowed my suspects down to your family."

"Here you go," Dawn said, handing Niki and Bobby Joe cups of steaming coffee. "It's hot. Be careful." She sat down beside her wife and put her arm around Niki's shoulder.

"I'm getting a search warrant for all three of their homes. If I can find a Glock that matches the bullet we dug out of your porch pillar, I'll file charges against them. I've got my best computer geek working to trace a connection between them and the murder-for-hire site on the dark web. That's a long shot."

269

"But didn't the truck driver say his target was Dawn and me?" Niki asked. "Why would my family want Dawn dead?"

"That guy is dumb as an armadillo," Bobby Joe grumbled. "I don't think he knows who he was supposed to kill. He just had an address."

"Bobby Joe, Niki has improved drastically over the past three weeks. We'd love to go home. Niki's been released, and we're tired of living in the hospital. The university has arranged for her to take the tests she's missed. If she passes them, she can return to her classes and stay on track to graduate.

"Our lives have been in such upheaval. We just want things to be normal—whatever normal is for us."

"I understand," Bobby said. "But until I make an arrest, I want to provide you police protection, and the hospital is the best place to do that. I don't have the funds to put several men with you. Here you also have the hospital security guards. I should be able to make an arrest next week."

After Bobby Joe left they sat side by side drinking their coffee. "I guess we're stuck here for at least another week," Niki mumbled.

"I'm afraid so, baby. It's for our own protection."

Niki walked to the door and locked it. "Then you need to get a soft throw for your sofa, Doctor."

Chapter 60

While Dawn was in surgery, Niki spent the morning searching the hospital for a room they might use as an apartment for the next week.

Darcus Martin led her to a room that was scheduled to be turned into a VIP intensive care room. "We've stripped everything out of it, repainted the walls, and added carpet. Look at this bathroom. It's nicer than mine at home."

"May we use it for a week?" Niki asked. "It's perfect."

"Sure. I'll have one of the new larger beds put in here," Darcus volunteered. "It's nice, but it's still a hospital bed."

"It'll work fine," Niki thanked her and hurried away to complete her mission.

She spent the rest of the day gathering things to make the room a sanctuary for Dawn, a place where she could relax. A place to shut out the rest of the world.

She bought flowers and scented candles from the hospital vendor and begged a beautiful bedspread and real sheets and pillowcases from housekeeping. She found an extra coffee maker stored in the doctors' lounge and bought gourmet coffee and cups from the on-site Starbucks.

By the time Dawn completed her last surgery, Niki had transformed the hospital room into their own bit of paradise.

Niki sat in Dawn's office studying for her nursing exams. As soon as Bobby Joe released them, she wanted to take the tests and get back into school. Her heart jumped when Dawn opened the door. It was funny how a room changed when Dawn entered it.

"Look at you, getting ready for your big tests." Dawn moved a book and sat beside Niki. "I've missed you today."

"I've been busy." Niki tilted her chin, welcoming the kiss she knew was coming. "Your lips are always so soft and delicious," she whispered.

"Mmm-hmm," Dawn murmured. "Yours are electrifying."

"Are you finished for the day?" Niki began gathering her books and papers.

"I am. I wish we could go home. I guess I need to see about a room for us, since you've been discharged."

Niki stood. "Darcus arranged one for us. I moved all of our things to it. Come on, I'll show you."

Dawn gathered Niki's books and followed her. "I promise you a real honeymoon when all this madness is over," she said as she followed her wife. "We should probably have a proper wedding too. I sort of forged your name on our marriage license. I'm sure your mother's attorneys could have a field day with that."

"Can we do that tomorrow on your day off?" Niki asked. "The sooner we're a hundred percent legal, the happier I'll be. I don't need a fancy wedding to know I belong to you. We can apply for the license and have Father Garza marry us on Friday in the hospital chapel."

"I'd like to invite a few friends and my family," Dawn said, getting excited about the idea of a small wedding.

"We can do anything you want, honey." Niki smiled as she opened the door to their home for the next few days.

Dawn gasped as she surveyed the transformed room. "Oh my! You did this? This is wonderful, and it smells so good in here. Not like a hospital."

"Do you really like it?" Niki beamed.

"I love it, and I love you." Dawn placed the books on a desk Niki had found and turned to slowly pull the redhead into her arms.

"You make me so happy. You always make everything better, nicer, sweeter." Her lips touched Niki's, and she relished the feel of their soft silkiness. The sensation of Niki in her arms was overwhelming. She was so soft and inviting. Dawn tightened her arms around her wife as Niki deepened the kiss.

"I've waited all day for this," Niki whispered as she broke the kiss. "You're going to love our bed."

"I'd love a blanket on the floor," Dawn said, her eyes sparkling, "as long as you were on it."

##

"You are incredible." Dawn gasped as she rolled onto her side and gazed at Niki. "Just incredible."

Niki snuggled into the blonde's softness and sighed. "You take my breath away," she said, willing her pounding heart to slow down. "You are . . . . I love the way you make love to me."

Dawn chuckled. "I'm glad. I'd be in deep trouble if you didn't. But you know if I do something you don't like, or you want me to do something that will please you more, all you have to do is tell me . . . or show me." Her lips captured Niki's again.

They made love, planned their future, and made love again. They fell asleep as the sun was flooding their world with light.

##

Dawn lay still beside her wife. She reveled in the feel of the smaller woman snuggled into her stomach. She fought the desire to pull Niki tighter against her. She wanted to wrap around her and protect her from the world, to erase the nightmares of the insanity Niki had left behind. The thought of Lucky hurting Niki sent a burning wave of hatred through her.

273

Thoughts of the pitiful little waif who had stood between her and the horrors of prison sent a fresh surge of love through her body. The heat was unbearable.

"Are you just going to lie here and do a slow burn,"—Niki turned in her arms and kissed her breast—"or make love to me?"

"What do you think?" Dawn whispered as she rose above her wife. "You must be quieter. Remember, we still have a guard outside our door."

"I can't promise anything," Niki said, giggling.

Chapter 61

They spent the next day applying for a new marriage license and arranging for their wedding. Father Garza was thrilled that they wanted to get married in his chapel.

Dawn called her family, Libby, and Bobby Joe Jones. She was surprised to find that she considered the detective a friend, but she did.

She mentioned inviting Val, but Niki vetoed the idea, saying she wanted nothing at her wedding that would remind her of prison.

"Is there anyone else you want to invite?" Dawn asked.

"The only one I care about being there is you." Niki tiptoed for a kiss.

"Wild horses couldn't keep me away." Dawn laughed.

##

They were eating lunch in the hospital cafeteria when Libby found them. "I've been doing a lot of digging and found some interesting information about you, Niki," she said as she joined them.

Niki's confused look let Libby know she had no idea what the attorney was talking about.

"Sears & Klienschmidt," Libby said. "The second largest online retailer in the world."

"Oh, that." Niki wrinkled her nose in disgust. "My family's business but not mine. My mother disowned me after Father died."

"It doesn't quite work that way," Libby explained. "Like your older brothers, you were gifted several million dollars in S&K stock when you were born. It's in your name. Over the past thirty years the stock has split and doubled numerous times.

"Your brothers and your mother have sold their stock to pay for palatial homes, lavish vacations, expensive cars, and anything else their hearts desired.

"You, on the other hand, haven't touched your stock. Guess what? You are the single largest stockholder in S&K. You own eighty percent of the company, enough to run it as you see fit."

Both Dawn and Niki gaped at Libby. "My wife is an heiress?" Dawn whispered.

Niki gasped. "I'm the largest stockholder in S&K? How did I not know that?"

"Apparently you dropped off the grid after college," Libby said. "Your family assumed you were dead until Ruth Fairchild called your mother and tried to persuade her to visit you in prison."

"My brothers . . ." Niki choked back a sob. "They intentionally got me hooked on hard drugs. By the time I graduated, I was a big-time user. That's when I received the letter from mother's attorney informing me I'd been disowned, and the family wanted nothing to do with me. I was too far gone to care.

"I didn't even respond to the letter. I just searched for my next fix. When my money ran out, Mother refused to take my calls, and my brothers cut all ties. I found other ways to get money. I was a drug addict."

Dawn covered Niki's hand with hers. "That's all over now. It's a past that we've put behind us."

"Niki's family is a very real threat," Libby continued. "They tried to buy me off and threatened me when I refused.

"S&K is a privately held company, and their stock isn't traded on the stock market. They have just over a

276

hundred stockholders who have snatched up the family's stock any time they offered to sell it.

"The S&K board is dying to take the company public. No doubt the stock will soar and split three-for-one, based on the amount of common stock they want to release. They can't go public without your consent.

"As it is now, upon your death your stock reverts to the family. If you marry or have children, your spouse or children inherit your stock. Your death would make your mother and brothers extremely wealthy. My advice to you is to set up a living trust with you and Dawn as the administrators. That will take you out of their crosshairs.

"Let me make this clear to you," Libby said, leaning across the table. "You are a billionaire several times over."

"Children," Niki whispered, smiling as she squeezed Dawn's hand. "I haven't given much thought to children. I'd like that."

"Children?" Libby snorted. "That's what you take away from this conversation?"

"We need to discuss this," Dawn said. "It's a lot to process. Can we call you later?"

"Of course," Libby said. "I'll see you at the wedding."

##

"Are we okay?" Dawn asked as Niki made coffee. Their walk from the cafeteria to their room had been a silent one.

Niki frowned. "Why wouldn't we be? Does it bother you that I'm an heiress?"

"No, of course not. The only thing that would bother me is losing you." Dawn sat on the sofa, and Niki crawled into her lap.

"You'll never lose me, honey." Soft lips reinforced Niki's statement. "I'm not with you for your money, and I know you aren't with me for mine, so nothing has changed in our lives except that we do need to marry legally."

Chapter 62

Val looked around her new office. *No wonder he was feeding the prisoners dog food,* she thought. *He had to cut somewhere to afford this office and expensive furniture.*

She opened a liquor cabinet and found it stocked with the most expensive liquors available. Priceless artwork graced the walls of the conference room off the office. The entire suite looked more like a boardroom at a country club than the office of one who was responsible for the well-being of criminals.

Opulence, Val thought. *I'll need to make this look more austere.*

"Director Davis?" the voice hummed over her intercom. "There's a Detective Bobby Joe Jones here to see you."

"Please send him in," Val said, smiling to herself. She couldn't wait to show off her new surroundings to Bobby Joe.

"Wow!" Bobby Joe exclaimed, suitably impressed. "You have definitely moved up in the world, Val."

"Thank you." Val gestured toward a chair for Bobby and walked toward the liquor cabinet. "How about a scotch to celebrate my promotion?"

"Maybe just a finger," Bobby said. "I'm on duty, but it's not every day my childhood playmate is named director of the Texas Department of Criminal Justice."

He took the drink Val handed him and held it high for her to clink her glass in a toast. Her jacket dropped back, exposing the gun she wore. "May you achieve all your goals, my friend," Bobby Joe toasted.

Bobby tossed down the smoothest scotch he'd ever tasted. He picked up the bottle to see what it was. "Macallan Sherry Oak Scotch Single Malt," he read, "aged 25 years. That's one expensive bottle of scotch."

"I didn't buy it," Val said. "It was left over from my predecessor. That's just one of the many reasons he's my predecessor."

Bobby Joe walked around, looking at the artwork and statues placed about the room. "I love your office. He did have good taste."

"Yeah," Val huffed, "but when you consider that while he was basking in this opulence inmates were eating dog food, his good tastes seem obscene."

"Good point."

"But you didn't pay me a visit to tour my new office," Val said, chuckling. "What can I do for you?"

"Have you heard the verdict in Richard Wynn's case?"

"Yes, he got seven years without parole." Val shrugged. "Unfortunately for him, he was tried before the same judge Dawn appeared before. He gave Wynn the mandatory two years for vehicular manslaughter and five years for aggravated perjury, plus a $10,000 fine."

"He's lucky," Bobby Joe said. "The judge could have given him up to ten years for the perjury charge."

"The judge said he was giving him two years for the death of my sister, two years for Dawn's time in prison, and three years for lying."

"So, when did you start wearing a gun?" Bobby Joe asked.

"When people began making attempts on Dawn's life. With Lucky on the prowl and the unsavory characters I've met on the job, I felt safer wearing a gun. It's become a part of me now."

"That's good," Bobby Joe said. "You're in a real snake pit now, and the snakes aren't in cages."

"Director, the Attorney General is here to see you," the intercom announced.

"I've got to run," Bobby Joe said as he got to his feet. "Take care, Val, and you know where to reach me if you need me."

After Bobby Joe left, Val poured herself another tumbler of the Macallan before greeting the Attorney General. *Bobby Joe is right,*" she thought. *This is the smoothest scotch I've ever tasted. Perhaps I'll always keep it on hand for dignitaries. I can't wait to show Dawn my new office. She'll enjoy having coffee with me here.*

##

"I'm as nervous as a virgin on her wedding night," Niki confided in Libby. "I'm so glad we're doing this again. I was barely coherent the first time."

"You make a much more beautiful bride this time around." Libby laughed as she zipped Niki's dress. "The photographer is here. I bet you're very photogenic."

"Is Dawn as nervous as I am?" Niki fidgeted with her flower bouquet.

"You've seen your wife in surgery," Libby scoffed. "She has ice water in her veins. I don't think anything shakes her except the possibility of losing you."

The wedding march echoed through the chapel. "That's our cue," Libby said as she caught Niki's hand. "Bobby Joe is waiting to walk you down the aisle."

"In a way, Bobby Joe and Val Davis are responsible for today," Niki said, swallowing hard against the lump in her throat. "If Dawn hadn't been wrongly accused, I wouldn't have met her."

"Lord!" Bobby Joe exclaimed as they walked toward him. "You are one gorgeous woman."

Niki ducked her head to hide the crimson that was coloring her face. Bobby Joe held out his arm. "Ready?"

Niki nodded, and they stepped into the chapel, walking to the swell of the music.

Niki couldn't take her eyes off the woman waiting for her with Father Garza. Dawn sparkled. Niki swore a light from heaven spotlighted the beautiful blonde. Her smile illuminated the room.

The ceremony was a little longer than their first, as Father Garza gave them the traditional Christian blessings. Niki was deaf. All she could hear was the beating of her heart.

"By the powers vested in me, I pronounce you woman and wife," the priest concluded. "The brides may kiss."

Dawn leaned down and chastely kissed her wife. The fireworks would have to wait for later. Niki wrapped her arms around Dawn's waist and hugged her.

They spent the next two hours posing for photos, visiting with their guests at the reception set up by the nursing staff, and dancing.

"Would it be rude if we left?" Niki looked up at her wife as they danced to a slow song. "We could simply slip away. I just want to be with you."

They danced their way to the nearest exit, and Dawn looked around to make certain everyone was entertained before pulling Niki into the corridor. "Quick, run for the elevator," she said, laughing.

They ran to their room, undressed one another, and fell into bed. "What a day," Dawn exclaimed.

"Are you as tired as I am?" Niki snuggled into her wife's arms.

"I'm exhausted."

"There's always tomorrow," Niki mumbled as sleep overtook both of them.

Chapter 63

Libby moved quickly to set up a living trust for Niki, who had decided to name Dawn, Libby, and herself as the administrators. She informed Libby that she wanted her to manage the trust. "I don't really want anything to do with it. If my family had been halfway decent to me, I would have signed the stock over to them. This way we can help others in need."

When the paperwork was processed to change Niki's stock from Niki Sears to Niki Fairchild Family Trust, Sylvia and her sons stormed into Libby's office demanding an explanation.

Libby informed them of how Niki's marriage and the trust affected the stock and, more importantly, them. Sylvia went into a rage. Libby had the fleeting thought that the woman would melt if she threw water on her. *I should be so lucky,* she thought.

"So, you can stop trying to kill Niki and Dawn," Libby declared, "because their trust would still live on."

"What happens if all three of you die?" Renfro sneered. At that point, Libby called Bobby Joe Jones.

##

"We ran search warrants on the homes of your brothers and your mother," Bobby Joe informed Niki, "but we found nothing to tie them to the shooting or the thug who was hired to kill you or Dawn with the truck.

"I'm not ruling them out, but I have no cause to arrest them except for Renfro's threat to Libby, and that turns into a big 'he said, she said' argument. Of course, the Searses are swearing it never happened."

"Bobby Joe, I think the danger has passed," Dawn said. "The Searses have no reason to kill me. They didn't in the first place. Richard, Lucky, and Merrick are all in jail now. So even if it was one of them, they're locked away. Niki and I just want to go home."

Bobby Joe gave her request several minutes of consideration then agreed that the danger to them had passed. "Okay." He sighed. "My captain is giving me hell over the cost of the guard detail, and you're probably right. Still, I do want the bastard that hired the hit man who almost killed Niki. The guard detail is approved for one more night."

"I have the next two days off," Dawn said. "We'd like to move home in the morning."

"Perfect timing." Bobby Joe grinned. "Can I help you relocate?"

"No, we can put everything in the back of our SUV. Thank you for everything, Bobby Joe. You've been a good friend."

"You've got my number in your cell phone." Bobby Joe hugged both women. "Don't hesitate to call if you need me. I may run by and check on you tomorrow."

Dawn turned to Niki as the detective walked away. "Ready to load the car?"

##

The next morning Dawn woke as the sun made an appearance. She opened her eyes to gaze into green eyes flecked with tiny sunflower petals. Red hair tumbled about the face of an angel, and kissable lips parted as a pink tongue darted out to moisten them.

Dawn could feel her heart rate increase as Niki threw her leg over Dawn's and eased on top of her. She wrapped her arms around the redhead. "Where do you think you're going, missy?"

"I'm going to make love to you." Niki giggled as she straddled her wife.

"Hmm. And I should let you do that, why?"

"Because you're dying for me to show you how much I love you." Niki brushed Dawn's lips with her own, letting her full bottom lip linger on Dawn's as she pulled away then pressed harder. Dawn parted her lips and welcomed the warm, pink tongue that was exploring her mouth. She slid her hands up firm, silky legs to grasp Niki's waist and hold her where she wanted her to be. Niki began to move against her.

Dawn moaned. "Baby! Oh Lord, Niki. Don't stop. You feel so good."

"I'll never stop loving you this way." Niki caught Dawn's nipple between her teeth and tugged on it before sucking it into her mouth.

Dawn threw back her head and arched her body to meet her wife's movements. "So good, baby," she moaned.

##

Later, they lay in each other's arms, whispering words of love. "Are you ready to go home and start living our lives?" Dawn murmured.

"I want that more than anything." Niki kissed her. "I'm just having a difficult time leaving your arms."

"I know," Dawn muttered as she gently massaged Niki's back. "You're such an armful of woman, yet you're so small sometimes."

"I love the way we fit together," Niki whispered against Dawn's lips. "We fit so perfectly."

Chapter 64

"Bobby Joe, I can't trace this to a specific computer, but I did trace it to this address." The police department's chief of cybercrimes pitched a sheet of paper on the detective's desk. "Unfortunately, there are hundreds of computers in that building."

Bobby Joe studied the paper for several minutes before replying. "If I can get on the computer I suspect, will you be able to tell if they've gone to this site?"

"If they didn't erase their browsing history I can, but if they went to the trouble to use the dark web, I'm sure they would erase the search. It's been months."

"It's the only lead we've got." Bobby shrugged. "I've got to follow it."

##

Val gazed around her office. Everything was perfect. Her life was perfect. She had achieved her goal, and her career was right on track. Of course, her end goal was to be US Attorney General. She already had Governor Addison's attention. She was certain he would eventually run for president. Then he would need a good attorney general. It was just a matter of biding her time. She'd make a difference while she waited.

She was tired of waiting alone. Her job had consumed all of her energy the past few months, but she finally had things under control and running smoothly.

She pushed the speakerphone on her desk console and autodialed Dawn Fairchild's office number. "Dr. Fairchild's office," the efficient voice answered.

"Dawn Fairchild, please. This is Val Davis calling."

"I'm sorry, the doctor is off today. May I have her return your call in the morning?"

"No, I'll just call back tomorrow." Val hung up the phone and decided to visit Dawn at her home.

As she drove to Dawn's house she tried to think of some reason to visit the gorgeous doctor. The last time they'd talked, Dawn had walked away from her without looking back. Val had told her she couldn't possibly go on television and accept any responsibility for Dawn's guilty verdict. "I'll say it was dark and raining, and that I'd suffered a blow to the head, but I won't say I was mistaken about seeing you exit through the driver's side."

"You've always known you lied about that," Dawn had fumed.

##

Val pulled her car into the driveway and admired Dawn's home. The yard and flowerbeds were immaculate. Val could see herself living in this house with the blonde doctor. She walked to the door and pressed the doorbell.

Dawn looked confused when she opened the door. "Val? What are you doing here?"

"I felt that we parted company on a bad note," Val said.

"It's water under the bridge. I've let it go and am moving on with my life. I'm the chief of staff, and you're the director of prisons—"

"Director of the Texas Department of Criminal Justice," Val said.

"Whatever." Dawn dismissed her correction with a wave of her hand. "The point is, both of our careers are on track, so we can just let it go."

"I'm glad you feel that way," Val said with a smile. "I want us to be friends. I miss talking to you. It's lonely at the top. Sometimes I'd give anything to get your input on a problem."

"I . . . um . . . ." Dawn didn't move from the doorway.

"Please, Dawn. Can we just talk over a cup of coffee like old friends do?" Val looked down and scuffed her shoe on the porch.

Dawn stepped back and let her enter the house.

"Whoa," Val exclaimed. "Something smells good."

"I'm cooking spaghetti sauce," Dawn said. "It's my mom's recipe. I mix several herbs and let it simmer all day, but it's worth it. It's delicious."

"I bet." Val looked longingly at the pot on the kitchen counter.

"I just made a fresh pot of coffee," Dawn said as she poured the steaming brew into two cups and motioned for Val to sit at the breakfast table. "Tell me what you've been up to."

Just like that, they were back at the prison, with Val discussing her problems and seeking Dawn's help in finding solutions. Neither heard Niki as she slipped into the house.

"Honey, I'm home," Niki called out as she walked into the kitchen. "Val!"

"Niki! I thought . . . I thought you were—"

"Dead?" Niki said, a wry smile on her face. "No, I'm very much alive and happily married to Dawn."

"Married?" Val sputtered, unable to maintain her composure. "When?"

"Three months ago," Dawn replied.

"I had no idea," Val said, pushing back from the table and scrambling to her feet. "I didn't mean to intrude."

"It's not a problem," Niki said. "I'll walk you to the door."

Dawn watched in wonder as her wife ushered Val out the door and locked it behind her. "That was rude," she said when Niki returned to face her.

Niki beamed. "I know. Can you believe she just showed up unannounced?"

Dawn laughed. "I meant the way you showed her out was rude."

Niki narrowed her eyes. "I'm not stupid. I know when another pussycat is making a move on my woman."

"I've been told that redheads don't share," Dawn teased, pulling her wife into her arms. "You're such a little thing. Are you sure you can take care of all this by yourself?" She waved her hand down her side.

Niki put her arms around her wife's neck and pulled Dawn's mouth to hers in a searing kiss. "My God!" Dawn gasped, trying to slow her heartbeat and catch her breath.

"Any time you aren't satisfied, I need to be the first to know," Niki scolded. "Are you sated, Dr. Fairchild?"

"Never," Dawn whispered as Niki led her to their bedroom.

Niki collapsed onto her wife. "You have deboned me," she said, giggling. "I don't think I can move a muscle."

"I'm just glad I'm lying on my back." Dawn brushed her lips against Niki's. "I don't think I have the energy to roll over."

"Mmm. I know, and I love it," Niki murmured. "At first I was afraid we weren't going to be compatible, but now I know we're perfectly matched."

"What made you doubt our compatibility?"

"In prison you never seemed to want me," Niki mumbled. "You kept a wall between us."

"I wanted you so badly I could taste it," Dawn whispered. "I just didn't want you to pick me because I was the best woman available at the time. I wanted you to have a choice outside of prison."

"I still picked you, silly." Niki nipped Dawn's shoulder. "But mostly because you make great spaghetti."

"Oh!" Dawn sat upright, taking her wife with her. "I forgot about the spaghetti."

"I turned off the burner." Niki pushed Dawn back down on the mattress. "I knew it would burn before I was through with you."

"I've also been told that redheads are insatiable," Dawn whispered. "And they like adventurous sex."

"We'll see." Niki lowered her lips to her wife's. "We have a lifetime to find out if all the redhead rumors you've heard are true."

Chapter 65

Niki grumbled as she pulled to the curb in front of the house. A black Mercedes was parked in the center of the driveway. Not to one side so she could pull into the garage, but right in the center, as if they owned the drive.

She grabbed her bookbag and computer and stomped into the house. She didn't see anyone in the living room or the kitchen. She checked Jacey's room; she was gone, as usual. Dawn wouldn't be home for another hour.

She dropped her books in their home office and went to look for the Mercedes' owner. "What are you doing here?" she demanded when she came face-to-face with her mother. "How did you get into my home?"

"Your friend let me in," Sylvia said. "We need to talk."

"I don't think we have anything to discuss." Niki backed away from the woman who had always made her life miserable. "I'd like you to leave."

"Not until you listen to me," Sylvia insisted.

Niki shrugged. "Make it quick and then get out."

"We need your help."

"Why does that not surprise me?" Niki's sarcasm was wasted on her mother.

"We're about to lose everything," Sylvia continued. "We barely have enough money to support our lifestyle. You've got billions and don't even use it."

"I don't want to end up like you, so I'm saving it for a rainy day," Niki said. Her mother just glared at her.

"Give me one good reason why I should care what happens to you," Niki fumed. "You never loved me. I can't recall you ever holding me on your lap or hugging me. If I fell or had a skinned knee, it was always Daddy who consoled me and put a Band-Aid on it. It was Daddy who showed up at all my school plays and functions. You didn't even attend my high school graduation."

"You were always a daddy's girl," Sylvia snarled.

"I was a daddy's girl because I had no mother. You made it plain that you never wanted me. The boys were all you cared about."

"You're right. You were entirely your father's idea. He came home drunk one night and forced himself on me. You were the result of that attack." Sylvia began to sob.

"Do you have any idea what it's like to be raped?"

"Get out of my home," Niki hissed through clenched teeth. "Take your self-pity and pompous attitude somewhere else. You have no idea what rape is. You have no idea what it's like to—"

"What's going on here?" Dawn slung her bag onto the sofa and moved to stand between her wife and Sylvia. "What are you doing here?"

"She wants money," Niki snapped.

Dawn never knew where the gun came from. She only knew that Sylvia was pointing it at her and Niki. "I could kill you both," she hissed, "and make it look like robbery. I'd take my chances in a civil court to regain control of your stock."

A gun racked behind Dawn. "I wouldn't do that if I were you," Val said, leveling her Glock at Sylvia. "You'll probably miss. Believe me, I won't."

Sylvia let her hand fall to her side, and the gun clattered to the floor. Dawn picked up the weapon. "I'm calling Bobby Joe," she said.

"No need to." Bobby Joe entered the room. "I was driving by to check on you two when I noticed the gathering of vehicles in front of your house."

"She tried to kill Dawn and Niki," Val said as Bobby Joe took her Glock and slipped it into his pocket. "You showed up just in time."

Bobby Joe quickly handcuffed Sylvia. She didn't protest as he radioed for backup.

"You shot at Dawn," Bobby Joe said to Sylvia. "You're not a very good shot. I'm betting ballistics will match the slug we dug out of Dawn's porch pillar to your gun."

"I want my lawyer," Sylvia barked.

"You'll get your lawyer, but tell me how you hired the hit man who almost killed Niki."

Sylvia snorted. "I don't hire idiots to do my dirty work."

"One of her sons probably did it," Val suggested as two more police officers entered the room.

Bobby Joe nodded for the men to take Sylvia away.

Then he turned to Val and clicked open a second pair of handcuffs. "I'd believe that if we hadn't traced the contact to your computer," he said as he slapped the cuffs on Val.

"You're crazy," Val snarled.

"Sylvia was willing to kill for money," Dawn said. "But you? Why did you want me dead?"

"You were going to ruin me," Val said, her face twisted with emotion. "You were going to report me for trying to kiss you. Then you wanted me to tell the truth about the accident. Yes, I know I lied and sent you to prison. How did I know I'd fall in love with you? How could you not love me back? If you'd only loved me back none of this would have happened."

Dawn shook her head in disbelief. "If you hadn't wrongly accused me, none of this would have happened."

Chapter 66

Dawn was bursting with pride as Niki accepted her graduation certificate. It had been two years of hard work and dedication, but Niki was officially a nurse practitioner.

Friends and relatives gathered around to congratulate the redhead. She leaned against Dawn as they visited with Bobby Joe and his wife. Flint had married Libby, and they were expecting their first child in six months. Ruth and Phillip Fairchild were thrilled about becoming grandparents.

"Everyone is invited to our house tonight for a graduation dinner," Ruth said. "This is all so exciting." As they parted, everyone promised to reassemble at the Fairchild home.

"I'm so proud of you," Dawn said, lacing her fingers with Niki's as she drove with her free hand. "Beauty and brains too. How did I get so lucky?"

"Don't forget the adventurous sex." Niki giggled as she kissed Dawn's knuckles.

"Oh, I could never forget about that. I think about it all the time."

"Good." Niki nibbled on Dawn's finger. "Then I'll always be the only one on your mind."

Dawn grinned. "That's a given. You're always on my mind and in my heart."

The End

Thank you for reading my book. If you have enjoyed it, I would be very grateful if you would consider taking a moment to write a brief review for me.

The review can be as short as you like. As a self-published author, honest reviews are the most powerful way to bring my books to the attention of other readers. Reviews also help encourage the Amazon system to include my book in the "Also bought" and search results. Thank you, Erin

Learn more about Erin Wade
and her books at www.erinwade.us
Follow Erin on Facebook
https://www.facebook.com/erin.wade.129142

Other #1 Best Selling Books
by Erin Wade
Too Strong to Die
Death Was Too Easy
Three Times as Deadly
Branded Wives
Living Two Lives
Don't Dare the Devil
The Roughneck & the Lady

Erin Wade writing as D.J. Jouett
The Destiny Factor

Coming in 2019
Shakespeare Undercover
Assassination Authorized!
Java Jarvis
Dead Girl's Gun
Doomsday Cruise

Shakespeare Under Cover
By Erin Wade

Below are the first five chapters of *Shakespeare Under Cover*. I hope you enjoy them. *Shakespeare Under Cover* will be released in the first quarter of 2019.

Again, thank you for being a reader of Erin Wade novels.

Chapter 1

Professor Regan Shaw watched her class file into the lecture hall. For the tenth time, today, she wondered why she had agreed to be the guest professor for the fall semester. *Burnout,* a tiny voice inside her head reminded her. *You're a has-been and right back where you started.*

A noisy group of students pulled her from her reverie. "Come on, Brandy, you promised." A six-four hunk in a football jersey pulled at a blonde wearing a matching pullover.

Must be going steady, Regan thought.

"Keep your hands off me, Joey Sloan," the blonde said as she yanked her arm from his grasp.

Joey grinned salaciously. "That's not what you said last night."

The blonde shot him a look that would have melted an intelligent man. "I have changed my mind. It's a woman's prerogative."

"You can't just yank me around like that," Joey growled.

"Why don't I just cut you loose?" the blonde threatened. "Why don't you go find someone else to—"

"Aww, look, Brandy. I'm sorry," Joey said. "I just want you to come to the frat party tonight. I like to show you off, baby."

"No, and that's final." Brandy spotted an empty chair on the front row between two geeky-looking guys and sat down, leaving Joey no choice but to sit somewhere else.

Regan got to her feet. "Ladies and gentlemen, welcome to Discovering Shakespeare. I'm Professor Regan Shaw."

"Hot damn," a male voice called out from the back of the lecture hall. "You're really something, mama."

Brandy jumped to her feet. "Who said that?" she demanded. "Joey, was that you?"

Regan quickly scanned the class roster for Brandy's last name. She had no Brandy on her list. "Miss, I am quite capable of controlling my class," she said loudly.

Brandy whirled around to face her. "Sorry," she said as she dropped back into her seat.

"How many of you studied Shakespeare in high school?" Regan continued. Everyone's hands went up. "So, you know his plays and prose were written over four hundred years ago?"

Nods and moans were the response from her class.

"Shakespeare can sometimes be difficult to understand," she said.

"That's the understatement of the day," Brandy interrupted. "Shakespeare is ambiguous."

Regan shot the class her million-dollar smile. The one that always captivated her audiences. "Part of the reason Shakespeare seems so ambiguous is because he made up his own words. If he had no word to express his emotions, he simply made one up. We can thank him for such words as addiction, archvillain, and bedazzled.

"I want you to read *A Midsummer Night's Dream,* and be prepared to discuss the symbolism Shakespeare uses.

"I will see you all next week."

Regan looked at her class roster again. "Brandy, may I see you for just a moment?"

297

The room emptied quickly. Brandy remained seated until Regan spoke to her.

"Are you supposed to be in my class?" the professor asked. "I don't have you on my roster."

"Brandywine," the girl said. "Grace Brandywine."

Regan smiled slightly. *Of course,* she thought. *Second name on my list.*

"I see," Regan said. She walked from behind her desk and leaned against it as she studied her student.

Grace Brandywinewas movie star beautiful. Everything about her screamed money. *Probably oil money,* Regan thought.

Brandy tossed her head and glorious blonde hair cascaded down one shoulder and settled on her perfect breast.

"I loved your last book," she said with a smile. "You're a wonderful writer. The movie didn't do it justice."

"Thank you." A slight smile played on Regan's lips. *You didn't see my last book,* she thought. *No one did. It was rejected by my publisher.*

"I can't wait to read your next book," Brandy said sweetly. "I've read all your books. You're my favorite author. That's why I took this class."

"Oh," Regan teased, "I was certain you took the class to study Shakespeare."

Brandy made a sound that was something between a giggle and a snort.

Damn, she's cute, Regan thought.

Suddenly, a handsome man in his midforties entered the lecture hall. "There you are. I had a feeling I would find you counseling a student. Did you forget we have a lunch date?"

Regan smiled. "I didn't forget. I'm just trying to get my roster in order."

"I'll grab us a table. Hurry. The SUB fills up quickly this time of day." He squeezed Regan's arm and left the room.

"I'm meeting Joey in the SUB," Brandy said. "Want to walk over together? You could tell me more about Shakespeare."

"I have to drop something off for Professor Fleming," Regan said. "I'll see you around."

##

"Want to go with me to the Delta Tau Delta fraternity party tonight?" Coach Danny Tucker asked hopefully.

"I don't think so." Regan frowned. "You know how I feel about drinking and frat boys."

Danny laughed. "Indeed, I do. The powers that be have instructed me to attend their first bash of the year. So, you're going to throw me to the wolves with no backup."

Regan watched as Brandy and Joey strolled into the Student Union Building. Joey had his arm draped around Brandy's shoulders. His hand sneakily brushed her breast, and Brandy slapped his arm away. "Joey Sloan, if that happens again, I swear . . . ."

Joey grinned mischievously. "Sorry, babe, it really was an accident. I know how you hate PDA."

Brandy rolled her eyes and stomped away from him. She raised her head and found herself staring into the deep brown eyes of her English lit professor. A twisted smile passed across her lips.

"Professor Shaw, Coach Tucker. I didn't expect to see you here," she said. The lie came easily. *Coach Tucker and Joey share the same lack of imagination when it comes to a date*, she thought.

"I'm trying to talk Professor Shaw into going with me to the Delta Tau Delta bash tonight," Tucker said.

"You should come." Joey joined them flashing a gleeful smile. "Brandy and I will be there. It'll be wild and

299

crazy. It will be hot!" He let his eyes wander down Brandy's slender body.

Regan tilted her head and caught Brandy's eye. The girl shrugged. "You should come," she said softly.

Regan smiled. "Three great recommendations. How can I go wrong? What time is it?"

"Starts at seven." Tucker grinned from ear to ear. "I'll pick you up at six thirty."

"Um, I'll meet you there," Regan said. "I may not stay till the bitter end."

Coach Tucker looked at his watch. "We gotta go, big guy. Football practice in ten minutes. You need to suit up."

Regan watched as the two men left, mumbling to each other and laughing out loud.

"Delta Tau Delta—is that the fraternity that has all the drug charges leveled against them?" Regan said.

"You can't believe everything you hear," Brandy grumbled.

Regan sipped her iced tea and studied the girl.

"I was under the impression you weren't going."

"Joey wouldn't stop hounding me, so I agreed to go to get him to leave me alone." Brandy cocked her head and surveyed Professor Shaw. "He's the president of the fraternity. Said I was making him look bad by refusing to attend his first party.

"You and Coach Tucker?" Brandy raised her eyebrows.

Regan blushed. "Tell me why you date Joey," she said, desperately wanting to change the subject.

"Probably the same reason you date Coach Tucker." Brandy smiled knowingly.

I doubt that, Regan thought.

##

Brandy paid extra attention to her appearance as she dressed for the party. She was in her I'm-gonna-knock-your-boots-off mood. She briefly wondered if Professor

300

Shaw wore boots. Loud honking in front of her sorority house told her Joey was demanding her presence.

Mom would kill me if she saw me tolerating Joey Sloan's rudeness, she thought as she skipped down the stairs.

The party was in full swing when the couple arrived. Joey parked his Porsche convertible along the curb, jumped out without opening his door, and started up the sidewalk.

Brandy sighed loudly as she opened her own door and got out of the car.

Coach Tucker and Professor Shaw were already at the party. A crowd of male students gathered around Professor Shaw.

"I'll get us a couple of beers," Joey yelled as he headed for the tubs of iced-down brew.

Brandy observed her professor. The woman was classy—hot, but classy. Dressed in a pair of formfitting black jeans and an open-necked, electric-blue blouse, she looked like one of the students. Her long, black hair curled around her shoulders, framing a face that dreams were made of. Brandy wondered how anyone applied makeup that perfectly.

Brandy ran the numbers through her mind, trying to figure the woman's age. She came up with thirty-four. Regan Shaw was young for one who had accomplished so much.

"Here ya go, babe." Joey held out a dripping bottle of beer to her.

"Thanks."

##

As the party grew louder and Joey got friskier, Brandy decided to leave. She had poured the beers Joey kept feeding her into the huge Mexican urn at the foot of the stairs. She was headed for the urn again when she saw Professor Shaw dump the contents of her bottle into it.

An inebriated Coach Tucker staggered toward Professor Shaw. "Obviously you don't like beer," he said with a chuckle. "Let me get you a glass of wine."

Ignoring Professor Shaw's protests, he weaved his way to the bar. Pretending to text on her cell phone, Brandy moved closer to him and watched as he put his hand into his pocket. To her surprise, he pulled out something and dropped it into Regan's drink.

Is that son of a bitch drugging her? Brandy thought.

She watched Coach Tucker swirl the wine until the pill had dissolved. Then he carried the glass to Professor Shaw.

"Come on, babe," Joey said, grabbing Brandy around the waist. "Let's go upstairs to my room."

"I want to dance," she insisted. "You never dance with me."

"Okay, okay. One dance then we go upstairs."

Brandy nodded. She watched Professor Shaw as the woman moved to the closest sofa and sat down. She finished half the wine before setting her glass on the coffee table. She leaned her head back and appeared to go to sleep.

"Joey, I think Professor Shaw is sick," she said.

"Nah, she's fine. Coach will take care of her." He shot her a salacious grin and jerked his head toward the staircase. "Come on, I'll take care of you."

Brandy smiled sweetly. "You go on up. I need to visit the ladies' room first."

Joey nodded and stumbled toward the stairs. Loraine Munoz grabbed his arm and clung to him all the way up.

Brandy walked to Regan Shaw. The woman was dead to the world. The blonde sat down by the professor and pulled Regan's arm around her shoulders. She slipped her arm around Regan's tiny waist and stood up, pulling the professor with her.

Regan was dead weight, but Brandy managed to drag her outside. She hoped the crisp night air would revive the woman. She felt in Regan's pocket for car keys and found a single fob. She pushed the button and prayed a car would respond. A car across the street flashed its lights.

"Bingo." Brandy smiled as she continued to drag the smaller woman toward her car.

"Hold your horses," Kiki Carson yelled as her roommate continued kicking the door. "Didn't God give you hands? Just turn the knob, for God's sake. It's unlocked.

"Holy crap!" Kiki exclaimed as Brandy carried Regan through the doorway.

"She doesn't look like much," Brandy huffed, "but the further I carried her, the heavier she became."

"Isn't that Professor Shaw?" Kiki whispered as if someone might hear her.

"Yeah, Coach Tucker roofied her at the frat party," Brandy growled as she gently placed the professor on her twin bed.

"You've got to be kidding," Kiki squealed.

"Does she look like I'm kidding?"

Kiki frowned. "Does he know you saw him?"

"No, and I was able to video it with my cell phone." Brandy pulled the phone from her pocket and showed the video to Kiki. Then she turned on her laptop and copied the video from her phone to the computer.

Kiki took the professor's pulse. "She's fine," she declared. "Just needs to sleep it off. How did you get rid of Joey?"

"Loraine Munoz was crawling in his pants, last time I saw him." Brandy grinned.

"I bet that really upset you," Kiki said, laughing.

"Better her than me. He's such an ass."

Both women watched as Regan stretched out on the bed.

"She's truly gorgeous," Kiki said. "Should we undress her and put her to bed?"

"Would you mind doing that while I shower?" Brandy asked. She rummaged through her dresser drawer for a couple of soft T-shirts. She tossed one to Kiki. "This should work for her tonight."

Regan woke with a splitting headache. It hurt to open her eyes. *I'm dreaming*, she thought. *Where am I?*

The urge to find a bathroom forced her to sit up in the bed. She tried to connect the room to anything in her life and failed. Thanks to her many book tours, she was used to waking up in strange bedrooms, but this didn't look like a hotel room. *This looks like a dorm room.*

A faint light from another room caught her attention. *The bathroom*, she thought.

She placed her feet on the floor and found herself standing on something soft, but firm.

"What the hell?" A drowsy Brandy rolled away from the professor.

Regan fell back onto the bed as Brandy turned on a lamp.

"Professor Shaw, are you okay?" Brandy was still on her knees, looking up at Regan.

The lamplight danced in the blonde's emerald-green eyes. *I have never seen a more beautiful woman*, Regan thought.

"I'm not sure," Regan said softly. "Where's your bathroom?"

Brandy scrambled to her feet and took Regan's hand to lead her to the bathroom. Regan noticed another woman sleeping in the other bed. A digital clock on the nightstand between the two beds showed seven a.m., Saturday, September 15.

When Regan returned, she walked to the bed where Brandy sat cross-legged. "How did I get here?" she whispered.

"Let's go to Starbucks for coffee, and I'll tell you all about it," Brandy whispered back. She handed Regan her neatly folded clothes and then put on clean clothes from her closet.

"I'll drive," the student whispered as she picked up her teacher's key fob.

Brandy parked the car and took Regan's elbow, supporting her as they entered the Starbucks. They ordered their coffee and sat at a table in the corner.

"I didn't drink at all last night, but I feel like I've been drugged." Regan pinched the bridge of her nose.

"You were," Brandy said bluntly. "Your boyfriend roofied you."

"Coach Tucker?" Regan gaped at her student. "Surely not."

Brandy pulled her iPhone from her pocket and showed her professor the video.

"I . . . I don't know what to say." Regan frowned. "The only reason I went to that party was to protect you. I figured something like this would happen to you, not me."

"Joey?" Brandy gasped. "You think Joey Sloan would rape me?"

"He is too aggressive with you," Regan said.

"He's no rapist," Brandy declared.

"Whatever." Regan shrugged, distressed that the girl would so easily dismiss the danger of being at a frat party with a drunk guy almost three times her size. "If he wanted to, I doubt you could stop him."

"Who says I would want to stop him?" Brandy grinned wickedly.

"May I have a copy of that video?" Regan asked.

"What will you do with it?"

"I intend to take it to the university security chief and file an official complaint," Regan said.

"Look, Professor, I don't want to get involved in anything with campus security," Brandy said. "They wouldn't do anything anyway. They never take any action. They will question Coach Tucker and take his word against yours. Tucker is a winning football coach. He took the team all the way last year. They won't even reprimand him. He's raped a dozen girls, and nothing ever comes of it.

"You're a visiting professor. They'll just pacify you and then tell you not to return when the semester is over."

"So we just let him get away with drugging me?" Regan whispered.

Brandy nodded. "No harm, no alarm. You're fine."

"What did Joey say when you left the party?" Regan asked, having difficulty accepting the girl's lackadaisical attitude.

"Nothing," Brandy said. "I doubt he even noticed, thanks to Loraine Munoz."

"What the . . .?" Brandy stared at the TV screen in the Starbucks. A photo of Coach Tucker filled the screen. The news ticker beneath the photo said, "UT head coach found dead early this morning."

The two women moved closer to the TV so they could hear what the newscaster was saying.

Regan gasped. "He was stabbed to death. Someone murdered him."

Brandy shrugged. "Must have roofied the wrong woman. He got what he deserved. He was a pig."

Regan cringed at the venom in Brandy's voice and the anger in her eyes.

##

Half of her students used Coach Tucker's death as an excuse to skip class on Monday. Regan carefully noted each one who was not in attendance. No one skipped her class without suffering the consequences.

She could see Joey and Brandy in the hall outside her room. Joey had his hands in Brandy's hip pockets, pulling the girl against him. He was whispering in her ear. She slapped him and charged into the lecture hall.

Joey rubbed his cheek as if he couldn't believe a girl had just hit him. He sneered and followed Brandy into the room. When she sat down between the two geeks on the front row, Joey leaned over to one of them and said a few words. The guy picked up his books and moved, and Joey sat down by his girlfriend.

Regan watched as Joey sketched something on his notepad. He folded the sheet of paper and grinned as he slid the note to Brandy.

Brandy glared at her boyfriend before opening the note.

"Miss Brandywine," Regan said authoritatively, "come here, please."

Still holding the note, Brandy walked to the professor's desk. Regan pulled the note from the girl's hand and opened it. She blushed slightly as she saw that Joey had drawn two stick figures copulating. He had written, *You and me, babe.*

Regan placed the note in her desk drawer. "Please return to your seat." Regan wondered how anyone as childish as Joey could hold the attention of a girl as beautiful as Brandy.

"Mr. Sloan," Regan said, "would you please give us a brief synopsis of *A Midsummer Night's Dream?*"

To Regan's surprise, Joey stood and gave an in-depth summary of the play. *He's obviously smarter than he seems*, she thought. Joey sat down and Regan cringed as Brandy ran her hand down his thigh and whispered something in his ear. He grinned like a fool.

Chapter 2

Regan slipped into a chair at the back of the lecture hall. The school chancellor had called a meeting of all instructors and administrators. The topic of conversation was Coach Danny Tucker.

"As you all know," the chancellor said, "Coach Tucker was murdered last night after a frat party at the Delta Tau Delta house.

"This is FBI agent Ryan King." She made a sweeping gesture toward a gorgeous strawberry blonde with brilliant green eyes. "Agent King will be questioning each of you. Please give her your fullest cooperation. Even if you didn't know Coach Tucker personally, simply answer her questions to the best of your ability."

Agent King floated to the podium and flashed a smile that would overshadow a spotlight. "I want to make this as painless as possible," she said.

"This morning I will interview those of you whose last name begins with *A* through *L*. The rest of you should come back after lunch." Ryan's mesmerizing voice floated from the speakers. "There's no need for you to waste time sitting around here all morning."

Brandy was waiting in the hallway when Regan emerged from the lecture hall. "What did they say?" she demanded.

"Nothing really," Regan replied. "Everyone will be questioned in alphabetical order. I am to return after lunch."

"Want to have lunch with me?" The gregarious blonde flashed her brilliant smile.

Regan shrugged. "I have things to do."

"I heard the killers cut off his penis," Brandy whispered.

Regan gasped. "Seriously? Where do you want to have lunch? Not the SUB!"

##

Regan was not surprised to find that Brandy drove a BMW. They drove to a nearby bar and grill.

"Did you get a good look at the FBI agent?" Brandy squealed as they found a seat in the crowed restaurant.

"You mean Agent King?"

"Yes, FBI Agent Ryan King." Brandy wiggled her eyebrows. "She's something! I bet she's great in bed."

"Miss Brandywine, I don't really care to indulge in this kind of conversation with you." Regan started to stand, but Brandy caught her hand.

"I'm sorry, Professor." Brandy smiled. "I didn't mean to be offensive."

"I'm afraid I find your uninhibited attitude about sex a little shocking."

"Really?" Brandy grinned seductively. "Then I suppose you would be doubly shocked to know I find you incredibly hot. Even hotter than FBI Agent King."

A pink blush started from the center of Regan's chest and spread up her neck to color her face. She was lost for words, distraught that a student would speak to her in such a manner.

"You may take me back to the university now," she said in her haughtiest tone.

"Don't be such a prude." Brandy laughed out loud. "I'm just jerking your chain." She waved the waitress over so they could order.

"I suppose you're upset over the death of Coach Tucker," Brandy continued. "We all are."

Regan raked her teeth over her bottom lip. "I didn't know him that well," she said, sighing. "He certainly wasn't the man I thought he was."

"They'll probably question you pretty extensively," Brandy noted, "since you were his date the night he was murdered."

Regan's mouth moved, but no sound came out. She hadn't thought about that.

"It's a good thing you were with me all night," Brandy said, her eyes twinkling.

"I wasn't exactly *with* you."

"You spent the night in my bed," Brandy said sweetly, clearly enjoying her professor's embarrassment.

Regan's brown eyes locked with Brandy's green ones. "I'm sure there are worse things that could happen to me," she said softly.

It was Brandy's turn to blush. She couldn't stop the warm feeling that spread over her body.

The blonde cleared her throat. "You know I'll verify that you spent the night in my dorm," she said, her tone suddenly serious. "I think we should show Agent King the video on my cell phone."

Regan smiled slightly. She knew she had won this round with her student. "I think we have to," she said.

"Can you believe Coach was mutilated?" Brandy squeaked as she salted her burger.

"Where did you hear that?"

"Joey told me," Brandy replied. "Joey knows everything that goes on around here."

"Yes, I'm certain Joey is a trustworthy news source," Regan huffed.

"Let's talk about something else. Tell me about your next book." Brandy took a bite of her burger.

"Right now I don't have a next book." Regan sighed. "I'm taking a hiatus from the computer."

"I know a thing or two about writers," Brandy said.

"Do tell."

"I know you always have several books working at one time." Brandy plunged ahead, undeterred by her professor's look of disbelief. "I know you haven't released a book in about eighteen months, and the literary world is expecting your next book to be your best."

Regan fought back the urge to shake Brandy and tell her she didn't know squat about the publishing business or writers. She didn't know how much it hurt when your agent returned the book you had poured your heart and soul into with a note that read, "This would kill your career."

"I know you're filthy rich and the talk show circuits adore you." Brandy was chattering. She knew Regan Shaw was miles away. "And I know for sure I'd like to go to bed with you."

Regan stared at her. "What? What the hell are you babbling about?"

"About your next book." Brandy's innocent look was laughable.

"The last thing you said." Regan glared at her.

"I was just checking to see if you were listening." Brandy stuffed a French fry in her mouth. "Apparently you were."

Chapter 3

"Professor Regan Shaw," Ryan King said, reading from the list in her hand. She blushed slightly as her heart skipped a beat when a beautiful brunette stood and walked toward her.

Calm down, Ryan chided herself. *It's been too long.*

"Thank you, Professor." Ryan shared her sweetest smile. "I appreciate you taking the time to speak with me."

Regan raised a perfectly arched brow. "Did I have a choice?"

"No, ma'am, you didn't. Please have a seat. This shouldn't take long."

Regan sat down and crossed her legs. Her skirt slid up to midthigh. Ryan couldn't pull her eyes away from the shapely legs. She blushed when her eyes locked with Regan's.

Ryan flipped open a file folder with Regan's name on it and studied the sheet of paper inside. "You were on a date with Coach Tucker last night?"

"Yes."

"Did you quarrel? Have a lover's spat?"

"Hardly," Regan huffed. "It was my one and only date with Coach Tucker. I assure you he was very much alive and falling-down drunk when I left the party."

"A fraternity party?"

"Yes."

"You left the party without him?" Ryan said.

"Yes."

"So, you did quarrel," Ryan insisted.

"Agent King, please stop putting tongue in my mouth." Regan scowled and blushed profusely when she realized what she had said. "Words. Please stop putting words in my mouth."

Ryan tried to suppress her smile as Professor Shaw struggled to recover from her faux pas.

"We didn't have words," Regan said. "He roofied me, and a student got me out of there."

"Drugged you? Coach Tucker drugged you?" Ryan was aghast. None of her prior interviewees had hinted at such activity on the part of the popular football coach.

"Professor Shaw, did anyone see him drug you?"

"The student who rescued me. She also videoed him doing it." Ryan pulled her cell phone from her purse, queued the video, and handed it to Agent King. "She sent me a copy. I didn't believe it at first either."

Ryan watched the video. It turned her stomach to think that the professor could be in an entirely different situation today if not for her student.

"May I have a copy of this?"

"Of course." Regan reached for her cell phone.

"I'll just add my number to your contact list," Ryan said, smiling. "Is it okay if I send myself the video?"

Regan nodded.

"I assume you'll be around campus if I have any more questions for you?" Ryan bit her bottom lip.

"I . . . uh, am I a suspect?" Regan asked.

"No, the question I have in mind is, would you join me for dinner?"

"I'm not sure I should." Regan hedged. "I was his last date and all, and—"

"You can say no, if you wish. I'm new to this area and thought you might be able to direct me to some good Chinese or Italian. It's not like I'm asking you out on a date. Since you were on a date with Coach Tucker, I'm assuming I'm not your type."

Regan laughed. "Of course. I'm just a little rattled. It's not every day one's date from the night before is found mutilated the next morning."

Ryan squinted at her. "How did you know he was mutilated?"

"I . . . I don't know. Wasn't it on the news this morning?"

"No. That's one of the things we're keeping out of the news." Ryan stood and paced around the room. She returned to stand in front of Regan. "That is something only the killer would have known."

Regan held her breath. *Then how did Brandy find out about it?*

"Who gave you that information?" Agent King's flirty demeanor was gone. In its place was a no-nonsense FBI interrogator.

"One of my students, I think." Regan didn't want to implicate Brandy, but King's chameleon-like change had disoriented her.

"Which one?"

"Ah, um, I'm not certain," Regan said. "I don't want to give you a wrong name."

"Why don't you give me a name, and I'll sort out whether or not it's wrong?"

"Grace Brandywine," Regan mumbled.

"Brandywine? Of course." Ryan snorted.

Chapter 4

Brandy watched the door of the building Ryan King had confiscated for her headquarters. She knew the FBI agent would be on campus until she caught the killer. King was tenacious. When she went after something, she always got it.

Brandy shifted her Beemer into drive and eased forward as Professor Shaw walked out of the building and started down the sidewalk. She pulled alongside the professor and rolled down the passenger-side window.

"Professor Shaw," Brandy called out. "Want a ride?" She leaned over and pushed open the passenger door.

Regan hesitated, but not for long.

"You look like you've seen a ghost," Brandy noted as she pulled away from the curb. "Was Agent King that hard on you?"

"Brandy, I mentioned that Coach Tucker had been mutilated, and she went berserk. She demanded the name of the person who gave me that information."

"So, you threw me under the bus?" Brandy quipped. "Is that the reason you're white as a sheet?"

"I feel so awful. I would never try to get you in trouble," Regan said. "I didn't tell her Joey told you. I'm certain she'll want to interview you.

"I would expect her to interview me," Brandy said, wrinkling her nose. "I saved you from a fate worse than death. I'm sure she'll want to know my relationship with you."

"We have no relationship," Regan scoffed. "I'm your English Lit professor, and you're my student. That's it."

"Yes, that's all it'll ever be." Brandy's woeful tone made Regan look at her in time to see a sly smile flit across her face.

"Brandy, sometimes you worry me."

"That's good." Brandy laughed out loud. "Where to for dinner, Professor?"

##

Pat Sawyer pulled the folder containing complaints filed on coach Danny Tucker. She debated shredding the incriminating evidence she had gathered during her past ten years as chief of security at the university. Always acting the part of the southern country gentleman in public, Tucker had been a vile human being in private. Now Tucker was dead, and there was no need to publicize her complicity in protecting the sexual predator.

Almost like clockwork, Pat had received at least one and sometimes two complaints every month from coeds claiming Tucker had raped them. Over 150 complaints had been filed against the winning coach. Some of the complaints had been so severe that Pat had instructed the victims to file a report with the Austin Police Department. Of course, the overworked APD had filled out a report and then informed the women they had to deal with the campus police force.

Pat was ashamed to admit that she had been forced to look the other way to keep her high-paying job at the university. With over 500 commissioned police officers serving under her command, the UT System police department was the third largest statewide police force in Texas, behind only the Department of Public Safety and Texas Parks and Wildlife.

Tucker's death would allow her to wash her hands of the whole sordid mess and start over. She would never again compromise her ethics or reputation. She tried not to think of what had led her down the dark, dismal road she had taken.

Heads would roll—including her own—if Tucker's file ever fell into the wrong hands. FBI Agent Ryan King would nail her tits to the wall if she ever got her hands on Tucker's file.

A loud knock on her office door interrupted her debate, and she slid the file folder into the bottom drawer of her desk.

The door swung open, and Ryan King in all her glory charged into Pat's office.

"Come in, Agent King," Pat said, smirking. "How can I help you?"

"I need to see your file on Danny Tucker." King never wasted time on niceties.

Pat eyed King as one would a wild animal about to pounce. "What makes you think I have a file on Coach Tucker?" Pat watched King's eyes to see if she was just guessing or had hard evidence.

"I already have a search warrant." Ryan's twisted smile told Pat she was in trouble.

"Go ahead and serve it," Pat said, calling her bluff. "We've no secrets to hide. You'll find nothing, so I'd appreciate it if you'd keep your suspicions to yourself until you find something to justify them. May I see your search warrant?" Pat held out her hand.

"It's on its way."

"Then you won't mind waiting in the lobby until it gets here." Pat stood and walked toward the door. "I'm trying to solve a murder case."

"You're off the case," Ryan barked. "It's my case now, and I don't have anyone's ass to protect or kiss."

Pat's eyes flashed. "Are you insinuating that I would look the other way when a crime is committed on campus?"

"It's been known to happen," Ryan said. "That's why universities shouldn't police themselves."

Pat shifted uneasily from one foot to the other and then opened the door so Agent King could leave her office.

King was as tenacious as a pit bull. She had arrived on campus two years ago when newly elected Chancellor Katherine O'Brien had requested the FBI investigate the disappearance of four coeds. King had moved swiftly, calling in all the personnel at her disposal, and located the women in the boxcar of a train headed for Mexico.

Both O'Brien and King had been heralded for their quick action, while Pat had spent the following months wiping egg off her face for failing to take the disappearance of the four women seriously.

Pat's intercom buzzed. "Chief, Chancellor O'Brien is on the phone."

Pat groaned as she mentally prepared to deal with the Irish spitfire waiting on her line. She decided to let O'Brien take the lead. "Chief Sawyer."

"Good morning, Chief. Please fill me in on your investigation of Coach Tucker's death."

Katherine O'Brien never wasted words on cordiality when her university was under attack.

"The case is out of my hands, Chancellor. The FBI is confiscating my files as we speak."

"Cooperate with them," O'Brien ordered. "Don't make them get a search warrant. That will make it look like we have something to hide, and we do not. Do we?"

Pat gulped. "No, ma'am. We've nothing to hide."

"Good, that's what I wanted to hear."

Pat leaned her head back against her chair and closed her eyes. She knew it was going to hit the fan when Ryan King got her hands on Tucker's file.

She looked around her office for a place to hide the incriminating file but decided King would find it no matter where she hid it. That would make her look worse than ever. She decided to hand the file over to Agent King. She pulled all the complaints from the file except the last four and hid them in another file.

Chief Sawyer opened her office door and stepped into the waiting room.

"We don't have our warrant yet," Agent King said, looking up from her cell phone.

Pat did her best to look amiable. "You don't need one. Chancellor O'Brien said to give you Coach Tucker's file." She held out the thin file.

"Is this all there is?" Ryan asked.

"Yes."

##

"FBI Agent Ryan King to see Chancellor O'Brien."

"Do you have an appointment?" the prissy secretary said.

"Seriously?" Ryan growled. "What part of *FBI agent* did you not understand?"

The secretary jumped to her feet and led the way to the chancellor's office. "FBI Agent Ryan King to see you, ma'am."

Katherine O'Brien drew herself to her full height of five-seven and walked around her desk to greet Ryan. "Agent King. How may I help you?"

"I wanted to thank you for the phone call that resulted in this." Ryan handed Danny Tucker's file to the auburn-haired beauty.

Katherine motioned for Ryan to sit as she returned to her chair behind her desk. "It's very light. I was afraid there would be more."

Ryan agreed. "Four complaints. It doesn't exactly jibe with this file from the Austin PD." Ryan placed a file that was over an inch thick on Katherine's desk.

Katherine frowned. "She's withholding evidence."

"We'll find it," Ryan said. "My people are going through her office with a fine-tooth comb."

"May I see what you find before you release any information?" Katherine asked. "I have a feeling this is going to be bad."

Ryan smiled "Sure . . . if you'll have dinner with me while I wait for my folks to finish. I have a video you need to see. I don't want you to be blindsided."

"That sounds like a fair trade," Katherine said. "Some place outside of town."

"I know just the place." Ryan opened the door and let her hand rest on the chancellor's lower back as she ushered her out the door.

##

Harvard educated Katherine O'Brien was the epitome of success. The University of Texas's first woman chancellor/president and the first Irish immigrant to head a comprehensive research university in the United States, her track record was incomparable.

Under Katherine's leadership, the Texas Advanced Computing Center had launched Stampede, one of the largest computing systems in the world for open science research that had led to mind-boggling discoveries in DNA by compiling input from genetic scientists all over the world, allowing them to consult and work together on their theories. The computer system saved universities worldwide from wasting valuable research funds duplicating work already completed by other scientists.

Katherine's most lauded recent accomplishment was landing the National Science Foundation grant to establish an Engineering Research Center (ERC) for research into nanomanufacturing, the first ERC designated at UT Austin and only the second in Texas.

At forty-five, Katherine O'Brien was exactly where she wanted to be, but she knew things weren't as they seemed. She was aware that beneath her firm foundation, something was wrong. Something was always causing a ripple that never quite reached her. The Texas good-old-boy confederates always seemed to cloud issues close to home preventing her from getting a clear view of seething problems. She feared that coach Danny Tucker's death was only the tip of the iceberg.

Chapter 5

Regan downed her last bit of coffee and got out of her car. She had spent a restless night thinking about Danny Tucker and Brandy's insinuation that he had raped several coeds over the years. She debated on whether she should tell Agent King.

Suddenly, a movement in a shadowy alcove caught her attention. Joey Sloan had someone pinned against the wall and was running his hands up and down her sides. The girl wasn't trying to fight him off. *God, don't let it be Brandy.*

She started to call out Joey's name then decided she didn't really want to know who he was crawling all over. She hurried to her classroom.

As she connected her laptop to the overhead projector, Brandy and Joey entered the room. They were arguing loudly.

"You promised you'd go home with me this weekend," Joey whined. "My folks are dying to meet you."

"It's too early to meet the parents," Brandy argued. "You know how parents get all excited when they think their offspring has landed a real catch."

"You are a real catch." Joey grinned as he placed his hands on her hips. "You're the only girl I want to catch."

"I bet you said the same thing to Loraine Munoz while you were banging her last night," Brandy huffed.

"I did not," Joey grumbled. "Babe, you know you're the only girl I love."

"I'll think about it, but we sleep in separate rooms. And no sneaking into my room after your parents go to bed."

The bell rang, and they continued to argue.

"Miss Brandywine, Mr. Sloan, would it be possible for you to find a seat and let me teach my class? Or I can just give you both a zero for today."

Brandy shot Joey a disgusted look and took a chair on the front row.

Regan waited while her class settled down. "I know that there is a lot of speculation about Coach Tucker's death."

A murmur ran through the room.

"I'm going to give you Wednesday off to finish reading *A Midsummer Night's Dream*. I'll post your study guide tonight, so you'll know what to expect on Friday's test."

Joey held up his hand. "Professor, do you grade on the bell curve?"

"Yes."

"What if we have a failing grade, but all of our other grades are really good? Will you allow us to throw out one grade every reporting period?"

"Yes," Regan replied. "Any other questions? If not, class is dismissed."

Regan wanted to avoid the SUB, so she walked across campus to the nearest kolache shop. She was surprised to see Brandy sitting alone in a booth reading a textbook.

Brandy looked up and smiled as Regan entered, motioning for the professor to join her. Regan stopped at the counter and ordered coffee and a kolache.

"I don't want to bother you," Regan said as she approached the booth. "Obviously, you're studying."

Brandy shrugged "Spanish. I was just brushing up. I heard the professor is going to give us a pop quiz this afternoon and a test on Friday. She's not as nice as you."

"She probably wants to gauge the level of her students so she'll know where to start teaching."

"Duh, Professor. It's beginner's Spanish 101. You can't get much lower than that."

Regan was fluent in Spanish, but Brandy didn't need to know that.

"So, join me." Brandy gestured toward the booth seat and Regan sat down across from her.

"Has Agent King questioned you yet?" Regan asked as the server placed her order on the table.

"After lunch she'll start interviewing students who had contact with Tucker. Joey is at the top of her list. He's captain of the football team."

"Does he know anything?" Regan said, fighting to hide her curiosity.

"Help me study for my Spanish test, and I'll tell you." Brandy's impish grin made Regan's heart skip a beat. She couldn't pull her gaze away from her student's beautiful face.

"Okay," Regan mumbled.

"What time?" Brandy beamed.

"What time for what?"

"What time should I come to your place so you can help me study?" Brandy looked up at her through long lashes and smiled.

"I meant right now . . . right here."

"No can do." Brandy stuffed her Spanish book into her book bag and slid from the booth. "I have to get to class. See you tonight. Six at your place."

"You don't know my address," Regan replied.

"Yes, I do." Brandy waggled her eyebrows. "You can cook dinner for me, if you'd like."

Regan watched the girl as she sprinted out the door. *Oh God. What have I gotten myself into? The last thing I need is Grace Brandywine in my home.*

##

"Joey Sloan, is that correct?" Ryan King watched the cocky young man sprawled out in the chair in front of her desk. He certainly overpowered the room. "You're dating Grace Brandywine?"

"Yes, ma'am." When Joey grinned, his blue eyes twinkled.

"Did you see Coach Tucker Friday night?"

"Yes, ma'am."

"Do you know what time he left your fraternity party?"

"No, ma'am." Joey hung his head and blushed slightly.

"What time did you last see him at your party?"

"A little after midnight. He was falling-down drunk and groping the girls."

"Do you know the names of the girls he groped?" Ryan had a feeling there was a brain beneath Joey's mop of unruly blond hair.

"No, ma'am. It all sorta runs together in my mind."

"Your date was Grace Brandywine, right?"

"Yes, ma'am."

"Did you leave the party around midnight?"

"No, ma'am."

"If you were at the party, why didn't you see Coach Tucker leave?"

Joey's blush deepened. "I was upstairs with someone."

Ah! I think I've just caught Brandy and Professor Shaw in a lie, Ryan thought.

"Who were you with upstairs, Joey?"

"I'd rather not say." Joey ducked his head lower.

"I'd rather you did." Ryan's stern, voice was flat. "We're you with Brandy?"

"Oh, no, ma'am. Brandy left early. She took Professor Shaw to her dorm. I later found out that Coach Tucker had put drugs in the professor's wine."

"So, who were you with, Joey? Who can provide you an alibi for the time of Coach Tucker's murder?"

Joey locked gazes with Ryan. "Surely you don't think I killed Coach Tucker?"

"If you don't have an alibi, I'm going to assume—"

"Loraine Munoz," Joey blurted. "Please don't tell Brandy. She'll kill me."

Ryan shoved her notepad in front of Joey and handed him a pen. "Please write Miss Munoz's phone number on here. I'll need to call her to verify your alibi.

"Joey, who told you Coach Tucker was mutilated?"

"I really can't say, ma'am. Everyone was talking about it in the frat house when I came downstairs that morning."

"Did Miss Munoz come down with you?" Ryan asked.

"Yes, ma'am. We spent the night together. Please don't tell Brandy."

##

Regan stopped by the supermarket on her way home. She had decided on spaghetti and meat sauce with French bread and salad. It was her go-to meal in a pinch, and her meat sauce was to die for, if she did say so herself.

An hour later, she surveyed her private sanctuary. Her apartment was immaculate, and wine was already chilling in the refrigerator. She put the sauce on to simmer while she took a shower. Everything was ready when Brandy rang the doorbell.

Regan wiped her palms on her apron. She was surprised at her excitement. The thought of spending the evening with Brandy was appealing to her. She opened the door.

Regan couldn't hide her smile. It was obvious that Brandy had taken extra care to look her best for their dinner. She nearly panicked. *This is beginning to feel like a date.*

"Wow! You're so hot." Brandy scanned her professor from the top of her head to the tips of her painted toenails. "I love the way those jeans hug your hips, and that sweater accentuates all your gorgeous curves." Brandy ran the tip of her tongue along her lips.

Regan stared at the brazen young woman without moving. *This is a bad idea*, she thought.

"I brought wine." Brandy moved into the apartment and closed the door behind her. "I pegged you as a red wine drinker. Of course, it might not go with what you've prepared for dinner."

Regan looked at the bottle of Bordeaux. "This is a Chateau Lafite Rothschild Pauillac. You shouldn't be spending this kind of money for wine."

"I didn't." Brandy giggled. "I took it from my dad's wine cellar."

Regan cocked an eyebrow. "Why does that not surprise me?"

"So, will it go with our dinner?" Brandy's smile was infectious.

"Yes, it's perfect. Give me your jacket. I'll hang it up."

Brandy followed Regan into the kitchen. "If you'll give me a corkscrew, I'll open the wine and let it breathe while we get dinner on the table."

"Top drawer on your left," Regan said as she stirred the spaghetti sauce.

"Oh my God!" Brandy sniffed the air. "That smells like heaven. How can you be so damn gorgeous and cook too?"

"Brandy, I don't think—"

"Sorry, Professor. I was way out of line. It won't happen again. I didn't mean anything by it. I just have a knack for saying what I'm thinking. If it's in my mind it comes out my mouth."

Regan served their food and carried it to the dinning table.

"Are we going to study Shakespeare the entire semester?" Brandy queried as she located glasses and poured their wine.

"It is a course on Shakespeare," Regan reminded her as they sat down at the table. "Or I could give you a break and have the class do a report on *The Purloined Letter*."

"No, no. Shakespeare is just fine. Don't give us Poe." Bandy groaned as if mortally wounded.

"You don't like Poe?"

"Some of his stuff is great. I mean, the story lines. Like *The Pit and the Pendulum, The Tell-Tale Heart,* and *The Masque of the Red Death.* Oh, and you must love *The Cask of Amontillado.* But *The Purloined Letter* is a trip to boredom.

"Honestly, Professor, if Poe submitted his writings to a publishing house today, they'd rubber-stamp Rejected all over them."

"I suppose you like *The Fall of the House of Usher* too." Regan frowned.

"It was interesting," Brandy said.

"Do you know what I find interesting?" Regan held out her glass for more wine. "That you're drawn to the ones where the main characters were obviously demented."

"So, what does that say about me?" Brandy made an evil face. "I could be a serial killer?"

"I doubt it." Regan chuckled. "You're too pretty to—" She stopped as she realized she was flirting with Brandy.

"You think I'm pretty?" Brandy's eyes twinkled. "Are you attracted to me?"

Hell yes, I'm attracted to you, Regan thought as she stood and walked to the living room. "Where's your Spanish book? Do you have a study sheet?"

"I should go, Regan." Brandy pulled her jacket from the coat tree. "Thank you for the best meal I've had in a long time and the most stimulating conversation I've ever had." She leaned down and kissed Regan on the cheek. "Good night, Professor."

##

Brandy tossed a thick envelope onto Ryan's desk.

"What's this?" Agent King asked, frowning.

"Just in case you haven't found them yet, it's over a hundred reasons why Coach Tucker was murdered—and that many people with motives."

King rolled her eyes. "I picked these up yesterday. What compelled you to get them?"

"I don't want you looking at Joey for Tucker's death." Brandy sat down in the chair across from the FBI agent. "He told me you really grilled him on that point."

"I've marked your boyfriend off my list," Ryan said. "It seems he has an airtight alibi."

"Let me guess, Loraine Munoz?" Brandy snorted.

Ryan nodded. "She swears they were awake all night long."

"Yeah, Joey could do that. He has the stamina of a racehorse."

"Do you know anyone who was molested by Tucker but didn't report it?" Ryan asked.

"If I did I wouldn't tell you." Brandy's eyes darkened. "The bastard got what he deserved. If he'd raped Professor Shaw, I would have killed him myself."

Shakespeare Under Cover will be available the first quarter of 2019. Don't miss it.

Contents

12732386R00184

Made in the USA
San Bernardino, CA
11 December 2018